THE BACHELOR and the BRIDE

OTHER PROPER ROMANCES

BY SARAH M. EDEN

Ashes on the Moor

Hope Springs

Longing for Home

Longing for Home, vol. 2: Hope Springs

Savage Wells

The Sheriffs of Savage Wells

Healing Hearts

The Dread Penny Society

The Lady and the Highwayman

The Gentleman and the Thief

The Merchant and the Rogue

PROPER ROMANCE

THE BACHELOR *and the* BRIDE

To Emily King,
a fighter, an inspiration, and a
fearless defender of the vulnerable

Visit us at ShadowMountain.com

Library of Congress Cataloging-in-Publication Data
CIP on file
ISBN: 978-1-63993-048-7

Printed in the United States of America
PubLitho, Draper, UT

10 9 8 7 6 5 4 3 2 1

CHAPTER 1

London, January 1866

London was no place for the faint of heart. Fortunately for Barnabus Milligan, he'd stopped listening to that organ long ago.

He was a doctor, tending to the illnesses and injuries and difficulties of people from all walks of life. When not treating patients, he divided his time between writing penny serials about medicine, doctors, and related oddities and assisting in the secretive work of the even more secretive Dread Penny Society, a group of fellow "penny dreadful" authors who went about the city looking after the vulnerable and undermining the efforts of those who exploited them. His time was well and truly filled. He preferred it that way.

Barnabus stepped through the familiar blue door of the DPS's headquarters, an outwardly unassuming London house. A meeting of the membership had been called, the second one that week. Their efforts on behalf of the poor and defenseless were being hampered by London's most notorious criminal, the Mastiff. There was neither time nor room for hesitation.

Nolan, the Dreadful's perpetually distracted butler, who tended to be either sleeping in his chair or perusing the *Times*, sat at his post in the entryway.

"Good morning," Barnabus said.

From over the top of his newspaper, Nolan offered a flat-jawed smile, the sort that emerged when a person hadn't many teeth left. Barnabus was well aware that most of London's struggling population, and a good number of the well-off folks, spent a lifetime visiting the teeth drawers.

Nolan offered his usual dip of the head. The butler was not talkative, but he was loyal. All the DPS depended upon him to help keep their headquarters and activities a secret.

Barnabus set his etched penny, the calling card of all the Dreadfuls, on a narrow table, adding to the pile already there. As the coin snapped against the tabletop, Nolan reached out and pressed the center of a carved flower on the entryway wall. That triggered a low scraping noise, followed by a wall panel sliding open, behind which was the DPS's meeting room, a small-scale replica of the House of Commons.

Countless voices echoed out, filling the sparse entryway. Barnabus tipped his hat to Nolan, who'd set down the newspaper, his eyelids drooping. The man'd be snoozing in another minute.

With a quick smoothing of his side whiskers and mustache, Barnabus stepped inside, the wall sliding shut behind him. Martin Afola, one of the youngest members of the DPS, stood nearby and greeted him as he passed.

Three tiers of chairs sat in rows on either side of the room with a throne-like chair in the middle used by Fletcher Walker, the acting head of their organization. Barnabus made his way down the second row, stopping at the third chair from the far end—his regular seat located between Brogan Donnelly and Stone.

The former of the two, a ginger-haired Irishman, greeted him with a grin, as was customary for him.

The latter, a Black man from America's South, greeted him with a silent nod, as was customary for *him*.

Barnabus set his cane under his chair, followed by his top hat. He hung his overcoat on the back of the chair, then took his seat.

"How is your wife faring?" he asked Brogan, both out of personal interest—they were friends, after all—and professional. Brogan's newlywed wife, Vera, was recovering from catastrophic injuries sustained during the last time the DPS had tussled with the Mastiff.

"She is better every day."

That was reassuring. "And how is married life treating you?"

"Married life is marvelous," Brogan said. "I heartily recommend it."

"You're wasting your breath, Donnelly," Stone said. "Doc's as confirmed a bachelor as this world's ever known."

That was more of an exaggeration than either of these men knew, but being the resident bachelor had served Barnabus well.

Fletcher stepped up to his "throne" and called the gathered DPS members to attention. "With me, gentlemen and lady."

Squaring his shoulders, Barnabus joined in the recitation of the society's pledge and guiding statement.

"For the poor and infirm, the hopeless and voiceless, we do not relent. We do not forget. We are the Dread Penny Society."

When Barnabus had heard their motto for the first time at his first meeting with the DPS, he knew he'd found where he belonged. They had summarized succinctly the principles that guided his own life. He'd vowed fifteen years earlier, upon the tragic death of his mother, to never relent, to never forget, and to save everyone he possibly could.

"Our first bit of trouble," Fletcher said, sitting casually in his very formal chair, "is the usual kind from the usual quarter: crime at the behest of the Mastiff."

The room kept quiet, tension thick all around them. The Mastiff ran London's underbelly with all the authority and precision of a general on the battlefield. He'd undermined the DPS's efforts time and again. He'd nearly killed Brogan Donnelly's wife. He held captive a woman the Dreadfuls were desperate to find and free. He threatened London's street children and blackmailed people in the highest level of the government. He was dangerous and growing more so every day.

"The bloke's suspected to have set another fire a few days ago," Fletcher continued. "Two people were caught in it. He's outmaneuvering us, mates. And people are dying."

"Everyone we know of in his network has gone as silent as the grave," Elizabeth Black said. She was one of their newer members, and no one outside of their membership knew the prim and proper headmistress of a school for young ladies was actually the reigning monarch of the penny dreadfuls, writing under the nom de plume of Mr. King. "If we can't even get a whisper of what they're doing, how can we possibly prevent these things?"

"The Mastiff is hiding his work better, but we're refining our network as well." Fletcher looked determined but not entirely confident. "Brogan's father-in-law is proving to be a shockingly good source of information."

Everyone's attention turned to their resident Irishman.

"I've not the first idea how it is he knows so much," Brogan said. "I've not even any clue where he's been the last two months, only that he is fully sure he and the children he's protecting would be in mortal danger if he weren't in hiding—enough so that he missed his own daughter's wedding. He sends me information regularly, so I'm hopeful he can discover what we, so far, haven't managed."

Mr. Sorokin's connection to London's underworld had been a source of great debate in the DPS. No one thought him a villain, but there was little else they were certain of.

Fletcher turned his attention to Martin. "Anything odd you've learned about this most recent blaze?"

Martin stood and tucked his hands in his pockets, not in a posture of uncertainty, but simply a trick for keeping himself more still than he usually was. "The Mastiff, assuming he is the one behind this, didn't wait for the people to be out of their shop, as he's done in the past. He set the premises ablaze with them still inside."

"This fire wasn't a *warning*," Stone said. "It was punishment."

Martin nodded. "Seems that way. He's getting bolder. People are terrified, and rightly so. He had been threatening them into compliance. Now he's just killing 'em."

Slipping women free from the unrelenting grasp of madams and bullyboys was Barnabus's particular emphasis in this organization. But a man who was heartlessly murdering people was everyone's concern.

"Ought we to be holding off on our efforts with the public-facing organization we've started?" Brogan asked.

Barnabus had asked himself the same question. The two of them had been charged with creating a front for the society, an acknowledged charitable organization the members' friends and families could be part of so the DPS needn't tell quite so many lies. It also served as a distraction to those who might be paying a bit too much attention to what the penny dreadful authors of London were doing in secret.

The work they'd dedicated themselves to involved hampering extremely dangerous and often powerful people, thwarting their crimes, helping their victims escape. Sometimes, the work they did was not entirely legal. It was crucial for their safety, their freedom, and their ability to continue their work that their activities be kept secret from everyone outside their organization. Even their own families didn't know of their efforts.

That secrecy, however, came with complications. Family members asked questions, pieced together unintended clues. Keeping the secret was becoming increasingly difficult. Some members had contemplated resigning from the DPS because they couldn't continue the ruse needed to protect those they'd saved and those they loved.

And so the DPS had created a sister organization: the Charitable Authors League of London. In full view of all and with the knowledge, blessing, and participation of their families, they would be undertaking efforts throughout London to ease suffering and want. Running two organizations simultaneously was difficult, but the survival of so many depended on yet another deception: the lie that "CALL" was the only thing this group of writers was involved in.

But did they dare continue with CALL given the Mastiff's growing threats?

"I think," Barnabus said, "we'd actually do best to push ahead. CALL's first charitable effort can be undertaken on the street where the fire occurred. We could do some good for people the Mastiff has terrorized, all while providing us cover for snooping around the ashes a bit, seeing what we can find."

"Excellent idea," Fletcher said. "And while we're sniffing about, we'll see if we can't sort out what happened to the victims of the fire."

"'What happened to them'?" Elizabeth repeated in confusion. "They were killed."

"Aye, that they were. Their bodies were recovered and then buried. But now those bodies have disappeared."

A weight settled in Barnabus's chest. Grave robbing was something every doctor was both familiar and uncomfortable with. It was a well-known secret that most medical school cadavers were obtained through the efforts of "resurrection men"; a bit of moral ambiguity most doctors struggled to make their peace with.

"Why would a resurrectionist bother with bodies that were damaged by fire?" Kumar asked. "No medical school or curious doctor would pay them for . . ." He let the commentary dangle, likely not knowing how to complete the sentence without sounding cruel or inhumane.

The whole group looked to Barnabus, he being the only doctor among them. Exhaling a tense breath, he offered *some* of the expertise he had on the matter. "If someone were studying the effects of fire, that person might be interested. There are, unfortunately, people with morbid interests and curiosities, but without true medical interest, who pay for bodies. Resurrectionists can also be employed for revenge. They also sometimes nip off with a body as a means of hiding something."

"Could it be the Mastiff felt something about these two unfortunate people needed to be hidden? Perhaps some odd clue that might lead to his true identity or whereabouts?" Kumar asked.

No one seemed certain.

Fletcher shook his head, not in dismissal of the idea but in growing confusion. "What could possibly be kept hidden by stealing their bodies?"

"Seems a question that ought to be posed to the fella that did the resurrecting," Stone said.

"I don't have any personal connections to resurrection men," Fletcher said dryly. "Do any of you?"

With a lump of apprehension, Barnabus realized he would need to make a confession he'd never intended to. "I do," he said on a sigh.

They all looked at him with wide-eyed surprise.

"From your days in medical school?" Fletcher guessed.

"Not exactly."

"Then what, *exactly*?" Elizabeth pressed.

"I know someone who is familiar with that line of work and the people who undertake it."

"How familiar?"

"Extremely."

"And how well do you know this mystery person?" Fletcher asked.

"Extremely well."

Brogan had that look on his face that always portended mischief. "How extremely well? A neighbor? A rival for some long-ago lady's affection?"

Barnabus pushed out a heavy, tense breath. "None of those things."

"Then how do you know him?" Fletcher asked again.

"I know *her*—"

That captured everyone's attention. He was known among them as the eternal bachelor, the doctor who had no interest in love or connections.

"—because she's my wife."

THE BACHELOR AND THE BRIDE

by Mr. King

Installment I
in which our Hero inquires of a Wise Woman and
receives Instructions of a most unexpected nature!

Centuries ago, in a quiet corner of the border country, a young man of medicine by the name of Duncan worked tirelessly on behalf of those who placed their well-being in his hands. Not having the expertise nor the implements of our doctors today, the pull he felt to protect the people in his care often sat heavy on his heart and mind. He dedicated himself to healing and comforting, but, as was far too often the case in years gone by—and, alas, in our time as well—he found himself as familiar with the churchyard as he was with his own cottage.

As had happened far too often before, he found himself tired, discouraged, and heartbroken after a harrowing few weeks of looking after impossible-to-cure patients, an illness having ravaged his area of the kingdom. One patient remained in his care, her recovery entirely in question.

The young girl was now an orphan, Duncan having

been unable to cure her parents of the very ailment that still threatened his patient. He had tried but failed in his attempts to cure the ill-fated family, and he had little hope of saving the child's life. Duncan was not one to simply declare defeat when faced with considerable obstacles, but he *was* the sort who was willing to admit when he had exhausted his own knowledge.

And thus it was that Duncan Endicott, man of medicine, donned his best linen shirt and doublet, though both were several years out of fashion, and smoothed his Van Dyke beard and moustache, before placing his capotain hat on his head. Satisfied he would make a favorable impression, Duncan undertook the rambling walk through the nearby forest to the cottage of an aged woman known to all in the area as Granny Winter, or *Geamhradh Seanmhair* as she was called in the ancient tongue of Scotland.

It was widely believed—and Granny Winter had never disabused anyone of the assumption—that she was, in fact, the legendary Wise Woman, the *Cailleach*, the figure from ancient tales who had come into existence shortly after the dawn of mankind, making her younger than the salmon but older than the eagle. The *Cailleach* was the bearer of great wisdom, the holder of great secrets, the creator of the hills and valleys, the queen of autumn and winter, the bringer of storms, the overseer of life on earth. She was revered, and a bit feared. Whether or not Granny Winter was the Wise Woman of old, she *was* an old and wise woman.

Her cottage was not hidden, neither was it difficult to reach, but few people drew near it. Whispers and hushed conversations about the mysteries of this aging woman revealed that arriving at her doorstep was not a quest undertaken by the faint of heart.

Duncan Endicott had never been the least fainthearted.

He knocked at the rough-hewn door of the thatched-roof cottage, a sprig of wildflowers in his hand, hoping the offering would convey to Granny Winter that he had not come with ill intentions.

His knock was answered by a young woman who had lived with Granny Winter for a handful of years. No one knew her origins nor how she had come to make her home there. Duncan had not been born in the area and had even less idea of her origins than anyone else did. It was widely acknowledged that Miss Sorcha Báirbre and Granny Winter were not actually kin, and yet, they looked upon each other quite as if they were.

Sorcha was near about Duncan's age. He had taken notice of her the first time he'd seen her after moving to this corner of the kingdom only two years earlier. He'd been struck by the sparkle in her deep-brown eyes and by the eagerness with which she undertook anything and everything. And he had hardly been immune to her soft and quiet beauty. Mystery surrounded her, yet she was clearly liked and embraced by the townspeople.

Seeing her at Granny Winter's door lifted his spirits and fortified his courage.

"*Geamhradh Seanmhair*," Sorcha called back into the cottage, "the doctor is here."

From within came the craggy voice of the old woman. "Call him in, lass. He has come on an important matter."

It was moments like this, when the wise woman seemed

to know things she ought not know, that solidified the belief that she was more fairy than human.

"She has been expecting you," Sorcha told him in her soft and reassuring way. She even smiled, which Duncan found particularly pleasing.

He removed his hat and stepped inside, allowing his eyes a moment to adjust to the dim interior. He approached the chair near the fire where Granny Winter sat watching him through her stringy silver hair. He presented his handful of flowers to her. For a moment, she didn't move. Was she displeased? Was his offering not acceptable enough to find favor with her?

At last, she spoke, but not to him. "Lass, take the offering and hang it to dry."

Acute relief passed through the young doctor. He had come to ask a favor; being deemed welcome was of utmost importance.

Sorcha accepted the flowers on the old woman's behalf. Voice lowered, she said to him, "Do not lose heart. She'd not have let you in if she didn't intend to hear you."

"Thank you," he said. "I'd not wish to make a nuisance of myself."

Again, she smiled.

Again, the sight buoyed him.

"Sit yourself down," the old woman said, motioning toward a three-legged stool. "Tell us what it is you have arrived to ask."

He moved to sit, his long legs bent at awkward angles as he lowered himself down. He faced her, his posture penitent and his expression humble.

"We have endured a string of illnesses of late, Granny Winter," he said. "I have done all I can, but my knowledge is limited, and my cures are insufficient. I have in my care a young girl, Donella. Her parents succumbed to the same illness their brave daughter fights fiercely all day and all night, clinging to life with ferocity. My heart aches to think her fire might extinguish despite my great efforts to save her."

Granny Winter nodded slowly. She spun in her hand an old and battered hammer. Beside her was a small stack of firewood. The cottage smelled of herbs and earth. There was something in the scene that was at once inviting and disquieting.

"What is it you wish for me to do for the lass?" Granny Winter asked.

"I have come to ask if you, in your wisdom, know of something that might help her, something I might do for her. I know I am presumptuous in asking you to give of your knowledge and time. Were I asking merely for myself, I would not do so. But I wish for the girl to live. I wish to see her restored to health."

"You have asked well," Granny Winter said. "That you inquire not to elevate yourself but for the sake of another speaks well of you."

"Will you help me save the girl?" Hope bubbled as it had not in weeks.

"Alas, I have not the answer you seek."

His heart fell to his feet. He knew not where to seek knowledge if she did not have it.

"Pick your face up, lad. I do not mean there are no

answers, only that they will not come from my lips. The answers to your questions must be sought at Loch Dreva."

On the other side of the cottage, Sorcha took in a quick, audible breath, something very near to a gasp. Loch Dreva was unknown to Duncan, but he hadn't a doubt Sorcha knew it well and not through pleasant recollections.

But if that was where he would find the answers he needed, then that was where he would go.

"I'm willing to make any journey, however long, however treacherous," he said. "But I do not know where Loch Dreva lies, nor do I know how to reach it."

Granny raised one bent and bony hand and waved Sorcha to her side. "Sorcha knows this land well. She lived her earlier years as a vagabond, traveling often and traveling far. She knows the mountains and valleys, the streams and meadows."

"Will you give me instructions on how to find this loch?" he asked the lovely young woman.

"It cannot be found by being told," Sorcha said. "One must be shown. But, be warned, Loch Dreva is a place frequented by fairies and monsters alike. Certain death awaits the ill-prepared traveler."

"I confess," he said, "I am quite ill-prepared for fairies or monsters or anything of their ilk."

"Sorcha knows the tales and warnings well," Granny Winter said. "I have seen to that."

"I do not know how much time I have before Donella will slip beyond saving." Duncan worried mightily for the young girl. "I will learn as quickly as I can and do whatever

I must to discover the location of this loch and gain the knowledge I need."

Granny Winter shook her head slowly, her silver hair wafting about her. A chill breeze rustled everything inside the cottage, though the door remained snuggly shut. "You must begin your journey now. Sorcha will lead you to Loch Dreva, and, as you journey, she will teach you how to escape the traps that await you."

Sorcha offered a humble agreement. To Duncan's relief, she didn't seem upset at the prospect of making the trek, though she'd not chosen it.

"But you mustn't set out without this." From beside her chair, Granny Winter produced a sack made of rough-hewn fabric, lumpy and awkwardly pieced together. "Everything you most need for your journey ahead lies within."

She held out the sack to *him*, not to Sorcha, which was surprising. She entrusted to him, whom she hardly knew, something he suspected was of value to her.

"I will guard it well," he promised.

Granny Winter shook her silver head. "Do not *guard* it well. *Use* it well."

"How long do you expect this journey will require?" Sorcha asked her. "It is nearly *Bealltainn*."

Bealltainn was a holiday of some significance in this corner of the world. It fell upon the first day of May, less than a week hence.

"Your wanderings can be concluded by then," Granny Winter said. "See that they are. I will look after the young girl, tend her until your return. But should you not take my place at her bedside by the going down of the sun on the first day of May, all will be for naught."

And thus began a journey into the world of fairies and monsters, walking a path riddled with danger in pursuit of answers to questions the two wanderers had not yet thought to ask.

CHAPTER 2

For three years, Gemma Milligan had sent a letter every few months to her one-time home in the Finsbury area of London, updating her husband-in-name-only on her whereabouts. He'd sent very few responses, none of which requested her to return. She'd told him before leaving that he needn't send for her unless he'd come to feel something more than a vague friendship for her. Absence was meant to make the heart fonder, she'd been told. After three years, she'd accepted that some people couldn't be absent enough to make any heart fond of them.

She currently laid her head in Wandsworth, a rough area of London south of Thames. She worked what odd jobs she could find. None of it would make her wealthy, that was for sure and certain. But she weren't starving, and she'd not needed to crawl back to her horrid father for a roof over her head. She couldn't have anyway. The man was dead, and good riddance.

Upon returning from a long day selling flowers on street corners, Gemma was met by her landlady, who tossed her a neatly folded letter addressed to Gemma. She recognized the handwriting and nearly dropped at the shock of it.

"Can't remember you ever getting a letter," Mrs. Woods said, watching her with all-consuming curiosity. "Hope it ain't bad news." On the contrary, the woman seemed to hope it were *exactly* that.

"Ain't got the first idea what it is." Gemma dropped it in her coat pocket. "I'd twig it's some job coming my way. Been hoping to leave off the flower selling."

On that Banbury tale, Gemma trudged up the tenement stairs toward the tiny, single-room flat she'd called her own for nearly half a year, which was a fair-sight longer than she usually kept to any one place. Her family's reputation had, miraculously, not caught up with her here. Yet.

She unlocked her door and stepped into the darkness that awaited her. The hour weren't overly late, but dusk came early in the winter. She hung her coat on the nail on the wall next to the door. With a flick of a Lucifer match, she lit a stump of a candle. She carried it and her letter to the kerosene lantern on the table and lit it. That was as bright as the space ever grew.

Gemma dropped her weary body onto her only chair. She broke the seal on her bit of mail and unfolded it under the spill of lantern light.

Gemma,

I am in particular need of seeing you. I realize Wandsworth is not an easy distance from Finsbury, but I hope you will be able to make the journey sooner rather than later. I am still at the same house and can be found there most of the time. If you choose to come—and I do hope you will—and I am out, the keys have not been changed. Let yourself in. Make yourself at home.

Yours, etc.

Barnabus

It was not precisely a declaration of love and devotion, but considering the agreement between them, it was nearly that. She'd waited years to hear anything from him other than "Received your letter. Hope all is well." He'd written so much more this time. He wished her to come home and not at a shambling pace. It was what she'd waited three years to hear from him. Three long and lonely years.

Make yourself at home.

Home.

Pleased as pudding, Gemma packed her few belongings into her well-worn carpetbag. She'd dragged herself so many places she hardly had to think about the ins and outs of it. Perhaps it was telling that she wouldn't miss this place or the people she'd come to know. If there was one thing Gemma was a dab hand at, it was moving along. Only once had leaving a place broken her heart. But now she was returning to that very place and the man who lived there. A man she adored to the depths of her soul. A man whose heart had grown tender toward her.

At last.

At long last.

The Finsbury house Gemma had lived in as a new bride hadn't changed much on the outside. Still tidy as seasons and neat as a new pin. The brass plaque on the door, kept polished to a shine, declared this three-story home a "Doctor's Infirmary." The peony bushes weren't in bloom, but she had no doubt they would in abundance when the season was right.

In this house, she'd been both the merriest and most sorrowful of her life. But she wasn't walking in as an interloper now. She was wanted, asked for, brought home. There'd be more of the happiness and none of the heartbreak. She was certain of it.

She *thwanked* the knocker against the deep green door. Her joy at being home again, her excitement that Baz—as she'd always called him—had asked her to return was warring with other, more difficult memories. Life had taught her that being stingy with hope saved a person from drowning in disappointment. That was too strong a lesson to shake even when her dreams were promising to all come true.

The door opened.

It was not Baz on the other side but rather a woman likely twenty years Gemma's senior and as much a stranger to her as would be the president of America.

She kept still as stone. "Is Baz—Dr. Milligan in?"

"He's not." The woman spoke gruffly but not unfriendly. "I'm his nurse. If you're ailing, I can help you."

"I ain't ill or injured." Baz's letter hadn't indicated this complication. "I'd like to pop in and wait for the doctor to return."

The woman shook her head. "I'll give him a message for you."

"Tell him I received his letter asking me to come and telling me that, if he were out, I was to make myself at home and wait for him and that I'd've very much liked to follow his instructions, but I weren't permitted to do so."

The woman's gaze narrowed. "He asked you to call on him here?"

"That he did."

"What's your name?"

"Gemma."

That didn't strike the woman as meaningful. "Do you have a surname?"

With shoulders set proudly, she said, "Milligan."

Finally, the woman seemed to think there might be something to Gemma's arrival. "You're kin to him, are you?"

Not the response she'd expected.

"He ain't never mentioned me?"

"He's never mentioned *any* family aside from his mother. And even she's only whispered about."

That hadn't changed, then. Baz had loved his mother deeply, and he mourned her with every ounce of himself. Perhaps he didn't speak of Gemma because his feelings for her were tender as well. That'd explain a great many things.

The woman motioned her inside, eyeing Gemma's carpetbag. Let the woman stare. Gemma was home at last, and she'd endure no clouds marring her sunshine.

"You'd do best to wait in the library," the woman said. "We might have patients drop in, and that'd require the use of the sitting room."

Gemma gave a single nod, then turned toward the library door.

"You know where the library is?"

"I've been here before," Gemma said.

"Not in the last two years. I'd know you otherwise."

"It ain't been in the last *three* years."

This woman, who'd worked for Baz for years and seemed intelligent and keen, hadn't the least idea who Gemma was. That sent a wash of worry over her.

Had Baz not ever mentioned his vagabond wife? Not even in passing? That weren't a comforting possibility.

He'd sent for her. He'd asked her to return, to come home again. On those simple truths she was steady as castles.

Gemma sat in a wingback chair, set her carpetbag on the floor beside her, and waited. Alone. The library contained more volumes than it had three years earlier but was still nowhere near full. Books came dear, and Baz had never laid claim to a fortune. The money his doctoring brought him went, in large part, toward his rescue efforts. She knew that firsthand. He had a heart as good as gold. She'd always admired that about him.

Her gaze fell on a shelf with a long line of thin, booklet-sized items. She knew what they were: penny serials. *His* penny serials. Baz's first had been published while this house had still been her home. Now, she saw his tales being read all over. She'd nearly burst with pride in him.

Voices sounded in the corridor. Gemma perked up her ears but kept still.

"Claims to be family," the nurse said. "But I know you don't have any living family. Leastwise, none you know of."

Gemma knew Baz hadn't the first idea who his father was or of anyone connected to his mother's family. But he did have family. He had *her*.

"Did she give you a name?"

That was his voice. She hadn't heard it in years but knew it in an instant.

"Gemma Milligan."

"Oh, brilliant." He sounded excited.

Gemma couldn't have been more pleased if she'd been given keys to a palace. *Brilliant.* Her Baz was excited to see her. She'd wanted that for three years.

She stood and faced the door as Baz stepped over the threshold. Hair still black as a stovepipe. Eyes filled with intelligence. Bearing tall and confident. Features so handsome even his thick side-whiskers did nothing to hide them. Her heart sighed.

"Gemma." He was one of the only people who didn't say her name as if it sat sour and distasteful in his mouth. "You—There wasn't—You didn't waste any time."

He carried himself with confidence, but she remembered well how he tripped over his tongue sometimes when he grew flustered. It was an endearing contradiction.

"You said you'd rather I didn't dillydally." She watched him, hoping he'd cross to her, pull her into a hug. She'd missed his embraces.

He smiled a little and motioned her to sit. She returned to the wingback chair, and he sat in the one nearest it.

"I've seen your penny dreadfuls all around," she said. "You feared no one'd take to them, but seems to me they've caught fire."

"A lot of things have been catching fire lately." The observation was made with too heavy an undertone to be a jest. He'd heard of those troubles, then, same as her.

"London's a regular firebox lately, i'n'it?" People were losing homes and businesses all over Town. "Have you doctored a great many burns?"

"A few. One patient was so bad off I wasn't certain she'd survive."

"It did always burden your mind when a poor soul couldn't be saved." Her heart had broken seeing how distraught he became, how much he grieved. Though he'd not confessed to it, she'd twigged that his grief over his mother was the foundation for all the rest. "I can't imagine you've stopped your rescue efforts. What flavor 'ave they assumed lately?"

"I—I am—" He shifted his gaze to the fireplace. "I still do what I can to thwart the underhanded madams and macks of London. And some of my fellow penny dreadful writers and I have started a charitable organization aimed at easing some of the suffering in the poorer areas of Town."

"You ought to put Wandsworth on your list. There's suffering and plenty in that corner."

He looked to her once more, growing entirely still. "Wandsworth is where you've been living." His eyes always had spoken louder than he did. In that moment, they were screaming with worry.

She tossed him the small smile she often had when he'd fretted over her. "I've made my home in shabby corners nearly all my life. I'd've been lost as a cow in a bog if I'd dropped m'self in a rum area of town."

Finsbury, where Baz lived, was finer than where she'd laid her head in the years before marrying him and in the years since they'd parted ways. She was finally leaving behind those seedier streets.

"Do you think you'll—think you'll ever stop wandering the world?" he asked.

Her partial smile grew to an amused grin. "I've never left London and the surrounding area, let alone seen all the world."

"But I suspect you'd like to." He had the loveliest smile, but he so seldom let it out to play. Seeing it in that moment wrapped around her like a blanket.

"At the moment," she said, "I'm happy as peaches to be *here.*"

"And I'm glad you came so quickly."

"You are?" Could he see how much that meant to her? How much she'd needed to hear what he was finally ready to say? She found herself leaning toward him.

Instead of drawing closer to her, he rose and paced a bit away. "There was an oddity attached to a fire a few days ago, and I'm hopeful you can shed a little light on it."

He meant to gab about a fire? Three years of waiting on the words she'd longed for, and he was leading off with gossip? Still, it was something. And *something* was a heap more than she'd had in a long time.

"I don't know a thing about fires," she warned, angling back into her chair.

He shook his head. "It's not about the fire itself but the people who died in it." So many doctors grew cold to death and dying, speaking of it as if it mattered little. Not Baz. "No one can sort the mystery of what happened to them after they were buried."

After they were buried. Her stomach dropped to her toes. "You suspect they were resurrected?"

"I'm certain they were, but I can't sort out why. What use or value would two badly burned bodies be to a resurrectionist?"

She took a calming breath, though her tension didn't ease. "Talkin' about the family trade don't give me pleasure. I ain't proud to be a Kincaid."

"I would never ask you to offer *detailed* recountings." He turned to look at her. "I—I am merely hopeful that you might have some insights into possible motivation."

Gemma swallowed the bile that rose in her throat. She hated that this was her heritage. "All resurrection men are motivated by the same thing: profit."

"Money?"

"Usually. Sometimes it's making or filling a debt. But most times, it's boodle, brass. Money talks louder than most anything to a resurrectionist. And they don't do anything out of charity." If her no-good father had taught her anything, it was that resurrection men like him never plied their trade for selfless reasons.

Baz rubbed his thumb along the edge of his mustache, his forehead creased in thought. "Someone wanted to get possession of those bodies."

"Or wanted to stop *someone else* from snatching 'em."

He nodded slowly. "But why?"

Gemma wrapped her arms around her middle, feeling

herself shrinking into the chair. "This topic's torture to me, Baz. Please don't belabor it."

He dipped his head. "My apologies. I forgot for a moment how abhorrent you find it all." A hint of a smile tugged at his lips. "I'd also all but forgotten that you call me 'Baz.' No one else does. I've missed hearing it."

A bit of relief washed over her. This was the ground she'd meant to be walking, not the slippery bog they'd traversed. "I've missed saying it."

His eyes darted from her to the carpetbag on the floor, studying it for the length of a breath. "Are you between places?"

Am I between places?

"You're welcome to stay here for a time if you need. The room you used is empty."

The room you used. Not "your room." The room she'd *used*. In a house she was welcome to stay in *for a time*. She wasn't "between places"; she'd come home because he'd asked her to. He'd finally sent for her.

"I'll tell Mrs. Simms however much you'd like," Baz said quietly, retaking his chair. "At the moment, she knows only that you're related to me in some way."

"You ain't told her that you're married?"

He shrugged. "Ours isn't a regular sort of marriage. And you're not ever here. It was far simpler to not explain over and over again."

"Have you told anyone at all that you've been churched?"

He sat a bit stiffer. "Very few people know that I am married."

Did he not want to admit to it? She'd feared that for a

long time. He'd no claim on a fine and fancy history. He hadn't lords and ladies and respectable people in his family; leastwise, none he knew of. But *she* was the daughter of a notorious resurrection man, one of three who ruled the Kincaid family with a violent iron fist. Baz hadn't ever said he was ashamed of being married to her. But not telling hardly a soul about her seemed to prove he was.

"Even after you sent word to me, you still didn't tell Mrs. Simms?" Surely he'd have made some preparations for her return now that he was ready to make something more of their marriage. It was the requirement she'd set—*they'd* set—for him writing to her at long last.

"It seemed a lot of explaining ahead of a brief conversation," he said. "If you need time to decide where you're heading next, I'll tell her whatever you'd like so you'll feel comfortable here for however long it takes to sort your situation."

For a moment, she sat mumchance, her mind too befuddled to allow a word to slip from her. He had *written* to her, asking her to return. Could it be he didn't remember their agreement and she'd misunderstood his letter? Or that he didn't remember the last day they'd spent together? How could he not? It was burned into her memory. But, then, she'd discovered three years earlier that many things in their shared life had meant more to her than to him. She'd felt more. And, in the end, had suffered more.

"I *am* needing a roof over my head." She managed the few words even with panic and despair swirling inside her. "Thank you."

He nodded. "It's good to see you again."

Is it, though?

He left the room without looking back. He seemed as content as could be, not put out or annoyed with her. He was pleasant but . . . indifferent. And that was terribly familiar. She'd seen it again and again during those early weeks of their marriage. She'd adored him, and he'd not shown any inclination beyond a general friendship.

For six months, she'd broken her own heart to pieces waiting for that to change. And for the next three years, she'd pasted the bits back together, all the while hoping his heart would soften and he'd find something in her to miss and long for. If her heart broke anew, she weren't certain she'd ever find a way to be whole again.

CHAPTER 3

Day dawned bright and promising the next morning. Barnabus quickly consumed his breakfast and retired to the library, as he always did.

He had a number of people to help today, though none of them would be his traditional kind of patients. Thinking of his responsibilities to the DPS inevitably made him think of his mother.

She had lived a tragic and short life, dying when Barnabus was only twelve. He loved and missed her. She'd taught him so much in the limited time they'd had together. She was the reason he worked as hard as he did to save women and girls from the fate that had awaited her when she'd come to London and the life she'd been forced to live from then on. She was the reason he never allowed himself to lose his focus.

"Our path can turn to misery without warning," she'd said to him as she lay dying of a fever. "Don't waste a moment of your life."

He hadn't. And he wouldn't. Her life had been full of struggles, but she'd done all she could to keep him safe and fed and to show him he was loved. Squandering away the life she'd fought so hard to give him was not and never would be acceptable.

And thus he had no intention of resting on this day. He needed to arrange for supplies to be delivered to two of his safe houses for the women taking refuge there. His publisher was awaiting the next installment of his newest penny dreadful. Mrs. Simms had the day off, and he meant to see to it she did not return the next day to find anything but pristine working conditions. And CALL was undertaking some charitable work later that day. There was no time for dawdling.

He'd only begun scratching out the opening paragraph of the second chapter of his newest tale when he heard the enthusiastic strains of "John Riley" floating into the library from the corridor. Gemma had always liked to sing. He'd all but forgotten how different the house was when she was in it. The brief months she'd lived here early in their unconventional marriage, the entire place had been filled with the sound of her singing, humming, and laughter. And near-constant moving about. She didn't merely not *live* in one place for long; she didn't *stand* in one place. She was constantly on the go. And yet, she wasn't exhausting the way people could sometimes be.

She breathed life into people and spaces. It was one of the many pleasant things he'd discovered about this resurrection man's daughter after they had wed.

Gemma bounced into the library. Her hair, though pulled up in a knot, looked as disarrayed as ever. He had never been able to decide if the chaos stemmed from her ceaseless moving about or if it had something to do with the temperament of her hair itself. What grabbed his attention most, however, was the threadbare state of her clothing and how worryingly thin she'd become. He'd noticed it the day before and hadn't been able to set his mind at ease on the matter.

When they'd first met years before, she'd not looked so down-at-the-heel. Her situation now couldn't possibly be as desperate as it had been then, could it? Yet she appeared to be living only a breath from absolute destitution.

Her gaze landed on him, and she smiled. The sight pulled his thoughts away from his worry and filled his mind with the memory of how very much he'd always liked her charming dimples. And how the sight of her so often left him tongue-tied. He never sounded less intelligent than when her smile or her dancing eyes or her dimples commanded his thoughts.

"I see you finally dragged yourself out of bed," Gemma said with her trademark amusement.

"Finally? It—It's only seven o'clock, and it is not yet light out."

She shook her head as if it were a great shame. "You missed absolutely everything."

He had always enjoyed her whimsy, though he'd not always understood it. "Did I?"

"You did, indeed." With a theatrical drop, she laid herself on the sofa. She pressed the back of her hand to her forehead, striking a pose even the most dramatic characters in Mr. King's penny dreadfuls would be hard-pressed to match. "A cat snatched itself a dead bird and went on parade outside the kitchen door. Meowed proudly for a full quarter hour, it did. You'd've thought it were the very king of tomcats rather than a coldhearted bird murderer."

He couldn't hold back the smile, just as he couldn't remember the last time such a smile had come so easily to him. "You haven't changed, Gemma."

In a quiet voice, she answered, "If only that were true."

He wasn't certain if she was speaking to herself or to him, but the sudden heaviness in her tone worried him. "Is something the—the matter?"

She hopped up with her usual vigor and energy. "Of course not."

Gemma crossed to sit in the chair across from his. She propped her elbow, almost visible through the worn fabric of her sleeve, on the tabletop, then rested her chin on her upturned fist. Her gray eyes danced with life and amusement.

"What jig are you dancing today?" she asked. "Doctoring or rescuing?"

"You seem quite convinced that I still undertake rescues."

She smiled, clearly not the least fooled by his misdirection. "I ain't the only one who's not changed, Baz."

He dipped his head in acknowledgment. "Today is a rescuing day . . . of sorts. Some of my fellow authors and I have started an organization, the Charitable Authors League of London. We bring food and supplies and other things to people who are in need."

"While still hampering the plans of the madams and macks of London." She shook her head, still smiling. "Don't you ever sleep?"

He chuckled quietly. "Not as much as I should."

Talking to her had always been easier for him than talking with others, though he did stumble about for words now and then. They knew so much of each other's history. So many of the things they usually kept hidden from others, they'd not needed to hide from each other. He knew about her family, where they came from, what they did. She knew his mother had lived her life trapped by the very sorts of people he'd dedicated himself to thwarting.

Her eyes settled on the parchment in front of him. "Is this your latest tale?"

"Yes. My publisher is hoping I'll have this installment finished soon."

"I've not yet read your newest story. I'm hoping to, though."

"You would like it," he said. "After all, you were the one who told me I ought to write about true medical marvels."

"You remember me saying that, do you?"

He nodded. "I've thought on it often these past years."

"Been thinking on anything else?" she asked, watching him as if she doubted he pondered much.

Surely she remembered that his thoughts were always full and heavy. "Plenty of things. My patients. My mother and what she'd think of me if she were still living. The poor people of London and what they need. Whether you were happy and safe."

"Because I'm one of the poor people of London?"

He couldn't tell if she was jesting. She *was* one of the unfortunates this city claimed in abundance. But she was also significant to him in a personal way. Theirs wasn't an ordinary marriage, but he did care what happened to her. He always had. He knew she'd doubted that in the days and weeks before she'd left three years ago. The reassurances he'd offered then hadn't been enough. He had his doubts they would be now. He didn't want to spend what little time they had together now arguing.

"Because I want you to be happy and safe," he answered, hoping she hadn't noticed his pause.

She seemed satisfied. "What's this latest tale about, then?"

"A fictional tale of a doctor searching out a mystery that's based on things that have, in actually, been documented and researched and wondered about."

Her eyes pulled wide as she listened to him, her interest never flagging. "I see it being read absolutely everywhere, but not a soul's been kind enough to drop their copy when racing after a train or leave it behind after having their shoes shined. Mark me, sometime someone'll be terrible careless, and I'll snatch m'self a copy."

Snatch one? "Do you not have any spare pennies, Gemma?" It would explain her current state, but not in a way that set his mind at ease.

"What is your charitable authors' group going to be doing today?" She made no effort at finesse when changing the subject, a sure sign she was uncomfortable with his question.

That told its own story, one that worried him. But he suspected questioning her directly would not get him the answers he needed. She did not confide in people easily. It was a trait they shared.

"We are bringing food and supplies to a corner of the city that recently had a fire."

"The same fire you was asking me about yesterday?"

He nodded. "That's how I happened to hear about the victims' graves being robbed."

"Ah."

The Dread Master had been right to direct the DPS to create this sister organization. It gave him a ready reason for knowing about things the DPS had discovered without having to outright lie to Gemma.

There were few things he disliked more than falsehoods and deception, both from himself and in others. He had seen the destruction it caused.

"Is this betterment ladle you've planned for today for authors only, or can friends and family and wives-not-seen-for-years take part as well?" she asked with a familiar air of mischief.

Life was so often heavy. Having a friend who lightened the load was a welcome thing.

"Many of the other authors will have family there," Barnabus said. "We'd welcome extra hands if you want to help."

Her dimples reappeared. She looked as if she meant to say something, but a knock at the front door prevented it.

"A patient?" she guessed.

It was possible.

Gemma walked with him to the door. On the other side stood Brogan Donnelly and Stone.

"We're not meant to leave for the CALL effort for another hour," Barnabus said. "What brings you around so early?"

"Stone, here, whacked his thumb with a hammer. 'Tis swollen three times its usual size. He objected, but I insisted he ought to have you look at it."

Brogan was remarkably good at hounding a fellow into

doing something he thought was ridiculous. He seemed to have managed it again this time.

"It's nothing," Stone said. "Brogan's being a pest."

Barnabus motioned them inside, closing the door behind them.

Stone held his hand out for medical inspection. His thumb was, indeed, quite swollen.

"The swelling will make moving it difficult, which makes that a poor clue as to the state of the bones beneath," Barnabus said.

Gemma said, "It's a blamed shame you cain't have a peek at the bones 'emselves. Without cutting the bloke's skin away, leastwise. I suspect he'd think that a bit too drastic for treating a hammered thumb."

"A far sight too drastic," Barnabus said. "But seeing the bones would certainly simplify things."

Brogan and Stone both eyed Gemma with unrestrained curiosity, though their expressions were quite different. Brogan grinned; Stone studied. Brogan looked ready to laugh; Stone looked ready to interrogate.

The members of the DPS were varied, which allowed for different thoughts, expertise, and viewpoints. And then there was the Dread Master. Their mysterious leader seemed to know anything and everything, and there wasn't a single corner of the sprawling metropolis he didn't have eyes and ears on. He ran the DPS from behind the scenes, directed their efforts, and had a tie-breaking vote in every significant decision they made. Fletcher, who acted as the head, answered only to him.

And no one knew who the Dread Master was.

Conjecture amongst the membership was vast and varied. Barnabus had his own guesses as to the Dread Master's identity. Stone was capable and secretive, intelligent and observant. And though it didn't reflect well on the general membership, prejudice was woven enough into the fabric of English culture that a Black man would realize he'd benefit from anonymity.

Barnabus's other guess, much more recently embraced, was Brogan's father-in-law. Mr. Sorokin, they'd discovered, had been secretly helping people throughout London escape dangerous and miserable situations for years. He'd shown himself to have connections all over the city and knew the comings and goings of people he had no reason to even be familiar with.

"I should warn you, Doc," Brogan said, "curiosity's always been m' besetting sin. If you don't make introductions where this lovey lass is concerned, I'll break with protocol and simply make them my own self."

He'd been so lost in his thoughts, he'd neglected to explain to any of the people in the entryway who the others were.

To Stone, Barnabus quickly said, "Be a bit ginger with the thumb until we know how badly it's injured. And when the nail falls off, be certain to bandage the thumb well."

"*When*?" Stone repeated.

Barnabus nodded. "It'll grow back." With a quick nod toward Gemma, he told his friends, "This is Gemma Milligan. My wife."

Brogan let his grin blossom fully. "I thought she might've

been, though I still haven't fully recovered from hearing that our eternal bachelor has had a bride this entire time."

"Don't be too offended," Gemma said. "He'd not told Mrs. Simms either, and she's here all the day long."

Stone folded his arms across his chest, somehow making the posture feel more stoic than intimidating. "I suspect there's a story behind that."

"There's always a story." Brogan laughed.

"But not all stories need to be told to all people," Barnabus said.

"Some stories, seems, ain't meant to be told to anyone," Gemma joked in an overly loud aside.

"Never you fear, Mrs. Mulligan," Brogan said with a twinkle in his eye. "We're experts at wriggling information out of the good doctor."

She offered a very formal curtsy, a gleam of laughter in her eyes. "Begging your pardons, sirs, I'm aiming to traipse about the site of a fire today and am needing to see that I'm well togged for the outing."

She bounced from the room. The visitors watched her go, then, in perfect synchrony, turned toward Barnabus.

"She's gorgeous," Brogan said. "And seems to be quite a ball of sunshine."

Barnabus nodded. "She is both."

"And you're fond of her?" Stone asked.

"Of course I am."

"And how long has it been since you've seen this woman you're so fond of?'" Brogan asked.

"Three years." Barnabus knew there was little point ignoring the question. As Stone had so aptly put it, Brogan knew how to make himself a pest. "Gemma doesn't like to stay in one place long. Explaining the oddity of our situation seemed more complicated than was warranted since none of you were likely to ever meet her."

"Where did *you* meet her?" Brogan asked. "She sounds like she's from South London, but you talk like you've had a fine upbringing."

"She *is* from South London. I didn't have a fine upbringing, but I taught myself to sound like I did so my patients would trust me."

"How long have you and Gemma been married?" Stone asked.

"Three and a half years," Barnabus said.

The confusion that immediately filled their faces reminded him, once again, of how strange his marriage truly was. Gemma had been gone for so long that he'd managed to convince himself it was what she wanted. *She* had left, after all. *She* had taken up the life of a vagabond, telling him she'd not care to return until he fell madly in love with her. He liked her and cared about her, but he'd never been top-over-tail in love with anyone. That wasn't likely to change because of an ultimatum.

She wanted what he couldn't give. There was no getting past that.

Bodies of Light

being a Fictionalization of Reported and
Corroborated Mysterious Phenomena

by Dr. Barnabus Milligan, physician

Chapter One

In recent years, in the area of London near Belsize Park, a young physician by the name of Sefton Palmer established himself as a reliable man of medicine and an individual of inquisitive disposition. Dr. Palmer was trusted by his patients, well-thought-of by his colleagues, and, it seemed, destined for extraordinary things.

Though his practice tied him to his particular corner of the metropolis, he was not opposed to travel and, thus, one day found himself in the countryside of Ireland, visiting with others of his profession. A detailed discussion of various medical discoveries with one colleague in particular had lasted longer than either had anticipated, setting him behind his intended time to make the journey over the then-frozen bogland toward the home of another colleague who waited in anticipation of his arrival.

Dr. Palmer and his trusted horse began the journey on a late-January evening long after the going down of the sun.

Reader, please bear in mind that bogs freeze in winter—they are nearly as much water as soil—and such bogs are easily disturbed by the pounding of horses' hooves, even when the beast is kept to a sedate pace. Failure to remember these well-established truths will render the following narrative perplexing in the extreme.

Dr. Palmer undertook his traversal of the boggy countryside with an eye to efficiency, not wishing to arrive at the home of his fellow physician at too late an hour. Thus, he set his horse to a quick clip, not as mindful as he ought to be of the dangers of a dark country lane with which one is not familiar.

The oddest of sounds reached his ears. He slowed his horse, to which the animal did not seem to object. In the dark stillness, he listened. Pops. And snaps. After a moment, he realized what he was hearing: the ice in the bogs was cracking. While he intended to remain on the road, it was easy to grow lost on a dark night, something he ought to have considered sooner. And growing lost in the bogland came with a risk of being plunged into a boghole or finding himself unknowingly riding into a lake and drowning.

As if to add to his sudden realization of the precarious nature of his situation, a thick fog began rolling over the land. The already dim landscape grew dark as ink. The cracking of ice grew louder and more frequent. He grew increasingly frustrated. And increasingly concerned.

"Slow and careful." He offered the instructions as much to himself as to his horse.

What little calm he'd managed to acquire disappeared as a sudden explosion of reddish-white light shot toward the sky. Followed by another. And another. Immense cones of fire appeared all around him. Their size and magnitude varied greatly. Some were six feet in diameter at the base, others five times that size. Their heights differed every bit as much—some no more than the height of a man, others reaching thirty feet into the air.

Two dozen, perhaps more, appeared and disappeared at unpredictable intervals and at vastly different distances. Some must have been at least a mile away. Even as he carefully led his horse onward, the cones of flame continued to appear and extinguish.

The effect was dazzling, shocking, and yet these columns of fire made little impact on the darkness, the light they produced being disproportional to their size. Neither did these pillars of fire add warmth to the frigid night. Dr. Palmer eyed them all with growing confusion and increasing interest. Though the blazes flickered without warning all over the landscape, each individual column stayed in place while it was visible, never wavering from its position.

What were they? What had caused them?

Rain began to fall, and with it, the columns of fire disappeared into the mysterious night.

The icy bogs continued to crack. But no more towers of fire appeared.

In three-quarters of an hour more, he found himself at the home of his colleague. Despite the shocking oddity of all he had seen, Dr. Palmer no longer felt upended nor worried.

His was, after all, a mind more predisposed to curiosity than to concern.

"Palmer," he was greeted, "I had nearly given you up."

"I left after my time." He set his hat on a hook near the door and pulled off his dripping wet coat. "The journey itself took longer than anticipated due to a most extraordinary experience."

He was forthwith shown to a bedchamber where he could change from his damp clothing. Though the hour was terribly late, his interest in all he'd seen proved greater than his exhaustion. While his fellow physician most certainly longed to seek his own bed, Dr. Sefton Palmer thought not of that possibility. A mystery weighed on his mind, and his mind never permitted itself to be ignored.

"Have you ever, whilst traversing the bogs, experienced anything odd?" Palmer asked his colleague.

"Odd in what way?"

Palmer proceeded to describe what he'd seen in as much detail as he could. Only after expending tremendous energy on the endeavor did he realize that his account might not be believed, that his colleague might deem him confused or even mad.

"Strange things are spoken of on the bogs," the other doctor acknowledged. "Though I cannot say I've heard tell of precisely what you describe, I would not dismiss the encounter out of hand. 'There are more things in heaven and earth, than are dreamt of in your philosophy.'" Ending his reply with a nod to the Bard was quite common for Palmer's colleague. He himself, though, was not so poetic.

"I know what I saw, but I do not know how or from

whence it came," Dr. Palmer said. "Neither do I know in what other forms it might occur. But, mark my words, good sir. I will solve the mystery of these sudden bursts of light even if I am required to dedicate the remainder of my life to doing so."

Such declarations should not be made lightly, for they have a most disconcerting tendency to come true in surprising and far too often destructive ways.

CHAPTER 4

Though Barnabus and Brogan were meant to be spearheading the efforts of CALL, they quickly realized, upon arriving at the location of the fire, there was not much for them to do. Family members of the Dread Penny Society had joined the cause and sorted the effort quickly. Kumar's wife was remarkably good at assigning tasks for maximum efficiency. Móirín Donnelly, Brogan's sister, kept a weather eye out for trouble. Hers was a good heart, but she was also a force to be reckoned with.

Hollis Darby's newlywed wife, Ana, was there, assisting in the efforts. All the DPS knew that she was secretly London's most capable sneak thief despite her outward appearance of a sweet and quiet society lady.

Elizabeth Black was participating, though anyone noticing her there would assume she had come as Fletcher's guest; their nuptials had finally been announced, and the two would be married in a few weeks.

All the participants were curious as to who Gemma was. Again and again, Barnabus gave the same answers to the same questions. She was his wife. No, she hadn't been around the place. Her long absence came about because she enjoyed moving around and didn't stay in one place for long. It must've been acceptable; Gemma never offered more details or corrected the ones he offered.

She dove eagerly into the day's efforts, making friends easily and conversing comfortably with newly met people. It was, no doubt, a skill that had served her well during her frequent wanderings. Barnabus hadn't the same knack for it. His early years had been spent in almost complete solitude.

His mother had been snatched by a pair of macks upon arriving in London when she was a young woman. With no one to save her and no means of escape, she'd lived her life tied to a brothel, held prisoner by a ruthless madam.

Barnabus had been born there and grown up there, seeing and hiding from things no child should ever encounter. His only escape had been wandering the streets for hours on end, sometimes digging bottles out of the mud of the Thames to sell for ha'pennies. But a child alone on the streets was hardly safe. By the age of five, he'd witnessed his first murder. By eight, he'd stopped being surprised by any of it. By twelve, he'd decided he meant to do something to change it all.

The CALL had borrowed carts to use for the day's efforts. The items they'd brought to offer the locals were set out. They had bread and produce. Someone had obtained second-hand stockings and gloves in decent shape. Barnabus knew a few other charitable-minded doctors who shared his desire to help the less fortunate, though perhaps without his zeal for it. They had contributed some medicine and supplies.

Barnabus's eyes briefly met Stone's and Fletcher's. They

meant to do a little snooping about while the charitable distribution provided them with cover. Barnabus didn't mind being left out of the search. He liked solving mysteries, and he liked helping people. But he got far more satisfaction out of *doing* things that addressed those problems rather than rooting out all of the reasons for them.

Fitzgerald Parkington, a member of the Metropolitan Police and an invaluable source of information for the DPS, stepped up beside Barnabus.

The man was hard as steel and good as gold, a rare combination. And, though he hadn't been told the entirety of the DPS's activities or identities, he knew more than nearly anyone else outside the organization.

Fletcher had even suggested he try his hand at writing penny dreadfuls. He had tales enough to tell, no doubt. And they'd heard him spin any number of good ones during the time they'd been working with him. If he would finally set pen to paper, they could let him in to the Dread Penny Society and stop keeping so many secrets from him.

For a time, Barnabus had thought Parkington might be the mysterious Dread Master. But Parkington, while willing to bend the rules when absolutely necessary, would balk at breaking them entirely, which the DPS did regularly.

"Fine thing the lot of you are doing," Parkington said. "A bit of a departure from the usual snooping, though."

"An author can't ever stop learning all he can about people and the world," Barnabus said. "And if that learning helps people in trouble, so much the better."

Parkington seemed doubtful that was the full truth, but

let it pass. "Brogan pointed out Mrs. Milligan to me." He narrowed his eyes on Barnabus. "She's a beauty."

"Yes, she is."

"Everyone says she ain't been around before, but she seems familiar." Parkington scratched the back of his neck. "I can't place her, though."

Barnabus's heart dropped to his shoes. Gemma's family were criminals, back generations, and she herself had been part of their criminal efforts, though not by choice. She was hiding as much from the law as she was from the Kincaids.

And he'd brought her face-to-face with an enforcer of that law.

Móirín and Gemma approached in the very next instant. Móirín's expression was her usual pointed perusal of everyone and everything. Gemma wore a look of mischief.

Parkington was studying her already. It'd only be a matter of time before he pieced it together. Barnabus's best course of action at the moment was to behave as if nothing was amiss.

"Why do I get the impression I might be in trouble?" Barnabus kept his tone light, looking from one woman to the other and back again.

"Because you are," Móirín said. "You've kept Gemma a secret from me. I'm not overly pleased about that."

With a barely suppressed smile, Gemma said, "I ain't best pleased either. Móirín and I could've been chums all this time, Baz."

Móirín hooked an eyebrow upward. "*Baz*?"

"Can't say I've heard you called that before," Parkington said with a chuckle.

Móirín eyed the policeman. "Don't you have some poor, unsuspecting soul to arrest, Parky?"

He tipped his hat. "I'm off duty, Miss Móirín."

"How fortunate for us," she said dryly.

Gemma didn't seem to be paying the least heed to the bickering but was watching Barnabus. Voice lowered and eyes worried, she asked, "Would you rather I not call you Baz when others are listening?"

He offered what he hoped was a reassuring smile. "It doesn't upset me."

Gemma threaded her arm through his. "I'm pleased as plums to hear you say that." She smiled at him, her dimples appearing, but then almost immediately assumed an overly dramatic look of displeasure. "I forgot. We's boiling mad at you." She pulled her arm free and assumed a combative posture that no one would have believed was truly aggressive.

Oh, how she lightened every situation. He'd missed that during the years she'd been away.

"You've not only denied me a friend, Dr. *Baz*," Móirín said, "but I've discovered Gemma is quite adept at giving Brogan a spot of difficulty, which is something for which I've needed a partner these ages."

"There are plenty of us that do that on the regular," Barnabus said.

"None of you do it well," Móirín replied with her familiar dry humor.

It made sense to Barnabus that she and Gemma had become fast friends. Gemma hailed from Southwark, an area of Town where being hardened and fierce was the only way a person survived. Furthermore, she'd grown up a Kincaid.

How she'd managed to escape from that heritage with any degree of tenderness remaining, he didn't know.

And everyone knew Móirín was always armed and formidable to the point that even the most violent roughs would be hard-pressed to match her fearsomeness.

To Gemma, Móirín said, "Are you at Doc's now to stay? It'd be good to know where to go when I invite m'self to supper."

Gemma glanced at Barnabus. "I ain't certain."

Móirín looked to him, clearly thinking he knew the answer.

"Your guess is as good as mine," he said. "Gemma comes and goes as she pleases."

Gemma smiled, but there was something strange in it. Something almost like hurt. Did she think he was poking fun at her? He wasn't. He'd offered that explanation all day to anyone who asked. It was easier than explaining that she'd left because their marriage simply wasn't working, that he wasn't what she wanted and didn't know if he'd ever be, that she preferred living in poverty in Wandsworth to living with him.

"Well, you're welcome to call on me whenever you'd like, no matter where it is you're calling home," Móirín said. "And that 'tisn't an offer I make lightly."

Gemma looked at him, and Barnabus nodded. "If Móirín's inviting you, that's a fine commentary on how highly she thinks of you."

That seemed to please Gemma to her very bones. With a broad, dimpled smile, she slipped over next to Kumar's wife and assisted in handing out handfuls of vegetables.

Parkington, though he'd moved a few steps away, was likely still aware of everything that was happening around him.

Móirín eyed Barnabus with a look that indicated she had

seen right through him to the things he didn't care for anyone to see. Barnabus didn't have time for her soul searching. He needed her help.

Turning away from Parkington, he whispered, "Do what you can to keep a distance between Gemma and our resident policeman, would you?"

"Jealous, are you?" Móirín whispered as well.

Barnabus shook his head. "That isn't at all the reason for my concern."

In an instant, understanding filled Móirín's expression. "Seems there's a great many things you've not told us."

"Not everything's mine to tell."

"Yet even those things that are, you keep tucked away. I'm fearfully good at digging, Doc." She was sharp, this intimidating Irishwoman.

"Watch over Gemma. That's all I'm asking."

"Aye. I'll not let anything happen to her." Móirín stepped away and rejoined Gemma, who was gabbing with Kumar and McCallister and their wives.

Parkington kept a keen eye on everyone. He wasn't the sort to make a person feel uneasy under his scrutinizing gaze—unless, of course, one had reason to be.

And Gemma, though only Barnabus was fully aware of it, had more than ample reason.

Not even a quarter hour had passed when Fletcher caught Barnabus's eye and motioned him to join him and Stone.

"We didn't find anything helpful in the rubble." With finesse born of experience, Fletcher managed to look as if they were having an insignificant conversation rather than a report regarding a clandestine search. "Gabbing with the people hereabout, it seems there were whispers that the couple who worked here and lived above the shop had been afraid on account of a letter they received."

That sounded worryingly familiar. "Brogan's wife received a great many unsettling letters before the fire that destroyed her home and business. The one set by the Mastiff."

"I suspect that ain't a coincidence," Stone said.

Fletcher nodded. "Blackmail and arson are among the Mastiff's specialties. I'd wager these people was being warned to do something or keep quiet about something, and they didn't heed it."

Barnabus took a moment to look around the area. He was somewhat familiar with it. "There's a coach stop not far from here."

He spent a lot of time near various coach stops and train stations. Young women often arrived in London by way of coaches and trains and were unexpectedly swept off by macks and madams before they even had a chance to piece together what was happening. His mother had fallen into that trap, which was why he did all he could to prevent others from living the life she subsequently had.

"The Mastiff's network regularly snatches women and girls from those coaches. It's possible the letters this poor couple received were meant to strong-arm them into aiding and abetting those efforts," Barnabus said.

"Or," Fletcher said, "they saw something and were being warned to keep mum about it."

Stone retained his usual expression of silent contemplation. He had a keen mind for solving puzzles but managed it without talking through the pieces. He sorted situations and decided on a course of action without discussion. Just as the Dread Master would.

"Did that energetic wife of yours have any insights about the reasons for resurrecting a badly burnt body?" Fletcher asked.

"She said a resurrection man plies his trade only if there's profit in it, be that money or favors. Usually money."

"So someone slapped down a bit o' brass or winked off a debt for whoever did the digging? Something of that sort?" Fletcher asked.

Barnabus nodded. "And she said it wasn't only the medical schools that paid money for bodies, which is why one that couldn't be used for teaching or examining could still have value."

Stone's gaze returned to the ashen rubble of the burned building. "Could be whatever made the poor souls valuable after death is the same thing that got 'em killed to begin with."

It was a direction, which was more than they'd had even a few days earlier.

"Piece it together," Fletcher said, "and we might happen on a few clues to the Mastiff's network."

"Assuming he is, in fact, behind this," Barnabus said. "He's not the only coldhearted murderer in London."

"Do you suppose we'll have more answers after all this?" Fletcher asked. "Or simply more questions?"

If Barnabus had learned one thing in life, it was that no matter how many answers he found, there were always more questions. Always.

CHAPTER 5

Hope was a terrible tease.

Gemma had felt it creeping about, whispering promises she wasn't certain it could keep. And, yet, she let herself believe the assurances that fickle friend dangled before her: that she was home and wanted and that everything would be different this time.

She and Baz had not wed out of love or attachment. Marrying her had been another in Baz's long list of heroics. And yet he'd never treated her like some pitiful, helpless waif. He'd shown her kindness and respect. He'd held her when she was sorrowful or fearful. He'd even kissed her a few times, though nothing beyond a friendly salute. She'd not known him from Adam when they'd first crossed paths, and he'd've been hard-pressed to pick her out in a crowd for some time after. But he'd proven kind. More to the point, he'd proven *safe*. So few people did.

A few days after the charitable endeavor in Shoreditch, Fletcher Walker and Elizabeth Black dropped in to take supper with them. Gemma felt almost like a regular gentry mort, playing hostess to fine guests. Except Fletcher sounded as London as she did. No one hearing the two of them would've believed they were anything but riffraff.

Elizabeth hailed from outside London, the only child of a fine-feathered family and now the headmistress of a respectable school in London. Fletcher and Elizabeth seemed terribly mismatched. Unless one watched 'em together—then it became clear how perfect they were for each other.

"I'm sorry I ain't read any of your novels," Gemma said to Elizabeth. "I ain't illiterate, mind you. I simply haven't coin for books. I'd likely not be able to twig what they was about as it is."

Elizabeth didn't turn up her nose at that. "Thank the heavens we live in a time when there are offerings available for all tastes and preferences and incomes. Stories are such wonderful things."

"I keep telling her she ought to chuck her bonnet in the penny dreadful ring. I'd wager she'd be proper good at it." Fletcher tossed a wink to Elizabeth, who shook her head at the tease and smiled.

Some of the fine and fancy writers would likely be offended by the suggestion, but Elizabeth didn't seem to mind.

"Iffen you're itching to dance that jig," Gemma said, "you'd do well to spin tales of something other than medical mysteries and oddities. I understand there's a writer what has already made a name for himself in that category." She twitched her head in Baz's direction, though not the least subtly.

"There is, indeed," Baz said. "But he's rubbish at it."

At that, laughter rang out from all of them. Baz didn't

always let himself join in a jest, but the rare sound of his laughter was one of her favorite memories of him.

"Was Barnabus publishing his stories when you two first met?" Elizabeth asked. "I confess, I'm not certain when either began."

"I had dabbled a little," Baz said. "But I hadn't had the right push to take the full leap until—"

"Until Gemma gave you that push?" Fletcher asked.

Gemma wasn't certain about that. She *had* nudged him.

Barnabus nodded. "Every time I told her that I was certain the story I was writing wouldn't go anywhere, she said I wouldn't know until I tried, that new things were always the most daunting before they were started, and that I oughtn't give up on myself. I don't know that anyone has ever expressed such faith in me."

Few things made Gemma blush, but hearing him speak so highly of her managed to put her to the glow. For most of her life, she weren't ever on the receiving end of kind words. It was little wonder she'd fallen so entirely in love with him, and further, why she held out hope that he'd learn to love her despite there being so little evidence of it.

"I, for one, am glad you chose to listen to her," Elizabeth said. "I've enjoyed your stories and feel I've learned from them. And your writing is the reason you know Fletcher, which is the reason I know you."

"You read his stories?" Gemma asked Elizabeth. She didn't think the Quality spent much time perusing the penny dreadfuls.

"I read a variety of things," Elizabeth said. "There is so

much to be learned and observed in life. It doesn't do to ignore chances to expand one's horizons."

Gemma moved a bit closer to Baz on the settee. "Do you remember when, not long after we were married, I heard some of your patients having a bit of a chinwag about dancing the waltz, and I didn't know what they were on about?"

He stroked his mustache, something he always used to do when befuddled. Did he not remember? That night had been magical. She thought back on it often, even now. How could it not've mattered as much to him?

She pushed ahead. Hoping. "You described the steps to me. I couldn't wrap my mind around it leftways or rightways. But you said it were likely one of them things a person learned by doing. You spent a whole heap o' time that night teaching me how to waltz."

"I do remember that." He nodded, seeming pleased at the memory.

Gemma leaned against him, slipping her arm through his the way she used to. "Dancing was the perfect escape from all our worries."

"Worries do—do seem to find us, don't they?" He hadn't tripped over his words nearly all evening. Why was he suddenly doing so again?

"Elizabeth made a try at teaching me to waltz," Fletcher said. "I proved about as good a dancer as an old mule."

That brought another round of laughter, followed by a few well-woven tales from Fletcher about bumbling his way through society gatherings. Through it all, Gemma kept her arm wrapped around Baz's. He didn't pull away, didn't look sour about it. He certainly didn't seem to dislike that she was snuggling up with him. They'd had a lot of nights like this during their first few months of marriage, when she'd felt at home with him and been so certain he was starting to feel for her what she was starting to feel for him.

Theirs had been an odd beginning, aye, but it weren't a bad foundation. Maybe she ought to've stayed longer, given him more time to see something in their future beyond what they had.

"One of Baz's patients brought some ginger biscuits today," Gemma said to the others. "It'd make a nice close to our evening."

Everyone agreed. Gemma slipped her arm free of Baz's and hurried toward the kitchen.

Mrs. Simms was at the house still, it being a day when patients knew they could drop in even late into the evening, but she'd said she didn't mean to leave the sitting room. So Gemma wasn't overly concerned about crossing paths with her. Every time the two of them came face-to-face, Gemma felt full sure the nurse was itching to tell her what she thought of her, and that what she thought didn't come anywhere near approval.

But Baz relied on Mrs. Simms. Gemma'd find a way to be in good mutton with the woman.

Gemma carefully unwrapped the paper from the ginger biscuits and set them right-tight on a platter. Her eye caught a few currant scones on the worktable. That'd elevate the offering. Though it'd be bang-up if she brought a bit of clotted cream and jam. Adding that meant bringing a few little plates and forks. So she added those to the growing heap.

Fortunately, she'd experience and plenty hefting odd and

often heavy loads. Still, she took care on her walk back toward the library, not wanting to overturn the platter.

She had not quite reached the open doorway when voices became clear from inside.

"I've not been able to sort out the connection between you two," Elizabeth said. "You care about her, and the two of you are obviously fond of each other, but I don't sense you are top-over-tail in love with her."

Gemma paused, unsure how Baz would answer. Explaining the whys of their marriage meant revealing much of her history.

"I am very fond of her," Baz said. "But ours isn't the ordinary sort of marriage, certainly not the kind that is celebrated in the *Times*: 'Dr. Barnabus Milligan of Finsbury wishes to announce his nuptials to the future Mrs. Gemma Milligan of Southwark in a ceremony performed in secretive haste inside a shabby chapel in Haggerston.'"

"You must've been more than fond of her to've married her," Fletcher said. "Or there's bits to this you ain't telling us."

Those "bits" involved her family and their chosen profession—something she'd rather these newfound friends not know.

"That history is not mine to tell in its entirety," Baz said. "But it can be summarized more or less as she was in a tough spot, and there wasn't anyone else willing to help her."

There wasn't anyone else willing to help her. Those words pierced Gemma's heart. She'd always acknowledged that Baz marrying her had been an act of heroism, but somehow hearing from his own lips that there'd been nothing else to the decision, no attraction or affection or tenderness, cut deeply.

"Marrying someone is taking 'helping' to an entirely new level," Elizabeth said. "Her difficulties must have been enormous to take such a drastic step."

"Believe me," he said, "had there been a less-drastic solution, I would have taken it."

It was the closest Gemma had ever heard Baz come to saying he regretted marrying her. She'd known he wasn't drowning in love for her, had known the desperate nature of her circumstances had pushed the matter forward quickly. But his explanation—that he'd been helping her because no one else would—held a painful note of pity and a hint of not having had a choice.

She'd come to love him all those years ago. She had always, in her heart of hearts, believed he felt the same but was simply struggling to say so.

But he hadn't. He'd pitied her when seeing that no one else was willing to do a blasted thing for her. He'd rescued her, but he hadn't loved her. How easily she'd let herself believe, when his letter had arrived, that he'd had a change of heart. She was thick as Tewksbury mustard, she was.

She needed time to sort this out. But simply disappearing when they'd guests to gab with would only make things worse. She pasted a smile on her face and stepped into the room, recognizing with a drop of her heart that she'd done this before. In the last few weeks she'd lived in this house before, she'd called on every acting skill she had, every ounce of endurance, every talent for pushing away heartache and fear and worry, and had gone about each day pretending she wasn't dying inside of a broken heart.

She very much feared Baz was about to break it again.

CHAPTER 6

Fletcher and Elizabeth didn't stay too late, which was fortunate for Gemma, who was struggling to keep up her cheery facade.

"You did a fine job as hostess," Barnabus said to her as he closed the door behind their guests. "I know you haven't done it often."

"I'm a quick study."

He gave her a little smile. "Perhaps we might have others over for an evening while you're still here."

While you're still here. He had no expectation that she'd stay for good.

That realization sat heavy on her mind and heart as she followed him from room to room, helping blow out candles and various flames. In the end, they had but one lit candle on a brass candlestick. He carried it as they walked up the stairs, lighting the way to Gemma's room.

He stepped inside with her, though not more than a couple of strides. Using his candle, he lit the lantern on the nearest table, lighting the space enough for her to prepare for bed.

"You are very quiet," he said, hovering in the doorway. "Is something amiss?"

"I've something spinning about in my mind, is all."

He set his candle beside the lantern, quite as if he meant to stay. "What are you pondering?"

She sat on the edge of her bed, studying him and debating whether or not to answer with the full truth.

"If it's something I can help you with, I'd like to," he said. "Or if it's just something you need to talk through, I'm good at listening."

He was, she had to admit. And, yet, on this topic she wasn't certain a "good listener" was what she needed.

"I'm in earnest, Gemma," he pressed. "What's weighing on you?"

She could tiptoe toward her question, she supposed, get a little insight without having to make too many confessions. "Are you happy I've come back?"

"Of course I am." There was no hesitation, no indication he was being insincere. "You brighten the house, Gemma. You make me smile, which I'll admit I don't do as often as I likely should. This house can be very lonely at times, but it hasn't been since you came back."

"Doesn't Mrs. Simms keep you company?"

He sat on the bed beside her. "She's not here always. And even when she is, it's not the same."

She liked that answer. "Then, would you mind terribly if I stayed for a time?"

"You've always been free to come and go as you'd like."

For one who'd not had the least bit of freedom in the houses where she'd grown up, she appreciated the sentiment.

But it still weren't what she wanted to hear from him. He'd married her because he couldn't think of any other way to help her. And he'd helped her because there weren't no one else who would. That he didn't wish her to Hades ought to've been a relief.

It wasn't.

"I've been hawking flowers in Wandsworth to keep coin in my pocket and my landlady from tossing me out on my ear. But I ain't living in that area now, and I don't have enough connections in Finsbury or anywhere nearby to find myself a new position."

If she were staying for good, she might've asked to be trained to help *him* in his work. But he didn't mean for her to lay her head there permanently. And she'd been in earnest three years earlier when she'd said she couldn't bear to stay if her love for him was truly one-sided. She couldn't put herself through such torture again. The situation hadn't changed, no matter that he'd written to her asking her to return. She needed to be moving along. But setting up somewhere else required coin, and she didn't have any.

"Is there anything in particular you're hoping to do?" he asked.

"I'll do any work that's respectable, provided it ain't in Southwark. I'd rather not cross paths with any of my family."

"That is understandable." He set his hand on hers. "Móirín Donnelly and Stone both work all over London. They've likely heard of openings."

"A good idea, that." She wove her fingers through his, allowing herself to enjoy the touch despite knowing it weren't being offered romantically. *Thick as Tewksbury mustard.* "I can drop in on Móirín and see what she knows."

"The two of you seemed to enjoy harassing me at the CALL effort."

Gemma bumped his shoulder with hers. "You're terrible fun to tease, Baz. When I lived here before, if you got proper flustered, your East End side would tiptoe out a bit."

The tiniest smile tugged at his lips. "It did?"

She nodded. "I enjoyed hearing it. Felt like getting a peek at you back before I knew you."

"I told you about my life before we met."

She squeezed his fingers. "I know, and it meant heaps to me that you trusted me enough to share it. I easily twigged you don't usually talk about your past."

"I thought you could understand the heaviness of having a difficult childhood."

"It's a crushing weight at times, i'n'it?"

He patted her hand. "The danger's behind you now. I'm grateful for that."

"So am I."

Baz rose and took up his candle. "If Móirín doesn't have a job idea for you, let me know. I'll send word to Stone. He'll know of something."

With that, he stepped out.

Her Baz could be so tender and sweet. But, oh, how easily he broke her heart. She could stay in this house where she'd been happy, but would staying make things better or worse? Ought she try to deepen the connection between them as she had during the last months she'd lived there? Or would she be wiser to find satisfaction in the simple friendship he offered?

Sometimes life's questions didn't have any good or easy answers.

Gemma rose long before the sun decided to make an appearance the next morning. She'd not been an early riser until after she'd married Baz. The Kincaid family trade was plied at night. But she'd not had to do that for years, and she'd found she liked watching the sun rise.

Watching it from the house where she'd first felt safe and welcome did her heart a world of good.

"Hearts are weak things, girl." She heard her father's voice return to her mind from across the years. "Best silence yours before it lands you in a heap of trouble."

It hadn't been a bit of fatherly advice, nor even a well-meaning warning. It'd been a threat and nothing else. She'd been ten years old and had sobbed when she'd heard they'd been hired to rob the grave of a neighbor she'd been fond of. Had she not dried her tears and moved forward with him, her father would've exacted his revenge on her. He always did.

She'd hated growing up as a resurrectionist's daughter. They'd barely stayed a step ahead of the law. Her father and uncles used threats and violence to silence anyone they thought needed it. She'd had only one friend in all of Southwark, but Gemma'd pulled away, not wanting her friend to be tainted by association with the Kincaids.

She'd been lonely.

She still was.

But she had a place to live for a time. She'd have money once she found a job, and with that money, she could move on again. London was overflowing with options if a person weren't too picky. There were enough houses and buildings that were all but falling over, held up by grumbled prayers and long wooden planks leaning across alleyways. Plenty of people with nowhere else to go hunkered down there, guarding what little they had with a wary eye. No one ever slept well in those half-fallen hovels, but it were better than nothing. Gemma could toss herself into one of those if need be. She'd done it before.

She knew of one in South London, not far from where she grew up, that only one other person beside herself knew about. If it came time to leave Baz's home before she'd another option, she could lug herself there.

She stepped up to the door of the humble flat the Donnellys called home at what she hoped was a reasonable hour. The jaunt from Finsbury to Piccadilly had taken some time, as she'd wound her way a bit, lengthening the journey.

Brogan answered her knock, looking awake enough for her peace of mind but more than a little confused. "Gemma? What brings you here this early?"

Perhaps she ought to have wandered a bit more. "I've come looking for Móirín."

"She's only been awake a quarter-hour at most. She'll not be down for a spell."

She felt about as awkward as a chicken in a ballroom. She *was* too early. "I'm happy to wait for her."

Brogan motioned her inside. He looked curious, but he

asked no questions. "Make yourself at home, Gemma." He indicated a small sitting room. "Sit wherever you'd like."

She chose an upholstered chair, while he sat on the arm of the sofa, studying her a bit.

"I can see you's dying of curiosity," she said. "I ain't one for sitting about long without something to do. I don't have a job, and I need one."

"And you're needing one before the roosters've even yawned themselves awake?"

She didn't know how long the Donnellys had been in London, but there was no mistaking they were from Ireland. It flavored every word they said.

"I ain't one for squandering even an hour."

Brogan laughed. "You mean on useless things like sleep?"

"Devilish waste of time. I avoid it whenever possible."

His smile didn't waver. "We're happy to have you here, no matter the hour."

Though she felt relieved at that, he'd not yet consulted the others in this house. Gemma wasn't worried about Móirín, but she hadn't the first idea about Brogan's wife.

"I know you're married," she said. "Give your missus my solemn word that I'll not make a habit of being here at this hour. I know well enough how to not make myself a burden on a household." Nothing had kept her safer over the years than proving herself both useful and unobtrusive.

"She'll likely be joining us in another moment. She heard you knock at the door just as I did. She simply doesn't move very quickly."

Gemma nodded. "I'd like to meet her. Everyone at the charitable event spoke highly of her."

"'Tis an easy thing to do," Brogan said with unmistakable fondness in his voice. "She's a wonderful person." He lowered his voice. "So you're not caught unawares—there was a fire at the shop where she worked, and while she wasn't caught in it, she was hurt by it. She moves with a great deal of difficulty and is still healing in a lot of ways. You'll not miss the stiffness of her movements or the way she winces now and then. I've found it helps to let people know 'tis nothing personal against them, simply the struggles of a person whose body is at war with itself."

That he loved his wife deeply was crystal clear. What would that be like?

Mere moments later, the sound of shuffling steps reached the sitting room. A woman slipped into the doorway. Gemma looked up and gasped in surprise at the sight that met her: Vera Sorokina.

THE BACHELOR AND THE BRIDE

by Mr. King

Installment II
in which our Hero learns much from our Heroine
of Things both odd and dangerous!

Sorcha and Duncan had long since left their village behind. The bag Granny Winter had provided them hung over Duncan's shoulder. Sorcha was not one to be left out of the difficult work of any undertaking and, therefore, carried another bag filled with food for their journey.

The two were not entirely unacquainted with each other, which made their arrangement more comfortable than it might have been otherwise. They'd spoken often at village gatherings when their paths crossed. Sorcha had burned her arm a few months earlier, and Duncan had tended to it. If she had to put a name to their connection, she would likely have attempted to think of a word somewhere between *acquaintances* and *friends*. What she would not have admitted, though, was that she deeply liked him.

He was a good man. Everyone who knew him felt that. But he was the respected and loved bachelor doctor in the area, and she was the odd, spinster woman who'd simply arrived one day and now lived deep in the woods in a cottage. The woman who was surrounded by whispers, who had passed the majority of her life without a home, without roots, and was now without family.

"How long will it take to reach Loch Dreva?" Duncan asked.

"We are likely to arrive on its shores this afternoon. The distance is not significant."

"And one truly cannot find the lake unless one already knows where it is?"

She nodded. "Everyone who knows its location has been brought there by someone who had previously been brought there by someone who had themselves been brought there by someone . . ." She motioned with her hand to indicate this was a pattern that repeated endlessly.

"Who, do you suppose, was the first to impart this knowledge?" He did not ask with mocking tones or dismissal but with genuine curiosity.

"No doubt a creature from the realm of fairies and monsters brought someone from the human realm there, and that person, in turn, brought someone else."

"And who was it that showed you?" he asked.

She did not always grow emotional when speaking of her family, but she found herself reluctant to answer on account of the lump forming in her throat. "My father."

Duncan must have sensed the emotion bubbling inside her. His expression filled with the same empathy and concern she had seen every time she'd watched him treat an injury or illness. "One never entirely recovers from the loss of one's parents." He spoke as one who knew.

She nodded, unable to add words to the sentiment. How sorrowful was her heart! How heavy were her reminiscences!

He managed to slip his sack from his back to his chest as they walked. He opened the bag, searching its contents. "I wonder what Granny Winter has provided us for this errand."

Sorcha had long since come to value the endless wisdom of the woman who had taken her in, but she was no closer to comprehending the enormity of it.

"I see a pair of soft leather shoes and a small stone butter crock. Odd items to be sure." He pulled from the bag a taxidermied vole. "This was certainly not expected." He set it back in the bag.

"Is that all?" she asked.

He shook his head. "There also appears to be a pair of spurs and a bottle of some sort."

Sorcha hadn't the first idea why Granny Winter had chosen those particular items, but Granny Winter seldom explained herself.

"There does not seem to be a single item in here that might aid in our defense," Duncan said.

"Seldom can the creatures that inhabit the realm of fairies and monsters be defeated by the clash of arms. Most are overcome through cleverness and an understanding of the laws that govern them."

Duncan peered inside his bag once more. "I cannot imagine a stuffed vole proving useful in a battle of wits."

"Somehow, it will," she said. "Granny Winter is as clever

as the fairies. I would wager that even the strangest things in that bag will prove absolutely vital."

"Even the vole?" Duncan asked with a raise of his eyebrows and a tip of his mouth.

She smiled in return; she couldn't help herself. She was often reserved, struggling to show lightness even in pleasant moments. He brought that out in her, miracle worker that he was.

As they continued on their journey, the land around them grew more untamed, more untouched. The trees grew taller. The thistles grew thicker. On and on they walked. Closer and closer they came to the first of many dangers such a journey must hold. Oh, courage! Oh, selflessness!

"Where did you live before you came to our village?" Sorcha asked as they walked along the edge of a crystalline river.

"I lived in a village in the north of England, not terribly far from the border country."

"Do you miss it?" she asked.

"A little. My family is no longer there, and they were the strongest tie I had to it."

Had her family a proper home, a place that was theirs permanently, that is where she would have felt a pull as well. As it was, she felt them everywhere and nowhere all at once.

"My family traveled a great deal," she said. "We spent most of our time in places like this." She motioned to the surrounding vista. "There were times when I would wonder if we were the only humans to have ever seen what we saw or heard what we heard. I grew up more acquainted with fairies than with children, more with monsters than with people."

"Were you scared?" he asked.

"Sometimes. My family taught me of their ways and kept me safe. Until the end, at least."

He glanced at her but didn't press. She suspected that he, good man that he was, meant to save her from the misery of recounting such a difficult moment in her life. But she was made of stronger stuff.

"I was fourteen years old. My family, in our travels, found ourselves at a crossroads. Those are dangerous places, you must realize. For while *we* might see only the meeting of two roads, crossroads are where the human world and the fairy world often meet as well. And not every creature that emerges into *our* sphere does so with good intentions."

"Was that the case on that day?"

She nodded. "We were intending to pass the night in a small, nearby cottage and regain our strength. We had only just come to the crossroads when an enormous dog appeared. It had the look of a wolf but the size of a calf. When the light hit it in precisely the right way, we could see something even more extraordinary about this canine. It glowed an otherworldly green.

"My father shouted to all of us to run, that we must reach the cottage as quickly as possible. We immediately obeyed and ran as hard as we could toward the shelter in the distance. One piercing, terrifying howl called after us. The sound filled me with terror like I had never felt before. I ran faster, more desperately. My family did the same.

"Another howl pierced the evening air. I didn't know

this creature well, but the sound of its horrifying cries told me in ways words could not that it was to be feared and for good reason. The terror I felt nearly stopped me in my tracks, nearly froze me to the spot. I sensed that one more howl would literally stop my heart.

"The time was approaching when it must, with surety, howl once more. I reached the cottage, threw open the door, and tumbled inside. In the very next instant, that third howl sounded. I huddled in the corner with my back against a wall, shaking, terrified for my very life."

"And your family?" he asked gently.

"I emerged the next morning after the light shining through the windows of the cottage revealed that I was in the home alone. I searched for my family but found nothing of them beyond my father's hat. For days, I wandered those roads, hoping to find my family but terrified I would only find that dog again. I kept at my search, going to places we had been before, all the while losing hope. It was nearly a year later when Granny Winter found me and took me in."

"You searched for a year?"

She nodded. "And I would be searching for them still if not for her. I told her all that had happened. She told me the creature we had encountered was the *cù-sìth*. It is, as I had suspected, from the realm of monsters. It hunts with howls. Humans who hear its terrifying cry but don't reach shelter under a protective roof by the time the third howl sounds . . . they die."

He took gentle hold of her hand and squeezed. It was a friendly and kind gesture. "I am so sorry for your loss."

"Granny Winter has spent these past years teaching me

of the dangerous difficulties my father hadn't time to explain to me. I suspect there is little of the fairies and monsters I do not now know. I have taken refuge in her cottage for a long time, afraid to return to the paths I once knew."

"Did this quest force you to do so before you were ready?" he asked.

She pondered his question. "I was ready, but I needed a reason to take that leap again."

"Well, I thank you for being willing. I could not bear the idea of losing Donella without having exhausted every resource I have. And I could not accomplish this journey on my own. Beyond not knowing the location of the loch, I know very little of what we might encounter while we are out here. My knowledge of fairies and creatures is limited to a vague understanding of will-o'-the-wisp and an even less-specific knowledge of hobgoblins."

"And I know very little of doctoring," Sorcha said.

"It's a fine thing for people to offer each other their expertise, is it not?"

His hand still held hers. He swung their arms between them. It was, perhaps, a childish gesture, but it lightened her heart and eased her mind.

"So, tell me," he requested, "have you any idea what we might encounter at Loch Dreva?"

Quick as that, her heart grew heavy.

"I know precisely what we will find. Though I understand why Granny Winter is sending you there, I was terrified to hear her speak the destination."

Her declaration did not appear to surprise him. "Is there a horrible monster at Loch Deva?"

"Not in the sense you are likely thinking. This particular creature has the appearance of a cantankerous old woman. She looks more human than monster."

"But she is not human?"

Sorcha shook her head. "She is the *Bean-Nighe*, the Washing Woman. She is often found at lakes and rivers, washing clothes."

"What is terrifying about washing clothes?"

"Her laundry is the death shrouds of people who are soon to die. And anyone who comes upon her is doomed to wear the shroud she is washing. Death will soon claim him or her."

"Granny Winter sent us to this bringer of death for answers?"

"The *Bean-Nighe*'s expertise is the realm of death. She knows the answers to many things about life, healing, death, fate. She will know how to cure Donella."

"How do I speak to her without seeing her?"

"There is a way," she said. "But it is difficult and dangerous."

"All the more reason for you to explain it to me. I need to be as prepared as possible to undertake whatever task is required of me."

His courage warmed her and impressed her. "The first thing to remember is that once you see her, you must not look away. If you do, the shroud will be yours. Further, if she sees you, the shroud will be yours. You must come up behind her, never looking away, making no noise that might give you away. You must snatch her up off the ground before she knows you are there.

"Once you've done this, you will have power to prevent her from declaring you the next to die. While you have her, she will ask you what you require of her to secure her release. Tell her you require that she answer three questions of your posing."

He nodded. "So if I manage to lift her off the ground without looking away from her, and without being seen by her, and, in response to her asking what my demands are for releasing her, I say she is to answer three questions of my posing, then I may ask her how I can cure Donella?"

Sorcha nodded once more. "She must answer all three of your questions, and you must be very careful how you ask them. The *Bean-Nighe* is very clever. She answers questions in unexpected ways, tricking her capturers into asking questions which will not give them the answers they seek."

He did not seem discouraged but also did not seem to be taking the task lightly.

"There is more," Sorcha said. "While you do have power over her and she *must* answer your questions, the laws of such interactions require you to answer three of her questions in return."

"This is quite an ask," he said, looking wary but just as determined as ever.

"Do you feel equal to it?" she asked. "For if you don't, I will undertake this in your place, though I will not necessarily know what to ask, especially if she proves as clever as legend says she is."

"Could we not help each other navigate her tricky questions?"

Sorcha shook her head. "Only one of us can approach her, else the other, having been seen by her, will die."

He took a deep breath. "Then it is something I must do alone."

"There is no other way."

"How am I to approach quietly? Even as we have been talking, I've been able to hear my own footsteps. I will not have the cover of conversation to hide the sound."

Immediately, the answer popped into her thoughts. "The soft leather shoes in Granny's sack."

The moment she said it, he seemed to understand the epiphany she'd had. It was precisely what was needed. His feet would be protected from the rocks and thorns and thistles, but his footfalls would be rendered much lighter and much quieter.

They talked over the difficulties and worked out a few strategies. They spoke of their worries and their hopes as they continued their journey toward Loch Dreva. Soon enough, Sorcha recognized the hill around which a path led to the loch where the *Bean-Nighe* could be found undertaking her gruesome washing.

Sorcha stopped. She could pass by the hill without making the turn and remain hidden from the Washing Woman, but Duncan needed to continue directly toward his fate.

"This is where we part, is it?" He looked to her for confirmation.

"If you follow this hill, you will see Loch Dreva—and the back of the Washing Woman."

He took a deep breath. "Do you mean to wait here for me?"

"I fully anticipate you returning, successful and ready to save your dear little patient. I will wait here for you to complete your mission."

"I suspect you have more faith in me than is actually warranted."

"So prove to me that it is warranted."

He raised her hand to his lips and pressed a kind and gentle kiss there. "I will return shortly."

With that, he slipped slowly out of sight.

In her mind, she could hear the howl of the *cù-sìth*, could feel the fear of sitting alone in the silence of the dark cottage, waiting for loved ones who would never return.

CHAPTER 7

Gemma was on her feet, feeling both confused and delighted. Brogan looked ready to jump to his wife's defense.

"It ain't what you seem to think, Brogan," Gemma said. "I'm gaping because I know Vera."

A smile spread across the woman's familiar face. "Gemma. I've not seen you in years. How are you?"

"Carrying on proper, i'n't I?"

Vera laughed lightly. "Are you, though?"

"Perhaps not full proper," Gemma answered, "but I'm staying out of trouble. I'd heard Brogan's wife's name was Vera, but not in a million years would I've twigged she was you. How'd a girl from South London and a man from Ireland meet each other?"

Brogan helped Vera sit on the sofa—a feat as difficult for her as he'd warned Gemma it'd be—and remained beside her.

"You'd already fled Southwark when my father and I sold our print shop there," Vera said. "We opened a finer one in Soho. Brogan earned a bit of boot at our shop for a time."

Brogan looked from Vera to Gemma and back repeatedly. "The two of you truly did grow up together?"

Vera nodded. "Her family were always on the move but kept to Southwark. Gemma and I crossed paths enough to become something like friends."

Something like friends. That was the long and short of it. Gemma's family had changed houses often, a step ahead of the blue-bottles and too slippery for loose lips to give away. Most everyone knew who the Kincaids were. That alone kept people at a distance.

And Vera's father had kept Vera tucked away and protected from everyone, so she'd not had friends either. That the two of them had managed to be "something like friends" was nearly miraculous.

"Where have you been all this time?" Vera asked.

Assuming as sunny and light an expression as she could, Gemma said, "I've moved about a lot, worked different jobs, lived in different parts of London."

"Married a doctor," Brogan added, dryly and with a twinkle in his eyes.

That brought Vera's wide-eyed look of shock to her husband. "Married a *what*?"

Brogan looked at Gemma. "Do you want to explain, or are you wanting me to?"

Gemma figured *she* ought to. If she told her own history, she could decide how it was painted. "I left South London to get married."

"You didn't tell me you was getting married."

Gemma rubbed the back of her neck. "We didn't invite

no one. Father didn't approve. Making him boiling weren't the best foot to start off on."

Vera nodded heavily. "We were all terrified of your father."

Gemma sighed. "I've heard whispers he's dead. Likely makes me a terrible person, but I'd rather he were under the ground than on it."

"If that makes you a terrible person, then I'm one too."

Brogan took Vera's hand, holding it gently but firmly.

Gemma pushed away the surge of longing she felt. Baz sometimes held her hand; he had the night before. She wanted that to mean something, but she weren't sure it ever would.

"So you and this doctor traveled a great deal?" Vera asked.

"Just me," Gemma said. "He ain't a wanderer."

"And you've come back to see him again?"

"For a spell."

"All this beating around the bush is driving me batty," Brogan said to Gemma. "She knows him. Might as well tell her flat-out who he is."

Again, Vera looked shocked and confused and curious.

Gemma didn't know why she was avoiding saying his name. She'd married someone who didn't love her. That wouldn't surprise anyone who'd ever known her. "He's Dr. Barnabus Milligan."

Vera looked as if she might fall over. "Doc?"

"The one and only," Brogan said with a slight chuckle. "Our bachelor doctor, who you and m'sister have been scheming to find a wife, had one all along. And, we discovered only now, you already know her."

Brogan might've found it entertaining, but Gemma didn't. Not at all.

"It is a small world at that, i'n'it?" Gemma hoped that would end the conversation, and she jumped quickly to a new one. "Would either of you object to me making breakfast for everyone? I suspect you ain't eaten yet, and gabbing with me is keeping you from doing so."

Though he narrowed his eyes on her for a moment, Brogan didn't push the matter. "That'd be kind of you."

Gemma slipped from the room and found the small kitchen. It was little more than a worktable, some shelves, and a fire. It was enough.

She pulled from the larder a few things and began piecing together a simple meal. Under other circumstances, she'd've been overjoyed to cross paths with Vera Sorokina again. Losing touch with her one friend had been a sorrowful thing.

But she'd have to make this reunion brief. She wouldn't impose on this household longer than she had to, and she'd leave them better than she'd found them. It was a life approach she'd embraced only after leaving her father's home. He certainly hadn't believed in that philosophy.

She had nearly finished preparing a humble soup while wandering through her own thoughts when Móirín stepped into the room.

"I've just had m'brother and m'sister-in-law spill a great many things into my ears," she said. "You're in need of a job, you know Vera from your years in South London, and you strong-armed m'brother into letting you make breakfast."

"Oi. That's the front and back of it." Gemma stirred the pot hanging over the fire.

"Well then, I'll begin with the easiest questions and make my way through the harder ones." She pulled over a chair, sat on it with her arms crossed, and began an interrogation Gemma knew was both serious and inescapable. "What are you making?"

"Cabbage soup."

Móirín nodded in approval. "Is there any type of work you'd prefer, or any area of town you're looking at?"

"Any work I can walk to from Baz's house without spending my entire day on the walking, and any job that'll earn me coins enough for finding a place of my own when the time comes."

"How long have you known Vera?" Móirín asked.

"We met when we were six or seven years old. We've had some semblance of a friendship since."

"But you didn't know she married my brother?"

"She had no idea I was married; I didn't know she were. I hadn't even heard about the fire, in fact," she said. Then something occurred to her. "Was her father caught in it?"

"Mr. Sorokin wasn't in the shop when it happened. Two urchins were working there for them, and Mr. Sorokin suspected there might be danger on the horizon, so he slipped them away. He's hiding them still. We don't see him anymore."

That was consistent with the man Gemma had known. He could be crotchety and off-putting and a bit paranoid, but he helped people in danger and in need. And he did so rather expertly. She felt full certain he was involved in a great many things he didn't admit to.

"I've one more question left," Móirín said. "Why is it you're already planning to leave Doc's house?"

The fact that everyone thought of it as his house, not *his and Gemma's* house ought to've answered that question.

"I ain't never been one to stay in one place long," Gemma said. "I'll get antsy again." That was just enough truth to ease some of her guilt in weaving such a Banbury tale.

Móirín didn't seem to fully believe her, but neither did she press the matter. "I know of places looking for cleaners. Sometimes 'tis backbreaking work, but 'tis reliable and safer than standing on a street corner hawking things."

"I know how to clean," Gemma said.

"I'll see what I can find."

"Thank you."

Móirín stood. "I hope you're planning to stay and eat some of that cabbage you're cooking up."

"I won't say no." Before Móirín could leave, Gemma posed a question of her own. "You said you don't see Mr. Sorokin anymore. Does Vera know where he is?"

Móirín shook her head. "No one knows. He's kept that a very close secret."

Gemma pondered that after Móirín left the kitchen. No one knew where Mr. Sorokin was. But Gemma suspected she did. He had, after all, hidden away another young person from a dangerous situation years ago in South London, the daughter of a resurrection man, whose life had been in danger. He'd tucked her away in an abandoned and dilapidated building no one knew of and no one could find without knowing what to look for.

She knew where it was, and she knew how to find it. And if she was right and he was there, she needed to find him. Because there was something she desperately needed him to do for her.

CHAPTER 8

"You're not fully yourself today, Doc." Mrs. Simms watched Barnabus with that stern-faced expression she so often wore. She cared about people but didn't always show it in the traditional ways.

"I have a few things on my mind." He sat at his desk in his sitting room.

"Like your wife, perhaps?" she asked with a pointed look as she folded bandages.

Gemma *was* on his mind, as a matter of fact. Something had been bothering her the night before, something other than needing a job. And though she'd slipped out early that morning, likely to go talk with Móirín about finding a position, he was certain she hadn't left permanently. But how long would it be before she did precisely that?

"Would it surprise you if I told you she is often on my mind, and not just this past week?"

Mrs. Simms gave a firm nod. "It would surprise me, but mostly because you've never said a word about her."

"It was complicated. It still is."

That didn't seem to satisfy her. "Nothing complicated about saying 'Mrs. Simms, I have a wife wandering about somewhere, and that's the reason I don't talk about things like getting married or courting anyone.' Would've been the easiest thing in the world."

She was right, of course. He'd avoided the topic because it was difficult to explain but also because, when he thought on it, he felt uneasy.

"I'm not the most tenderhearted of women," Mrs. Simms said, "but I don't like the idea of you being hurt."

She was forever discounting her own benevolence. "Caring about people is nothing to be ashamed of."

"Then why do you tuck your heart away as if you haven't one at all? Seems to me, you think it something worth feeling shame over."

Mrs. Simms continued folding bandages. Her criticism was not entirely unfounded. Leading with his heart had proven a poor choice in the past, making difficult decisions as a doctor impossible. It meant the pain of losing people was almost too sharp to bear. Keeping a clear head and his heart at a distance was far more advisable.

"Are you pleased to have Mrs. Milligan here?" Mrs. Simms asked, echoing the very question Gemma had posed the night before.

Why did either of them think he would be displeased? He couldn't imagine anyone who wouldn't enjoy Gemma's company.

"It is good to see her again," he said. "If nothing else, I don't worry about her while she's here."

"And is that the only reason you're glad she's staying at

the house for now?" Mrs. Simms never let a topic lie before she got the answers she wanted.

"I like Gemma. She brightens the house, and she makes me smile, which I appreciate."

Mrs. Simms made a sound of pondering but no further comment. They worked for a while without talking. They both tended toward companionable silence in conversation when it was just the two of them.

Into the midst of this pause, a boy of about twelve years old rushed inside. "There's a fire, Doc. Not too far off. Fletch told me to come get you."

Fletcher's network of street urchins was as efficient as they were invisible to the people who passed them every day.

To the urchin, Barnabus said, "Tell me exactly where the fire is while I scratch a note."

The boy did exactly that, and Barnabus wrote a quick line to leave for Gemma should she return before he did. He left it on his desk in the sitting room with instructions to Mrs. Simms to direct Gemma to it.

He pulled on his coat, popped his tall hat on his head, grabbed his cane—a sword concealed inside—and took up his doctoring bag. They were out the door and on their way with hardly any time having passed at all. Familiarity bred efficiency.

The fire was not difficult to find, the smoldering remnants of it, at least. The smoke still spilling from the charred remains of the shop could likely be seen by a good portion of London. A fruit monger stood beside his cart not far distant. Two men, laborers by their appearance, leaned against a wall across the street. A man and woman stood at the mouth of an alley. Another man, more finely dressed than the others, sat on a bench with a newspaper on his lap. All within a few feet of the ashy skeleton of a building.

Fletcher was nearby as well, watching the embers. Today, he was dressed in his lower-class attire, which allowed him to go unnoticed around these poorer corners of London. Fletcher was a chameleon in every sense of the word, and it served him well.

Barnabus reached him. "Did the fire brigade not arrive?"

"The locals were warned not to send for the fire brigade."

"Warned? You mean 'threatened'?"

Fletcher nodded slowly. The tension around his mouth belied his devil-may-care appearance.

"Any injuries?" Barnabus indicated his doctoring bag.

"The man what worked there."

"*Worked*? Past tense?"

Fletcher adjusted his hat while he pushed out a deep breath. "Whispers have it he might've been dead before the fire started."

The Mastiff, no doubt, was behind this latest trouble. "Any idea why this particular man might have been targeted?"

"He was an undertaker who'd been bragging about being able to identify the resurrectionists who've been digging up fire victims."

Barnabus looked at the blackened undertaker's shop. "The question, then, is who silenced him? The resurrectionists or the one paying them?"

"Don't matter in the end," Fletcher said. "The sour's coming from the same lemon."

Stone arrived beside them. He eyed the scene with weariness. "Another fire."

"I'd wager from the same source," Fletcher said.

Stone's expression remained pensive. His eyes remained sharp. "We oughta sniff around a bit. See if we can sort out which churchyard this poor fella gets buried in."

Fletcher looked to Barnabus. "Has Gemma ever mentioned whether resurrectionists dig up people as a matter of revenge?"

She had told him that her family had once been paid to dig up someone they knew, and it hadn't bothered her father or uncles one bit. Digging up someone they *didn't* like would probably be a thrill for them.

How could he answer Fletcher's question without giving away her actual connection to the resurrection trade? He'd been fortunate that, thus far, no one had pressed for further information on that front. Fletcher was sharp, though; he'd have it sorted if Barnabus offered too much more. If Barnabus's hypothesis about Stone was accurate, he might already know.

"She did say sometimes the payment for a grave-snatching is settling a debt," Barnabus said. "I imagine if they felt someone owed them a debt of honor—or *dishonor*, as the case might be—they wouldn't hesitate to settle it that way."

Fletcher looked to Stone. "Most of the churchyards in this area are full-up—don't take new burials. He'll be laid to rest farther afield. Let's sort out where."

Gemma likely knew the location of every churchyard in London. But he'd avoid asking her if possible. The topic wasn't a pleasant one for her, and he didn't like to see her hurting.

The man with the newspaper was no longer watching the smoking embers; he was watching *Barnabus*. Nothing in his expression looked threatening or fearful. He seemed to be puzzling something out.

That happened now and then. The reason was usually that he had been the person's doctor at some point, or the one studying him had been present when Barnabus had undertaken a rescue. As there was no anger in the man's expression, Barnabus felt confident the reason was the former.

Out of the corner of his eye, his attention was caught by the woman who'd been standing at the edge of the alleyway. She was alone now, and she looked anxious. He watched her, trying to ascertain if she was in some sort of trouble.

Stone seemed to notice the same thing. A ray of sunlight lit the woman's unwashed face. She looked so familiar. Where did he know her from? Was she someone he'd rescued before?

Under his breath, Stone said, "Familiar, ain't she?"

Barnabus nodded. "But I can't place her."

Her eyes met his, and she studied him too. Was he as confusingly familiar to her as she was to him? Quite without warning, her uncertainty turned to fear. She spun about and began to run.

"That's the woman the DPS has been looking for," Fletcher said. "Serena. The one being held by the Mastiff."

In a flash, Barnabus knew he was right. They rushed off in pursuit of Serena.

The DPS had first become aware of her plight months earlier. She was being forced to work for the Mastiff, held by threat of violence against herself and her two children. The Dreadfuls had not yet been able to rescue her from the grasp of the criminal mastermind, though they'd tried.

They followed her down the alley. She was quick, likely because she was afraid. But if they could just talk to her, they might be able to help her escape the Mastiff's clutches.

Serena disappeared behind the ruins of what had once been the back wall of the building. Stone and Fletcher followed her path. Barnabus cut through a gap in the wall. It was a risk, as the slightest bump could send scorched walls crumbling down. But he'd spent all his childhood slipping in and through dilapidated buildings—still did sometimes—and he felt certain this one would hold.

The shortcut set him beside Serena.

"Please," he said. "I'm here to help."

She stopped and turned to look at him. Barnabus had seen terror and despair in the eyes of many in this city, but seeing it heartrendingly bleak and bare in her gaunt face shook him. He'd grown too accustomed to the suffering that hung in the air of London; the reality of it seldom struck him with the force it did just then.

"No one can help," she whispered. "He's always watching. He'll know."

"I have safe places you could go," he said. "Away from his grasp."

She shook her head, walking away from him. "No one escapes him. Not anyone." Fear filled every word.

"We can help."

Her movements made jerky by panic, she backed herself into a wall. "I can't. He'll hurt my children." She felt her way to the next haphazard gap, not looking away from Barnabus, her expression both fearful and pleading.

Then she ducked into the darkness between barely standing walls and disappeared.

"Ah, fly me," Fletcher growled from behind Barnabus. "I thought for a moment you'd convinced her."

"The Mastiff has her too terrified to even try escaping," Barnabus said.

"I'd guess he's behind the fire too," Stone said. His gaze swept over the area, searching and studying.

Barnabus followed suit, but his eyes settled almost immediately on something that sent a chill down his spine.

With his cane, he pointed to the dilapidated wall. "I'd say the Mastiff is definitely involved."

Scrawled on the wall in what appeared to be ash was a horrifyingly familiar warning: The Tempest is coming.

Bodies of Light

being a Fictionalization of Reported and Corroborated Mysterious Phenomena

by Dr. Barnabus Milligan, physician

Chapter Two

The question of lights appearing without warning or explanation took root in Dr. Palmer's mind in the months that followed his shocking experience on the bogs in Ireland. He had formulated more theories than he had produced on that night, but he still had no definitive answers.

What he'd seen had not been a reflection. Though the lights had looked like fire, they were nothing of the sort. He had not eliminated the possibility of phosphorescence as was rumored to occur in marine life. He was also determined to learn more of any oddities peculiar to organic matter. He had heard of a very odd sort of lightning he meant to investigate. He had every intention of raising the question at the next meeting of the Royal Society.

Late of an afternoon, whilst his mind spun on the question of the reddish-white cones of fire-like light, Dr. Palmer was summoned to the bedside of one of his patients, a woman of heartbreakingly young years whose health was severely impacted by pulmonary consumption. Though he hoped to be proven wrong, he suspected she was approaching the end of her short earthly sojourn.

The door at Lavinia Abbott's home was answered by her ever-faithful maid, Jane. Dr. Palmer was shown to Miss Lavinia's bedchamber, where she had spent the entirety of the past three months unable to leave her bed, her condition deteriorating.

"I fear I'm not long for this world, Dr. Palmer."

He crossed to her bedside and sat on the edge. Death was part of doctoring every bit as much as life was. That did not, however, render the experience less heartbreaking.

"What has convinced you of your imminent departure?" he asked her.

"I was earlier today seized with a horrible suffocation. How I resumed breathing, I do not know. I fear the next time I will not be so fortunate."

Palmer evaluated her condition as she spoke and continued doing so in the silence that followed. Her pallor was significant. Her breathing was shallow and belabored. Her body had grown thin and frail.

"Are you in pain?" he asked, entirely willing to provide for her powders or tisanes to assure her comfort.

"Pains of mind," Miss Lavinia said. "I fear I shall suffer another suffocation and you will be far away. I'll not have you near to aid me."

He took her hand in his, careful of her paper-thin skin. "If you wish," he said, "I will remain here throughout the day and into the night to keep close watch on you."

She smiled weakly at him. "You are a good man and a good doctor."

"I try very hard to be." He did, indeed. The matter of unexplained lights had distracted him of late, but he was determined to focus his attention on his ailing patient.

He settled himself in the room, keeping watch over Miss Lavinia.

Jane brought her broth and made certain the bedside pitcher was well supplied with water. She cast sad eyes upon the woman she'd looked after for a half decade, clearly agreeing with Miss Lavinia's assessment of her own mortality.

Truth be told, Palmer agreed as well.

The remainder of the evening passed without incident. Miss Lavinia drifted into a light sleep not long after the sun dipped beneath the horizon. The lamp in the room was lit, casting a soft glow.

Dr. Palmer sat upon the edge of the bed once more as a cot was placed upon the floor. He meant to pass the night there, recognizing that the woman was fading. He'd only just checked the rhythm of her pulse and watched the rise and fall of her chest when the lamplight flashed bright and sudden upon her face, illuminating it in odd and unexpected ways.

"Jane, please move the lantern. Its light upon her face will wake her, and she needs as much rest as her body will allow."

From behind him, the maid replied, "The lantern ain't casting any light on her face, Doctor."

Palmer focused his powers of observation once more upon the countenance of his patient. Unmistakable light darted over her features. It flashed and danced, producing enough light to illuminate her head but cast no light upon the room in general.

He stood once more, taking a step back and observing the unexpected sight from more of a distance. He was not mistaken in what he saw. A silvery light, not unlike that seen when moonlight is reflected on water, danced upon her face. The curtains in the window were drawn, eliminating that possible source. The light rendered her skin so white one might believe it to have been covered in paint. Indeed, the skin took on a look of having been glazed. All the while, the mysterious light continued to dart about.

The learned and curious doctor spoke not a word, even as his heart pounded in anticipation and wonderment. There was no heat emanating from the light, nor did it shine beyond the precise location where it emerged.

Though the color was different, it put him immediately and fully in mind of the columns of fire-like light he had seen on the bogs months earlier. This time, though, the inexplicable phenomenon had made itself known on the face of a human being.

"This ain't the first time I've seen this happen, Dr. Palmer," Jane said.

"When have you seen it before?" he inquired.

"This morning," came the reply. "Miss Lavinia's face lit in just this way. I found it quite dazzling, I did."

"And did you tell anyone else what you'd seen?"

"Blimey, no. None of the other staff'd believe me, and Miss Lavinia would likely say I were being superstitious.

Fine folk are always assuming that about us lowly folk. But I won't never forget what I seen."

Palmer checked the position of the lantern once more, confirming to himself that it was, indeed, not in such a place as to be the source of the lights which continued to appear on Miss Lavinia's face. For an hour, the phenomenon continued before disappearing as suddenly as it had begun.

He stayed at Miss Lavinia Abbott's side for the remaining days of her life. The lights returned twice more, though he could determine neither cause nor source nor pattern for their rising and extinguishing. The evening before her passing, the lights returned for a final time, fainter than on the previous occasions and lasting a shorter interval.

Palmer had theorized the lights he'd seen on the bog were the result of the freezing and thawing of organic material. As Miss Lavinia lived out her remaining days, her condition deteriorated. Perhaps it was her deterioration that had caused the mysterious light to appear. Perhaps it was deterioration in the bogs that had done the same.

He would have answers. He vowed that he would. For, as much as the bog lights had sat upon his mind, this experience added weight tenfold.

People could glow. And he would not rest until he knew why.

CHAPTER 9

Mrs. Simms had left for the day by the time Barnabus reached his home. For three years, that would have meant returning to an empty, echoing house, but instead, he opened the door to the sound of Gemma happily singing "Fairlop Fair." Though his mind remained heavy with thoughts of fires and of resurrection men and of women trapped in horrible situations, her voice lightened his heart and eased some of that burden.

He hung up his hat and coat, leaned his cane against the wall, then crossed into the sitting room to put away his medical bag. Mrs. Simms had left the examination area pristine, as always. Until recently, he'd had two nurses working for him, alternating which days they were present. He was so stretched for time now, though, that he didn't see as many patients as before, and he couldn't justify a second nurse.

He hoped his most recent penny dreadful proved a success. He needed to increase his income somehow if he had any hope of keeping his safe houses operating.

"Baz, you're home!"

He turned toward the sound of Gemma's voice. She looked delighted to see him. He'd forgotten how nice that was to come home to. He'd not had it in years.

"You'll never twig what happened to me today." She bounced across the room to him. How could anyone not be buoyed by her joyfulness? "Móirín found me a job. It ain't terrible far from here, and it pays a nice lump of coin. And it ain't dangerous."

"That *is* good news." He held out his hand, and she took it without hesitation. "Where and what will you be doing?"

A bit of uncertainty entered her expression. "It ain't a four-liner job."

He squeezed her fingers. "If it's made you happy, that alone makes it important, no matter what others might say."

Her smile returned. "Few people hearing you would have the least suspicion you understand South London *and* East End talk."

He shrugged. "I am, essentially, multilingual."

She sat on the sofa, keeping hold of his hand so he sat beside her. "Are you ever tempted to return to your East End speaking?"

"Tempted? Not really. Though I do dream in East End speech."

"You do?"

He nodded. "I've not really thought about it before, but it makes sense; East End was in all the voices I heard growing up, other than my mother. She spoke like someone from the country. She never told me where, though." His heart grew heavy, as it often did when he thought of her. "I wish she had. There are so many things about her I never knew."

Gemma slipped her arm around his and leaned her head on his shoulder. "What *did* she tell you?"

He took a breath, not a strained one or a tense one but almost a cleansing one. Gemma had asked him about his mother before, and somehow talking with her about his sorrows was easier than with anyone else. She was a cheerful person and brought excitement and energy to any room, but she could also be peaceful and calming. "I think my most cherished memory of my mother is that she told me every day that she loved me."

"How could she not love you? I can't imagine anyone being a better son than you."

He slipped his arm free and wrapped it around her shoulder, tucking her up close to him. "You always did say rather flattering things about me."

"I don't merely say them, Baz. I *mean* them. That's an important difference."

"Oi. I always was your chuckaboo, weren't I?"

The breathtaking joy in her smile filled him. "I do love when you let your East End shine a bit. I know you think you've got to keep it tucked away, but it's part of who you were. And who you were is part of who you are, and you oughta be proud of the man you are."

He pressed a kiss to her forehead, something he'd done often in the past but not once since she'd returned. "I'll try to remember that, Gemma."

"I hope you do."

He leaned back on the sofa, his arm still around his wife, feeling more at ease than he had in some time. "I'm glad Móirín found you a job so quickly."

"So am I." She pulled in an excited breath. "Oh, and I met Brogan's wife."

"How is Vera?"

"She was in pain but also in good spirits." Gemma sat up straight and turned, facing him almost directly. "But, also, Baz, I know her!"

"You do?"

Her eyes lit with excitement. "She is from Southwark. We knew each other growing up."

"How remarkable! Were you friends?"

"As near as any Kincaid comes to having friends."

In an instant, he knew of a difficulty. "She knows your history."

"Oi, but I talked with her before I hopped off. She twigged why I'd rather the Donnellys not know what sort of people my family are. She said she'd keep mum on it, but if her husband asked her direct, she'd not care to lie to him. I told her I thought that was fair enough."

"I can tell you this: the Donnellys are good people. Even if they discover your past, they'll not hold it against you. They have ghosts of their own; they know life gets complicated."

"Do they know about your mother's 'complicated' life?"

He nodded. "Brogan has helped me with some of my rescues. During one of them, I explained why I want to save as many women as I can from the life my mother was forced to live."

She placed a kiss on his cheek. "You saved *me* from having to live that life. And you gave me freedom I'd never known before."

"You deserved to be free. You'll always deserve that."

Before she could answer, someone knocked at the door.

"Go see who it is," she suggested. "I'll put the kettle on."

She headed for the kitchen while Barnabus made his way to the front door.

Brogan stood on the other side. "Might I steal a moment of your time, Doc?"

Barnabus motioned him in. "Is something the matter with Vera? Gemma said she seemed to be in pain today."

"She's still hurting," he said, "and 'tis difficult for her to move about, but she grows stronger every day. I've come on another matter entirely."

Barnabus hooked his thumb in the direction of the library.

"You look a bit worse for wear, if you don't mind my saying so," Brogan said, following Barnabus into the room. "Have you had a difficult day?"

Barnabus nodded. "Another fire, one likely connected to all the others. While looking it over, Stone and Fletcher and I caught sight of Serena. We tried to convince her to let us help her, but she's too terrified of the Mastiff to take the risk."

"'Tis a frustrating thing when a person's in too much danger to even contemplate running from it," Brogan said.

It was, at that. But it also wasn't the only thing weighing on Barnabus's mind. "Scrawled on one of the walls of that alley, in ash of all things, was 'The Tempest is coming.'"

Brogan whistled low and long. "It couldn't have been a warning for us. The Mastiff wouldn't've known you'd be there."

Barnabus dropped onto a chair. "Perhaps we aren't the only ones the coming storm is meant to overtake."

"Your discovery, though, makes me ever more curious

about *this.*" Brogan pulled from his coat pocket a sealed note and held it out to Barnabus.

"It's addressed to the both of us," Barnabus said, taking it from him.

"'Tis the reason I didn't open it up. Fletcher dropped it at m'place. 'Tis from the Dread Master."

Brogan had received direct messages from their mysterious figurehead before, but this was Barnabus's first. Had Fletcher delivered it to Brogan before or after their time at the fire? Had it anything to do with that? To do with Serena?

"Gemma's in the kitchen making tea. Let's read through this before she returns." Barnabus broke the seal and unfolded the stiff, red-edged parchment. He read out loud but in a whisper.

B and B—

I've learned the Mastiff's last ten victims have all been taken up by resurrectionists. My network suspects the stealing of bodies is a cruel warning to anyone considering defying the Mastiff and his associates. Resurrection men seldom limit themselves to crimes against the recently departed.

They are dangerous.

Barnabus pushed out a tense breath. He knew firsthand the dangers of resurrectionists. Gemma's family had not always obtained from graveyards the bodies they sold. He had worried about that for months after marrying her. Her family's revenge could easily have turned violent.

Arrange for a CALL charitable endeavor

near St. Leonards in Shoreditch. That is where the resurrection man plied his trade last night against one of the Mastiff's known victims—this time a man stabbed to death by the one known as "The Protector," in what my contacts insist was punishment for refusing to bend to the Mastiff's demands. With any luck, there'll be a clue in the churchyard.

Whispers of something more on the horizon are all over London. Worries and uncertainties among some; heinous triumph among others. I suspect our foe does not mean to remain quiet much longer.

Be careful. Be vigilant.

—DM

"St. Leonards is in a hard-hit area," Brogan said. "'Twon't be difficult thinking of something that's needed there that we can help provide."

"And it's not terribly far from where we saw the ash-written warning today," Barnabus said. "I never have been one to dismiss coincidences out of hand."

"Neither am I," Brogan said. "The words had to have been written there for a reason."

"To scare people, or maybe to remind them of their duty," Barnabus thought out loud. "It was certainly etched in Serena's mind as she stood there. We may have stumbled across not merely a randomly scrawled cryptic message but a hideout or gathering place connected with the Mastiff and his people."

"Could be. And Shoreditch'd be the place for it."

"Considering all the fires, writing the message in ash doesn't seem accidental."

"Ain't terribly bright, either," Brogan said. "At the first rainfall, all that'll be left is a dingy puddle on the ground."

The Mastiff, or whoever wrote it on his behalf, must have been certain the words would be seen quickly by whomever it was meant for. More evidence that the crumbling walls and dark alleys were a location of some significance.

Another knock echoed off the front door.

"Have you been busy all day, Doc?" Brogan asked.

"Yes, but not with patients. It's been an odd day."

"Well, offer my apologies to Gemma, but I'll slip out the back door while you're seeing to whoever's at the front. It's a fair jaunt back to Piccadilly."

Barnabus walked from the library to the front door. He didn't usually have so many visitors on the nights his surgery was closed.

A man stood on the front stoop, his hat in his hands, looking a bit upended. He was dressed nicely if not elegantly. He might have worked as a clerk or a merchant. Nothing was obviously the matter with him.

"May I help you?" Barnabus asked.

The man's gaze narrowed, not ominously but in confusion. Something about his expression made him look familiar.

"I'm feeling a touch poorly," he said. "Was hoping you could take a minute and let me know if it's anything I ought to be worried about."

Barnabus motioned him inside and directed him to the sitting room where he saw his patients. As the man passed him, Barnabus spotted a folded issue of the *London Times* tucked under his arm. That one clue pieced together the rest of the mystery. This was the man who'd watched him on the street earlier that day, the man who'd sat with a paper on his lap.

"I'm Dr. Barnabus Milligan," he said. "What's your name?"

"George Snelling."

"Mr. Snelling, what is it that ails you?"

"I—There is . . . I . . ."

There was no mistaking he was trying to think of something. Most patients could tell him quickly, if in vague terms, what they were experiencing. Those who were afflicted with something potentially embarrassing would generally start by identifying it as such. This hesitation was neither of those things. And through it all the man kept watching him, studying him.

"My throat," Mr. Snelling finally said. "I fear it might be the beginnings of a putrefaction."

Barnabus decided to humor Mr. Snelling. The man had watched him very closely on the street only to show up, mere hours later, pretending to be ill. Barnabus knew full well that coincidences could happen, but he always took care to connect any dots that needed connecting.

He made a quick examination of the man and, as expected, found nothing wrong with him.

"I'd advise a bit of lukewarm tea before bed tonight," he said, keeping his suspicions to himself. "Choose soft foods for a couple of days, and the irritation in your throat should ease. This shouldn't become anything alarming."

He waited to see if the man would push his act any further. He didn't. He popped his hat on his head and slipped a few coins into Barnabus's hand in payment for the examination, then left as oddly and quickly as he had arrived.

Barnabus had occasionally interacted with people who were awkward by nature. Mr. Snelling was not one such person. The man had come looking for him; Barnabus was certain of it. What he didn't know was why. And he didn't like that. Not at all.

Mind still spinning over the confusing and worrying visit, he wandered back into the library. Brogan had slipped out, as he'd said he would, and Gemma hadn't come back from the kitchen.

The room was quiet, as was the house. It so often was.

And when Gemma decided to leave Finsbury, it would be quiet again. He'd been lonely these last three years, and for many years before that, but loneliness was not reason enough to tie her to a life with him when he knew perfectly well he wasn't what she wanted.

"I've lived all my life in houses where I weren't loved," she'd said three years earlier, standing in the entryway with her carpetbag in her hand and determination in her eyes. "I'd hoped this house would be different, Baz."

"You're safe here, and you're wanted. That's an improvement."

His logic hadn't softened her expression. "I asked you this last night, and I'm terrified to ask it again, but I need to. Do you love me, Barnabus Milligan?"

They'd covered this ground quite extensively. "I care for you a great deal."

She shook her head. "That ain't what I'm asking."

Frustration had bubbled. "We entered into this agreement without that expectation. To demand it of me now is unfair."

The slow creep of sorrow into her eyes remained one of his most vivid memories. It had torn at him.

"Life taught you to be careful who you grow attached to," she said. "Life taught me that expecting fairness is a fool's dream."

"Is living here with me so terrible?" He'd thought she'd at least been content, maybe even a little happy.

"I've been safe, which I appreciate. And, heaven knows, I'm indebted to you for slipping me free of the life I'd been living."

She felt *indebted*. They were at a painful impasse: she felt for him something he didn't want, and she wanted from him something he didn't feel.

Gemma had taken firm hold of the door handle. "If your feelings ever change, Baz, send word."

And she'd left.

Life taught you to be careful who you grow attached to. It was both a true and incomplete summation of who he was and who he'd learned to be.

He was utterly attached to Gemma. He cared what happened to her. He missed her when she was gone. He was sorely tempted to beg her to stay despite knowing she'd be settling for less than she wanted.

That was what life had taught him to be careful about: asking more of people than he was able to give, making promises to them, however inadvertent, that he couldn't fulfill.

Gemma deserved to live the life she wanted on her own terms. Earlier that very night, she had acknowledged she'd never been free before, and she valued having such freedom now.

He would not take that away from her by tying her to a man who was less than she needed him to be.

CHAPTER 10

She told me every day that she loved me.

Gemma hadn't been able to clear that from her mind. *Every day.* Before his mother died, Baz had been told by someone every single day that he was loved. No one had ever said that to her. Literally no one.

She'd always assumed that was because the Kincaids were a collection of no-account slubbers who hadn't affection for anything but money and power. And she'd told herself Baz had never said he loved her because he'd had a difficult upbringing as well, that he likely didn't realize what it'd mean to hear that.

She told me every day.

He knew. He just didn't feel that for her.

Gemma's heart had broken three years earlier, waiting for those words. A pathetic part of her had fully believed he'd say them to her eventually. Even if it weren't a romantic-type love, she'd expected he'd at least come to care about her beyond someone he'd rescued.

She was a regular codshead, she was, thinking things'd be different this time.

Her father had been wrong about most things, but he'd been bang on the mark in saying that hearts were foolish things. She'd appreciate that misguided organ keeping quiet and minding its own business.

Baz had married her out of pity, her head would remind her. But pitiful people were sometimes endearing, her heart would insist. And, it would add, maybe Baz had a secret weakness for that particular combination.

Pathetic.

He liked having her around; she knew he did. He was friendly and kind, and they got on proper well. It made it all the worse that her heart broke so easily at knowing there weren't likely to be anything more between them than that. She'd have given almost anything to have a bit of kindness these past years. From anyone else, it would've been more than enough.

Three days after starting the job Móirín had found for her, three days of pleasant evenings with Baz that never tiptoed beyond a comfortable friendship, Gemma ended her workday early and spent a few of her coins to take a hackney to Southwark, a place she'd vowed she'd never return to. She and Baz had been invited to supper at the Donnellys' flat and planned to meet there in the evening. This was her best chance of making a much-needed journey south of the Thames with no one the wiser.

Gemma asked to be let down a bit away from her actual destination, not wanting to risk rigging the jig. She walked down the street, knowing how to avoid attention.

The Kincaids were brilliant at it. A person could be jaunting down the pavement and not realize a member of her infamous family was within arms' length. Gemma was as good at it as the rest of them. Some families passed down heirlooms; hers bestowed on their children a talent for criminality.

Why wouldn't Baz be ecstatic to tie himself to that for a lifetime? she asked herself dryly.

Gemma eyed the people she passed, though none of them noticed her. Her father was dead, but he had two brothers who were still living. He'd never been the most dangerous of the three. It'd be best not to cross paths with either of her uncles if she could help it.

She slipped around the back of the workhouse, following Marshalsea Road to a quieter area, a darker area, a corner of Southwark where people could hide with ease. Blimey, but there were a lot of dark corners.

With her hands in her coat pockets, she likely looked as if she were trying to keep warm, when, like any South Londoner with half a brain, she had a chiv in her pocket. Knives were handy things, especially when wandering the back alleys.

And, like any South Londoner who'd been brought up by the Kincaids, she ducked down the first back alley she came to. The dim passage led to another—one with a low brick arch and rooms built above. The only points of light were at either end.

The arched walkway spilled into a walled courtyard, overgrown with weeds and grass, without a single cobblestone or bit of discarded glass to remind Mother Nature that London was no place for her. Few people came to this hidden bit of the city. And those who did were careful to leave no trace.

Gemma moved along the edge of one of the walls to where it appeared to meet another. But if a person looked closely enough, like she always did, it was clear that the two walls only touched at the top. Nearer to the ground there was a gap that seemed far too small for a person to pass through. But it was all a trick of the eye. Even the walls in Southwark knew how to lie.

Gemma stepped through sideways, as that was the only way to manage the thing.

The space beyond was a hodgepodge of fallen walls and supporting beams. The building was only standing out of sheer stubbornness. But that had been true for many years; something in it must've been sturdy and steadfast.

Gemma slipped carefully around leaning walls and the thick, rough-and-tough beams holding them up. Halfway through the maze of building carcasses was an overhang, another puzzle piece one had to know about to find. She slipped under and turned left. Tucked beyond a barrier of almost complete darkness, a length of fabric hung from the sagging ceiling.

"*Leti, soroka,*" she called out softly. Mr. Sorokin had told her to use that Russian phrase if ever she needed his help but couldn't risk anyone knowing.

While she waited for a response, she didn't make a sound. Resurrectionists depended on stealth, and she'd learned to be as silent as the very graves they'd dug up.

She heard footsteps, but only because resurrectionists also learned to listen very, very closely. On the other side of the curtain was someone as skillfully quiet as she.

The fabric pulled back, revealing a silhouette. Taller than she was—a decided advantage. And the man's eyes'd be adjusted to the dark—even more of an advantage. She had her knife, though, and she'd a knack with it.

"*Leti, soroka,*" she repeated.

"Gemma Kincaid?"

They'd each said only two words, but both had twigged the other. She'd found Mr. Sorokin, and he'd remembered her. Blimey, that was a relief.

"I'm in bad loaf," she said. "I need help wrigglin' out of it."

He took her by the arm, then pulled her into the darkness. He kept firm hold, guiding her into an open space, broken up only by more hanging fabric. Old windows missing their glass were covered with thick burlap. Peepers wouldn't manage to see in, but a bit of light did slip through.

"It's a friend," Mr. Sorokin said, the flavor of Russia seasoning his voice. "All's safe and well."

Two children climbed out into the open from hidey-holes she'd used herself years earlier. One child was a girl, likely thirteen years old, with hair as black as night and eyes that trusted no one. The other child was a boy, eight at most, with sand-colored hair jutting out in all directions and an expression that said he saw more than he let on and knew more than he ought.

"This is Gemma," Mr. Sorokin told them. "I've hidden her here before. You have no reason to fear her."

Gemma kept mum. His word would hold more power with these urchins than hers ever would. Trust and distrust were opposite sides of the same coin, and it could be flipped without warning.

The children nodded. The boy laid on his stomach and opened what looked like the latest from Baz's "Bodies of

Light" series. The girl held Mr. King's most recent offering, its peach cover giving it away.

Mr. Sorokin hooked his thumb toward a rough-cut table with a few rickety chairs around it. They both sat. Gemma loosened her grip on the chiv in her pocket, knowing she was safe. She'd only ever felt that with one other person, and he thought she was pitiful.

"What is it that you need, Gemma?"

"The front and back of it is, I need to die."

Mr. Sorokin was not the sort to be discombobulated by much of anything. "I don't kill people."

"I ain't needing to be dead literally. I just need certain people to think I am."

His intelligent eyes narrowed on her. "Which people?"

She shrugged. "The government. The church. My . . . husband."

"When did you get married?"

"Three years ago. I had a bit of time on me hands, thought, 'Ah, toss it,' and went and done it."

He almost smiled. She didn't remember him doing that often. "This husband of yours isn't in your family trade, is he?"

Gemma shook her head. "He ain't. And I ain't anymore either."

"There are a great many whispers just now about resurrectionists," Mr. Sorokin said. "They're awful busy, and not in the usual ways."

"There ain't nothing 'usual' about resurrection men. And nothing's beneath them." It was not a pun she'd intended to make, but she let it sit just the same.

"There's a man who runs London's underworld, and it is

rumored he has resurrectionists on his side and is paying well to terrorize the city into bowing to his demands."

"My uncles would enjoy terrorizing people. They'd enjoy making a pile of coins even more."

"The rumors hold that they are thoroughly enjoying both."

Of course her family was part of the campaign of horrors. The Kincaids were part of most every horrific scheme that took hold in London's underbelly. They helped think up most of them.

"Bung your eye," she muttered. "Are the Kincaids sweeping in a lot of brass with this arrangement?"

"They seem to be," Mr. Sorokin said. "And they'll bring in even more money if the scheme continues. That, however, depends on them having enough hands to do the increased work."

"I've cousins enough."

Mr. Sorokin shook his head. "Your uncles are getting a lot of work, Gemma. A lot. And it's worth a great deal of money. They need hands with more experience than your cousins have. They need someone who can take the lead on a resurrection."

Her lungs turned to stone. With what little breath she could manage, she asked, "Someone like . . . me?"

He didn't answer aloud or nod. He didn't need to.

She rubbed at her forehead. "I ain't crossed paths with any of my family in years. I've made blasted sure of that."

"Be very careful, Gemma. If the whispers are true, and I suspect they are, the Kincaids are the Mastiff's resurrection men."

A shudder rushed through her body. The Mastiff. She

knew who that was. Anyone who lived in poor neighborhoods and worked on the dangerous streets of London knew who he was. Feared him.

"Are you hiding the stork bundles here because of the resurrection men?" she asked. Resurrectionists sometimes saved themselves a spot of bother by creating a corpse rather than searching one out. And she had yet to meet a resurrection man who had any qualms about plying the trade against children.

"The Mastiff is the one who threatened them, but he has tentacles everywhere. I've kept these little ones hidden because I don't know the entirety of the threat. I suspect the Mastiff is not at all what he seems."

That was the way of the world of crime, death, and terror. Nothing was ever what it seemed.

"Now, why is it you need your husband to think you're dead?" Mr. Sorokin asked.

"Not just him."

Again, a hint of humor touched his expression. Few things gave her more joy than making people laugh, even silently. "Him and the government."

"And the church," she added. "Cain't forget that."

From behind them, one of the children laughed. She'd take that as a success.

"My husband didn't marry me on account of wanting to," Gemma said. "And now there ain't no way of wriggling out of it unless one of us takes a pine-box ride to the churchyard."

"Ah." Mr. Sorokin nodded. "You need to be declared dead so the man could marry again, if he wanted, without the law objecting."

"Or the church," the girl behind them tossed out. "Cain't forget the church."

Mr. Sorokin smiled fully. Despite the heavy topics they were tossing around, Gemma's heart lightened. There weren't anything in the world quite like seeing someone happy. That's what she wanted for Baz. And, blast it all, for herself too.

"I'm guessing you need a forged declaration of death," Mr. Sorokin said. "And, so you can find yourself work under whatever name you assume afterward, some forged letters of reference." He had done this kind of work often for people needing to create new identities; it's why she'd sought him out.

"The death declaration needs to be dated about three weeks from now, giving me time to earn enough coin for making the jaunt away from London." And time enough to see, one last time, if there were any chance of something deeper growing between her and Baz.

"I have a press I can use," he said. "It'll take me a few days, maybe a week. Maybe more."

She nodded her understanding.

"You'd be taking too great a risk coming here again. Not only might you be recognized, there's a chance someone would see you and find us. It wouldn't be safe for these children to be moved any sooner than is necessary."

"What did the children do to earn the Mastiff's wrath?"

"It wasn't anything they did. It's that they are associated with someone who did not bow to his threats."

"And they'd either be bait or indiscriminate casualties."

Mr. Sorokin nodded again. "He threatens poor people into doing his bidding and blackmails influential people into hurting each other and punishes anyone who stands up to him. He's gained power quickly and is using more tactics than we can keep track of."

The little boy approached with near-silent steps, though Gemma heard him. She looked in his direction, as did Mr. Sorokin.

"Miss Gemma," he said, his dust-sprinkled brow tugging low. "Are you really one of them Kincaids?"

There was no use denying it. "A right shame, i'n'it?"

"People are afraid of the Kincaids. More than they used to be."

The girl approached their table as well, watching Gemma with a knowing look and an expression too tired for someone so young. Poverty and pain did that to children on the streets of this city. It had done it to Gemma by that age.

"I was out fetching us food the other day"—the girl looked quickly to Mr. Sorokin—"real carefully, like you said." Her gaze returned to Gemma. "The Kincaids is looking for someone. No one knows who, but that family—your family—don't stop when there's something they want."

The little boy nodded his agreement. Mr. Sorokin asked him something in slowly spoken Russian. The boy answered in the same language. The children were shooed away, and when Mr. Sorokin looked back at her, his gaze was even heavier.

"They're looking for me, ain't they?" she asked.

"As soon as you have these papers, Gemma, get out of London. Your family has more power than they used to. You won't be safe from them for long."

He'd never been one for exaggerating, and he knew from experience what it meant to be in danger. "Have you heard any whispers that they've twigged where I am? My father knew where I went when I left Southwark, but I cain't say if he told anyone else before he went six feet under."

"If they knew, they'd have found you already."

Baz, then, was safe. At least for a time. Some of her panic eased. Cutting the ties between them and getting herself deemed dead would free him from more than just a marriage he didn't want. It'd keep the Kincaids off his doorstep.

"Tell me where I can find you," Mr. Sorokin said, "and I'll see to it you get the papers."

Gemma allowed a lopsided smile. "Have I got a wheeze to crack on that matter. I'm at Dr. Milligan's house. I'd wager you know him, as he's been looking after Vera."

For a moment, he didn't say anything. "Have you seen her lately?"

"I have. She seems very happy. That husband of hers is a good 'un, i'n't he? And Móirín's fearsome in the best sort of way."

"They're fierce protectors," Mr. Sorokin said. "I hate being away from her while she's hurting. But she stood up to the Mastiff, which is why he burned down our business, why he attempted to kill her, and why he would kill me and these children in a heartbeat if given a chance."

"So you have to keep tucked into the shadows."

He nodded. "I can keep the children safe here. Should danger find Vera, she will be quite thoroughly protected."

As much as Gemma would welcome a bit of that "thorough protection," she'd not make things more dangerous by hanging about Town too long.

"Why is it you're at the doctor's house?" Mr. Sorokin asked.

He needed to know her name if he was to forge her a document. "It's him I'm married to."

The tiniest surprise showed on Mr. Sorokin's face. She didn't mean to let him interrogate her on the matter.

"Do you want me to tell Vera I've seen you?" she asked him.

With a heavy sadness, Mr. Sorokin shook his head. "If she knows that you know where I am, she'll press you. Should anyone overhear who ought not . . . There are people who would stop at nothing to get such information."

Stop at nothing. "You must know more than you're spilling if the Mastiff and his associates would take such pains to find you."

"It is not merely what I know but who I've helped. I know secret identities, schemes, hiding places. Information that unravels important people. And I know the identities of those who are, in all reality, the only people capable of bringing down the Mastiff and those he works with."

"Like my family."

"They stand to gain both wealth and power through their connection with the Mastiff." He paused. "Whatever you do, Gemma Kincaid Milligan, don't let them find you."

CHAPTER 11

One advantage of Gemma being back for a time was that Barnabus wasn't spending his evenings alone, or even always at home. That evening, they were to have supper with the Donnellys. Fletcher and Elizabeth had come for supper already. Kumar and his wife had suggested doing the same. Perhaps after Gemma left again, he would have forged enough of a friendship with some of the Dreadfuls that they'd still spend time together. That would help stave off the loneliness.

He'd still miss her. He'd missed her every moment of the last three years. But he might not be so alone.

He knocked at the Donnellys' flat.

Móirín answered. "Brogan owes me a shilling."

An odd greeting. "A pleasure to see you as well, Móirín."

"We had a wager between us," Móirín said, "on which of the Milligans would arrive first."

"Gemma's not here yet?" He'd left home later than he'd expected to. She should have arrived far ahead of him.

"Not yet." Móirín twitched her head toward the inside of the house. "While we're waiting, Vera could use looking at."

"Has she taken a turn for the worse?" he asked, stepping over the threshold.

"She's having a difficult day."

Barnabus followed her into the humble sitting room. Brogan and Vera rose to greet him. Vera moved with obvious pain.

"You're hurting more," he said.

"In my back, a little south of center," she said. "The ache lingers there most days. It's just deuced bad at the moment."

There had been some debris lodged deep in her back after the explosion at her family print shop. He'd removed everything he safely could, but one last bit had sat so near her spine that he'd not dared attempt to dislodge it. He'd known she would be in pain with it left inside, but she wouldn't have been paralyzed. While he knew, intellectually, it was the safest and most sensible choice, he still wondered if he perhaps should have tried to remove it, if maybe he'd given up too quickly.

"I can give you a recipe for a tisane that'll offer a bit of relief. Pain powders do the most good, but you've told me they make you sleepy."

She nodded. "Some days the sleepiness is welcome. But there are days I'd rather not sleep through but still don't want to be in agony."

He wished he could do more to make that possible. "I'll jot down the recipe."

"Thank you, Doc."

As he made his way to the table near the window, someone knocked at the door.

"That'll likely be Gemma." Brogan rose and left the sitting room.

"Wonder what kept her so late," Vera said. "She didn't have as far to come as you did."

"Yes, but I took a hackney. She likely walked." That had been a worry about their decision to meet here, knowing she'd need to walk. But Gemma could be as stubborn as she was sunny.

Gemma stepped inside the room, and Barnabus was struck again by the gauntness that still hung about her. She must have struggled to eat regularly for weeks before returning to Finsbury. Would that happen again if she decided to leave?

She offered no greetings to the room, looked at no one, but there was no mistaking the heaviness in her expression. Something was worrying her, and she so seldom let that show.

He moved to where she stood. "Gemma?"

She seemed only a little startled, likely on account of how softly he'd spoken. She looked at him. Worry and hope collided in his chest, setting off an explosion of confusion.

"What's the matter, Gemma?"

"Nothing I cain't sort out."

He took her hands in his. "You've trusted me before," he whispered, uncertain how much she wanted the rest of the room to overhear. "You can trust me now."

Gemma watched him, emotions battling in her eyes. She looked to Vera. "Have you a room we could slip into for a moment?"

"Any room at the top of the stairs."

She kept her hand in his as they left the sitting room but let go as they climbed the stairs. She stepped into the first room on the landing. He closed the door behind them.

Her breathing was so tense he heard it.

"My family is looking for me," she said, her voice shaking.

Fear seized his heart. "Your father's dead."

"He ain't the only Kincaid. They're all terrors. Every blasted one of 'em." She paced away, though she couldn't go far in the small room.

He watched her, his mind spinning. Was she safe? Did she need to be hidden? Ought he to involve the DPS? "Tell me what you've heard."

"The Kincaids've come into a heap o' work, not the 'snatch a job as you're able' variety. There's a man, a dangerous man, who's hired them on to resurrect people on the regular. This rum cove what hired them, he hushes people, then has my family dig them up to make everyone else that much more afraid of him."

A shiver tiptoed down Barnabus's spine. She was talking of the Mastiff; he was certain of it.

"They've steady work now, but if they're to keep pace, they need more hands that know how to do the job without needing to be taught."

She had been forced into their trade from a young age. He knew from countless conversations and late nights when nightmares had plagued her that she'd hated it.

"Whispers are hovering all over South London that they's looking for someone. That someone ain't likely to be anyone but me." She pressed her fingers to her forehead. "If my family finds me, either I have to go back to that life or I'm dead where I stand."

Her eyes met his once more, and it wasn't weariness or mere concern he saw there. She was afraid. He held his arms out, hoping she would accept the offering. That she did so without hesitation proved both a relief and a worry.

"My job ain't terribly far from Southwark. I cain't be too close to that area of town. It's where the Kincaids all still live."

He rubbed a slow circle over her back. "You could—You don't have to—" He'd not gotten tongue-tied until now. How was it that she still managed to upend him sometimes? "We'll find you something else, Gemma. Something nowhere near Southwark."

He felt her sigh against him. "That could take time, though. I cain't make my next start without coin in my pocket."

That dropped like a weight on his heart. He'd always known she'd leave again, but he'd held out hope that she'd stay long enough to find a means of making things work. She had to have been deeply unhappy to want to leave a safe place when she was in such danger.

"What did you do, Baz, when you were younger and you were in trouble, but you couldn't go back to where your mother was . . . working, and you had nowhere else to go? What did you do when you didn't have nowhere else to hide?"

She was the only person he'd ever told about the terror he'd felt when, at only six years old, he'd been tossed out on the street. The cruel woman who'd run the bordello where his mother had been trapped had declared he was too old to stay, that he was costing the woman business and money—no matter that his mother had provided ample coin for the food he ate, coin he'd supplemented himself by his efforts on the streets each day. When at the house run by that unfeeling woman, he'd kept to the attics, out of sight, out of the way. There'd been no reason to toss him out other than cruelty.

"There was safety in not being alone. I kept to crowds during the day and the urchins' hovels at night."

"But what did you do when you were full spent and hadn't a day's worth of survival left in you?"

He closed his eyes, better able to remember without agony while she was in his arms that way. "I met my mother every morning at the back wall of that house. I'd get to see her and talk to her, and that helped."

"And that was when she'd tell you she loved you?"

Barnabus smiled at the memory. "That meant everything to me. I could survive a difficult day on the streets easier knowing someone loved me."

She set a hand on his chest. "I wish I could've known her, Baz."

"So do I," he said softly. "You'd have liked each other. I'm certain of it."

For a moment, they stood in silence, his arms around her, Gemma leaning into his embrace. A wave of memories rushed over him, moments like this one in which holding her had felt peaceful and . . . bittersweet. Mingled with them all were the difficult, painful, dangerous moments of his childhood, the piercing pain of losing his mother, the feeling of failure at never having rescued her from the life she'd hated so much.

After a time, Gemma spoke. "Do you suppose Móirín will be upset if I stay up here and rest for a spell? I know we're meant to be supper guests."

"I'll tell her you've had a difficult day and need a bit of peace and time to yourself. She'll understand."

Gemma stepped back, breaking the embrace. Her quick smile was forced. He could tell it was.

"Gemma?"

She shook her head. "I'll be fine. I only need a lie down." She sat on the edge of the bed.

He closed the door behind him and made his way quickly down the stairs. Móirín was at the bottom, watching him with a question in her eyes.

"Gemma's had a shattering day. She's asked to be allowed to rest for a time."

"Of course. That's my room you were in. She can stay there all night if she needs to."

"Thank you." He popped quickly into the sitting room. "I'm going to be just a touch rude," he told Brogan. "I need to deliver an urgent message."

Brogan watched him with narrowed gaze.

Barnabus pulled a single penny from the pocket of his vest and, making certain Brogan saw it but not Vera, flashed the coin to his fellow member of the Dread Penny Society.

Brogan gave a quick nod. "God speed."

THE BACHELOR AND THE BRIDE

by Mr. King

Installment III
in which our Hero encounters the *Bean-Nighe*!

Duncan paused as the trail he was on began to turn. Before he knew it, he would be facing Loch Dreva and the feared Washing Woman. Now was the time to switch his sturdy boots for the soft shoes Granny Winter had provided for him. How much quieter they would be!

The shoes fit him perfectly, which would have been surprising had they come from anyone other than Granny Winter. There was a reason she was so widely assumed to be the *Cailleach*.

He slung his sack on his back and once more began walking carefully and slowly toward his destination, amazed at how quiet his steps had become. However, as he began to hear the sounds of water, his heart pounded so loudly he wasn't certain the soft-soled shoes would help at all.

Once I see her, I must not look away. Mustn't make any noise. Mustn't let her see me. Must snatch her up off the ground. Must require her to answer three questions.

He silently repeated the list as he walked, hoping that by making the instructions quite clear in his mind, he would be able to adhere to them without difficulty. He would have but one chance.

His heart ached as he thought of Sorcha waiting for him on the other side of the hill. She had waited alone for her family all those years ago, not realizing they had been unable to escape the monster as she had. He didn't want her to suffer like that again. And he most certainly didn't want to die.

His footsteps, silent under the influence of his borrowed shoes, took him closer and closer to the sound of water. After a time, the swishing sound of water being agitated joined the cacophony. That, he would wager, was the *Bean-Nighe* washing her terrifying shrouds.

Duncan searched the area, determined to know where she was so he wouldn't accidentally give himself away. Closer and closer he drew. Nearer and nearer he came. A slight rise in the path afforded him a view of the entire loch—its pristine, luminous waters, the mountains on every side. And what appeared to be a haggard old woman hunched over on the shore, her back to him, washing.

The *Bean-Nighe*.

He stepped closer and closer. How he wished he could look down to make certain of his steps and avoid disturbing any rocks underneath his foot. But looking away meant certain death, so he kept his eyes on her.

She was muttering to herself, though not in any language he understood. Her voice was just loud enough to mask what little noise his footsteps made. He drew closer, keeping extremely quiet.

Don't let her see you.

So long as he didn't distract her from her gruesome task, she wouldn't look in his direction.

Careful.

Quiet.

He was closer than ever, close enough to hear the clink of rocks hitting each other, no doubt being used to scrub shrouds.

Lift her off the ground, or the shroud will be mine.

He was so close. One more step. He held his arms out. He could not afford even the tiniest mistake. He swung his arms together and wrapped them around the twisted figure, lifting her immediately from the ground.

The *Bean-Nighe*'s piercing scream was harrowing and unnerving. She was so light that she felt almost like nothing in his arms. It was a trick, no doubt, meant to convince people they'd not actually taken hold of her so they would release her without their demands being met and their survival secured.

She squirmed and screamed at him, in what language he knew not.

"I'll not release you until you meet my demands," he said firmly and authoritatively.

Her voice crackly and grating, she said, "And what are your demands?"

He recalled perfectly what Sorcha had told him of this part of the interaction. "You must answer three of my questions, and then I will release you, and you will allow me to leave unharmed."

"Someone has taught you our ways."

Unsure if conversation was permitted, he simply repeated himself. "You must answer three of my questions, and then I will release you, and you will allow me to leave unharmed."

"Very well," she said. "You must answer three of mine in return."

He knew that would be required of him. "Very well."

The Washing Woman ceased her wriggling and wailing.

"My first question is this: How do I cure Donella's illness?" he asked.

"And my first question is this: How do you define 'cure'?"

He held his peace a moment, remembering what Sorcha had told him of the woman's cleverness. The way he defined the word, he didn't doubt, would change the answer he received. "I define it as treating an ailment or injury or other such difficulty in such a way that the person being treated makes a full recovery."

"Then my answer to your first question—How do you cure the girl's illness?—is this: through great difficulty."

She had, indeed, answered the question, but she'd not done so in any helpful way. He had to think of a different manner of posing his question so that she could not escape answering it. "My second question is this: What are the *precise* means, methodology, and anything else necessary to the accomplishing of it, that will cure Donella?"

"You learn quickly." The *Bean-Nighe* sounded none too pleased. "My second question for you is this: How much are you willing to risk for this cure?"

Not wanting to give her reason to make his efforts more dangerous than they had to be, he was careful in his reply.

"My answer to you," he said, "is to observe our current situation and allow that to serve as your answer."

She growled in her throat. "Then my answer to you is this: You must travel to the churchyard in Carrifran and gather water from the mouth of the gargoyle. If the girl drinks it, she will be cured according to your definition."

He was not familiar with that town. How many days would be required to reach it? How many days to return home? How he wished he were granted limitless questions so he could learn all he needed to know. Instead, he asked what seemed the best question for obtaining the most pertinent information. "My final question is this: What is the most important thing for me to know if I am to make this journey and return home safely?"

"My final question is this: How do you define 'safely'?"

Again, she meant to trick him into limiting what she was required to do for him. "I define it thus: to be made and remain whole in body, mind, and spirit."

"And *my* answer is this: the most important thing to know is that no one emerges whole from a harrowing journey when that journey is undertaken entirely alone."

It was not at all the helpful bit of advice he'd hoped for. It was, however, true to her nature. Still, he had asked his allotted three questions and had answered hers. He felt certain that, were he to not honor their agreement, the consequences would be dire.

"Having obliged me in my requirements, and I in yours, I will release you, and you will permit me to go on my way."

"As agreed," she said.

His heart pounded, but he trusted Sorcha's knowledge

of these things. He lowered his arms so the *Bean-Nighe*'s feet touched the ground once more. He released his hold on her and stepped back. She picked up the shroud she had dropped when he'd grabbed her, and she returned to her washing, muttering to herself and not looking at him.

He hadn't thought to ask Sorcha if he was required to keep looking at the *Bean-Nighe* as he made his way back. It seemed best to do so rather than risk being wrong.

He walked carefully backward away from the loch, over the rise, and out of sight of the Washing Woman. Only when he was certain she could no longer see him, and already knowing he could not see her, did he truly breathe again.

Water from the mouth of the gargoyle in the churchyard at Carrifran.

Duncan did not know where that journey would take them, but he suspected the danger was far from over.

CHAPTER 12

My family is looking for me.

That single sentence had struck fear deep into Barnabus's heart, and he was seldom frightened by anything. The Kincaids inspired horror in most anyone who knew them. That they had joined forces with the Mastiff changed everything.

Barnabus rushed toward the DPS headquarters. The Donnellys lived near enough that he could make the journey on foot. His rushed walk took him past the place where most of Fletcher's urchins spent their days. It was a benefit in that moment; Barnabus needed to get word to Fletcher to meet him at headquarters.

Fortunately, it wasn't very late in the day, and many of London's street children were still about. Barnabus kept his eyes peeled, hoping to see one he knew was part of Fletcher's network.

Fate seemed to be on his side: Henry, an eight-year-old bootblack who often whispered things to Fletcher, stood on a corner, his shoeshine kit tucked firmly under his arm.

"Care for a shoeshine, guv'nuh?" Henry asked.

"If I toss you a half-crown, would you give a shoeshine to a friend of ours when next you see him?"

Henry nodded. "If I think of it." Though he gave no indication he understood Barnabus's request, there was no doubt he did.

"Any chance you'll see our bloke sooner rather than later?"

Henry tossed his satchel over his shoulder. "Could be. He lingers about this corner now and then."

"His shoes are in urgent need of shining."

Henry gave a single, quick nod. Though the boy casually sauntered off, Barnabus knew he could be counted on to see to the matter urgently. Barnabus continued his path to the DPS headquarters.

The front door was unlocked when he arrived, a sign that Nolan was at his post. The man lived at headquarters, making his room in what would have been the butler's rooms if this had still been used as an actual house, but Nolan's employment didn't require him to sit all day and night by the door. During his hours off duty, members depended on Fletcher to let them in. Only he and the Dread Master had a key. And no one other than Fletcher knew who the Dread Master was.

Barnabus stepped through the door and into the entryway. Nolan was in his seat. This time, though, he wasn't sleeping or reading the newspaper. In fact, he had the most recent installment of Barnabus's own penny dreadful in his hands.

Before Barnabus could decide if he wanted to ask if Nolan was enjoying "Bodies of Light," the man coughed, and not the light variety arising from a dry throat or a bit of dust causing a fuss. The rumble sat deep in his chest.

"I don't like the sound of that, Nolan. Are you feeling poorly?"

"I were a couple days ago. Better today." He'd always been a man of few words but of absolute reliability.

"Are you feverish? Fatigued? Pained when you breathe?"

Nolan shook his head. "Not now."

Barnabus leaned against the wall near Nolan's bench. "I mean it when I tell you that you should send for me if you're ever feeling even a little ill. None of us would want anything to happen to you."

His toothless smile popped up. "I ain't going nowhere anytime soon, Doc. I'm looking after the lot of you."

"On behalf of the lot of us . . . thank you."

Nolan gave a quick nod, then took up his reading once more.

Barnabus set a penny etched with his initials on the table where they always set them upon arriving at headquarters, whether for a meeting or simply to pass the day. There were no other pennies on the table. The house, then, was empty.

He stood at the foot of the stairs, pondering. Where ought he to wait? The library was a comfortable and familiar place, but his mood did not match the calm feel of that space. The boxing saloon would certainly allow him to work out some tension, but it was not conducive to conversation. He could slip into the pub—having an actual pub inside a clubhouse was an odd thing, but the Dread Penny Society never did anything in the usual way—but he would be tempted to sample what was on tap there, and he didn't dare. Gemma's life, after all, depended on them getting this right.

His stomach rumbled, answering the question of his

destination. The kitchens. That meant taking the back stairs all the way down to the below-ground level. He didn't overly mind; he was still waiting for Fletcher to arrive.

It was strange being alone at headquarters. He wasn't one who spent long hours here. He hadn't the leisure time. Even then, when he knew Mrs. Simms would make certain any patients who happened by the surgery were looked after by her or sent to another doctor for care, he felt a pull away from headquarters. And not always to work on his next "Bodies of Light" installment.

He felt that same pull tonight, urging him to return to the Donnellys and sit with Gemma. He wanted to talk with her. Try to comfort her. But she was in too much danger for him, alone, to address it. He needed a word with Fletcher.

The larder was never entirely empty at DPS headquarters, though the offerings were modest. He started a fire in the fireplace, heating coals enough for roasting a potato and warming a bit of smoked pork.

He'd only just placed his humble meal on a plate when he heard footsteps approaching. He turned his attention to the doorway just as Fletcher and Stone stepped inside.

Fletcher's mirthful smile was firmly in place. Barnabus didn't doubt he understood this was an urgent manner; the swagger was simply his way.

"We debated where we might find you," Fletcher said. "Stone, here, owes me a guinea."

Stone didn't look angry but also didn't join in the jest.

"Henry found you quickly," Barnabus said. "Seems I chose the right messenger."

"Steady in a storm, that Henry." Fletcher shook his head

in appreciation. "If I thought he'd take up writing, I'd stand him for DPS membership in a heartbeat."

"Put a bug in Hollis's ear," Stone said. "Educating little ones is that fella's lifework."

Stone wasn't wrong about that.

The two men took seats at the rough-hewn table where Barnabus sat with his supper. Though they were waiting patiently, Barnabus suspected they were as anxious to hear what he had to say as he was to tell them.

He took his final bite of potato, then pushed his plate away. "This'll take some explaining, but it's necessary to truly understand."

Both men nodded.

"Gemma grew up in Southwark. Though it's not widely known, and I don't think she'd appreciate me telling you this, she comes from a family of resurrectionists. They've been doing it for generations. They're blasted good at it. And they're dangerous, violent."

"Blue bashers." The creative curse whooshed from Fletcher. "She's a Kincaid, ain't she?"

Barnabus nodded. "Her father was the oldest of the three brothers."

Fletcher looked to Stone. "The Kincaid family've been London's most feared clan of resurrectionists for ages. I grew up hearing tales of them and the three brothers that run the family in this generation. They're very nearly as feared as the Mastiff himself, though I'd say it's a hair's breadth difference."

"And your wife," Stone said to Barnabus, "is one of them?"

"She is. My marrying her was part of helping her escape her family."

Stone nodded as if Barnabus had solved a great mystery for him.

Fletcher waved a hand, encouraging him to keep explaining.

"Resurrectionists are a hard and dangerous lot. Sometimes, when money is tight or they're looking to be a bit more comfortable, they obtain bodies without waiting for them to—"

He knew he didn't have to mince his words with these two—they understood the realities of poverty and crime—and yet he was talking about Gemma's family, the life she'd been forced into. He hated the idea of tying her to it in any way.

"They snuff the bloke's candle themselves," Fletcher said, finishing Barnabus's explanation bluntly.

Barnabus nodded. "The Kincaids are known for murder almost as much as for resurrections. She escaped that life and, it seemed, her family's clutches. But she's heard that they're looking for her."

"Any idea why?" Fletcher asked.

Barnabus stood and began pacing. Too much was bubbling inside for him to sit still. "Her family is working for the Mastiff, and apparently, they anticipate their workload increasing. That means two things." He held up a finger. "One, the Mastiff intends to increase his efforts, killing more, resurrecting more, threatening more."

He held up another finger. "And two, more work means more money for the Kindcaids. They are desperate for trained hands to help with the effort. Gemma knows the trade; her father gave her no choice in the matter. She'd be an asset to them. They know Gemma's in London, and they are searching for her, no doubt to strong-arm her back into their ranks. If she refuses, I have no doubt they will kill her."

Fletcher and Stone exchanged a glance.

Barnabus rubbed at his face. "I can't keep her safe on my own. She's found a job, but it takes her too near South London, and that's where all her family lives. She won't go back on account of the risk, but not having a job will eat at her. Even the daughter of a resurrection man has her pride."

"I can find her a position," Stone said. "There's work where I'm toiling most days, up near Marylebone. I can keep an eye on things. Quietly, of course."

"That's a far spell to go from Finsbury." Gemma would either have to spend hours walking each day or hop a hansom cab, which would take money. "But I'll let her know of your offer and see what she thinks."

"I'll gab with the Dread Master about all this," Fletcher said. "Might be there's more we ain't heard."

"Do you think he knows the connection between the Mastiff and the Kincaids already?" Barnabus tried not to be too obvious in his question, but there was every chance the Dread Master already knew. Stone was listening to everything they said. And Mr. Sorokin had known Gemma even before Barnabus had.

Fletcher nodded. "There's very little escapes the Dread Master's notice."

"Do the Kincaids know of *your* connection to Gemma?" Stone asked.

Barnabus shrugged. "Her father did. It's possible he didn't

say anything to anyone before he died, feeling embarrassed that he'd been thwarted. But he might just as easily have denounced me to every last one of them."

Fletcher and Stone exchanged another silent look, but they had clearly communicated something.

"What was that about?" Barnabus asked.

Stone answered for them both. "Only that your Gemma ain't the only one we need to safeguard."

Gemma walked up New Bond Street with Móirín on one side and Stone on the other. Baz had asked Stone to find her a job, and he'd managed the thing in less than a day. But that job was in Marylebone, too far for walking every morning. She'd stayed with the Donnellys that night, not going back to Baz's house in Finsbury.

Part of her worried that he preferred it that way.

"Might as well ask her your question, Stone," Móirín said. "Little point putting it off."

Stone had a question for her? He had not shown himself to be the gabbing sort. Still, people talking or not talking changed from time to time and from place to place. Sometimes Baz talked to her with ease. Other times he tripped over his words as if they were stray cats and he was a drunkard attempting to navigate a dark alley. She never had sorted the mystery of that.

"Doc never told anyone you were married," Stone said. "Did that bother you?"

Gemma blinked. That hadn't been anywhere near what she thought the man might ask.

"Have you a particular reason for asking? You don't seem the sort to pry."

"I ain't," Stone said.

"Are you fretting over Baz?"

"Not on account of this," Stone said.

Gemma looked to Móirín. "Care to shine a light on this?"

"If he wants answers, he needs to do the asking."

"But you know why he's asking?"

Móirín nodded. "We're good friends. I suspect there's not much about him I don't know."

Stone neither confirmed nor denied it. His expression had, however, grown more earnest. Something about his question was important.

"If I thought he'd kept me a secret on account of being ashamed of me, that would've hurt, for sure and certain," Gemma said to Stone.

"Then you don't mind that it's been a secret?"

She had minded a little. "It stings that he didn't even tell his friends. It's enough to make a person wonder if she's been forgotten."

Stone nodded as they walked, his brow furrowed in a look of deep pondering.

"Same as I told you," Móirín said. "Keeping a secret from people who aren't owed your confidence is one thing. Not telling your friends . . . 'tis a hurtful thing to do."

"I've told *you*," Stone replied.

"But you've not introduced me."

Gemma was piecing a great many things together. "Do you have a secret sweetheart?" she asked Stone.

He didn't offer any verbal response, but she was sure she'd guessed right.

"Why is it you ain't told anyone?" Gemma asked.

"Because he's stubborn as a duck," Móirín said.

While Gemma suspected that was true, her own experience made her wonder. "Are you ashamed of this secret love of yours?"

He shook his head firmly. "There's parts of my life that I like keeping to myself."

"Most of your life you keep to yourself," Móirín corrected.

Stone smiled a little, something Gemma'd not seen him do, though he didn't seem sour. "Then how is it you know so much?"

Móirín flashed a grin. "I'm exceptionally bright."

Coming their direction was the policeman Parkington. Gemma had met him at the CALL charitable effort, but she'd kept her distance, kept turned a bit away from him. She didn't think he'd connected her to her family, but he'd likely manage to if given too close a look.

She held back, moving closer to the iron fencing outside the row house they were walking past. This area of London, not quite all the way to Marylebone, was home to nibs and swells and people of rank and importance. Parkington'd likely haul her off simply for clashing with the local flavor. She tucked herself at the corner of the building and pretended to be buttoning her coat.

"Something the matter?" Móirín asked.

"It's that blasted copper." Gemma titched her chin in the man's direction.

Móirín recognized him quickly. "Parkington. Shame such a handsome man chose to be a Peeler."

Gemma could smile at that. "You think he's dimber, do you?"

"Even the biggest troublemakers can be fine to look at."

Stone was, at that moment, talking with the "troublemaker." He seemed to be on as good terms with the man as Baz was.

"Why is it you don't care for blue-bottles?" Gemma asked.

"'Tisn't so much that I don't care for them but more that they don't overly care for me. Or wouldn't if they knew a few things I make pains to keep to m'self."

Gemma nodded, understanding the predicament in an instant. Out of the corner of her eye, she spotted something odd on the walls of the building. Something dark in the shadows. Something hard to make out.

"Do you see that odd smudge just there?" She motioned to it as Stone reappeared at her side. He was tall and might manage a better look.

"Oi. Someone's written something on the wall." He touched it with his finger, then inspected the residue. "Looks to be ash."

Her heart dropped to her feet. "Can you make out what it is?"

"Nothing that makes sense: two vertical lines and a letter *K*."

Bung your eye. "In what order?" Gemma attempted to swallow her rising panic.

"The *K* is in the middle."

She rubbed her hand over her mouth, her heart pounding.

"You know this mark?" Móirín asked.

"The Kincaids sign their work. Three vertical lines for the three brothers. The one made into a *K* indicates which of them led the effort."

"Which brother's mark is in the middle?" Móirín asked.

"My uncle Silas." She couldn't stop the shudder that rushed over her. "Are there any lines under the *K*?"

"None," Stone said.

"Then it weren't someone in the family working on his orders. Silas, his own self, was here on a job."

Stone looked around. "There's no cemetery here."

Gemma pushed out a breath. "He was doing something else, then. Something he oughtn't be."

"What is in this building?" Móirín asked, her voice pitched low, her gaze searching.

"I don't know." Gemma looked away, out at the street and the people passing. "But he was terrible far from Southwark."

"Is it too dangerous for you to be here?" Stone asked. "We'll sort out another job if need be."

She shook her head. "This ain't his usual haunt. I'll keep my eyes peeled, but I ain't ready to toss it yet."

"Do you think we ought to send word to Barnabus?" Móirín asked.

"I'll drop a word in his ear," she said. And, in the meantime, she'd sort out how quickly after getting Mr. Sorokin's papers she could flee London altogether.

CHAPTER 13

Gemma made the return journey to the Donnellys' flat quickly but carefully that night; she and Baz were meant to have supper there again. She saw no familiar faces and no symbols written in ash. That didn't mean they weren't there. The people or the messages.

She needed to keep herself on this side of the ground until Mr. Sorokin's papers gave her an escape. It was a peculiar thing, striving to stay alive just long enough to be declared dead. And it was disheartening to have no other goal than to simply not die.

What else could she do but bide her time? No one had ever defied the Kincaids and lived to tell the tale, except for her and Baz. Her tale weren't finished being told yet, and she didn't mean for it to end with *him* paying the price for her disloyalty to her family. The best way to manage that was to do as little as possible so no one took the least notice of her.

She hated feeling useless. She hated *being* useless.

Gemma stopped at a costermonger's cart and bought herself an apple. She suspected the Donnellys weren't so plump in the pocketbook as they'd like to be. A quick bite on her way to their home would fill her stomach a bit so she'd not be tempted to eat more than she ought of their offering.

She ate as she walked, and she walked as she formulated a plan. Might she do a spot of good in the fortnight or so before she piked off? Something at the Donnellys' flat, maybe? Or a word of encouragement to Stone in the matter of his secret sweetheart connection? Maybe something to help Baz with his rescue efforts?

It wouldn't change where she came from or the trade her family had forced her into for a time. But she might tip the balance a little and leave things better than she'd found them. That was worth something.

She'd not settled on a firm plan by the time she reached the Donnelly home, but she'd a few ideas rattling about in her knowledge box. Her spirits were light enough to offer a genuine smile and a growing bit of hope when Vera opened the door and welcomed Gemma inside.

"How did your new job treat you, then?" Vera asked.

Gemma moved slowly, keeping to her friend's pace. "Weren't a terrible day, and it ain't a terrible bit of work."

"Will you keep at it, then, do you think?"

That was the question tickling the back of her brain. "The distance is too far to cover every day from Finsbury." But that distance also put her far from Southwark, which was safer. Still, Uncle Silas's mark had been on that building nearly all the way to Marylebone.

The aroma of cooked potatoes and onions filled the house. Gemma thought she smelled bacon as well. If not for the apple she'd eaten, her stomach would've rejoiced far too loudly.

"Are you certain I ain't imposing—two suppers in two nights?"

Vera shook her head firmly. "For my part, I'd have you eat with us every night. I see few people now that I ain't got m'print shop. I like having company."

They stepped into the sitting room where Baz was gabbing with Brogan.

"You're meant to be seeing patients for an hour yet," she said when he looked up at her.

"Dr. Fairbairn agreed to tend to anyone who came by the house. I've put up a sign letting visitors know." He moved to where she stood. "I wanted to make certain I had supper with you."

Her heart started fluttering, seeing as it had no sense of reality. Love wasn't part of this; she knew that well enough. People in difficulties had always pulled at Baz's compassion. And he was a good and loyal friend. She'd not let herself see more than that in any of this.

"Were you in need of something?" she asked.

He shrugged. "Of knowing that you were safe, of knowing if this new job will work out, of seeing for myself that you're less burdened than you were last night."

Baz was making it devilishly hard to remember what was best for her heart. He'd always been kind, but she knew herself to be just molasses-brained enough to believe that kindness was something deeper.

"Are you certain you didn't come on account of being full

clammed and knowing everyone in this flat can cook a filling meal?"

"I *am* hungry," he acknowledged. "But I also can cook a filling meal. I came for the company more than the food."

Brogan, who was sitting on the sofa beside Vera, tossed in his thoughts. "Does that mean I can take your share of supper? I'm 'full clammed'—" He looked to Vera as he repeated the phrase, having tacked on something of a question mark at the end. Vera nodded, and he looked to Baz. "I'm full clammed m'self, you know."

"I'd be happy to challenge you to a bout of fisticuffs with the winner taking the other's portion, if you'd like," Baz said.

A laughing smile pulled at the Irishman's face. "You do remember I grew up a child of the streets and survived by my fists for most of that."

"And, though I've worked hard to stop sounding like it, so did I." Baz hooked an ebony eyebrow upward.

"Did you?" That clearly intrigued Brogan.

In a voice filled with the East End, something he seldom allowed, Baz answered, "These hands ain't always been used for mending. They've known times when *creatin'* the need for mending were a much better use."

The two men laughed, and that seemed to be the end of it. Gemma wondered if Brogan realized, though, how light Baz really was making of the situation. He'd adopted fine manners and speech so his patients would trust him, but she knew details of her husband's childhood that had sent shivers down her spine. Few things did that to a Kincaid.

Móirín poked her head inside in the next instant. "Food's on the table."

Brogan helped Vera to her feet. She winced as she moved. Gemma didn't know the extent of her friend's injuries, and she'd not been nosy enough to pry, but anyone watching could tell those injuries were extensive. Brogan kept an arm around her as the two of them walked from the room.

"I wish I could assure her that she'll improve with time." Baz apparently knew where Gemma's thoughts had gone. "This, though, is likely to be her experience from now on. The pain I'll address as best I can, but her body won't heal much beyond what it has."

"That must knot her temper something terrible. The Vera Sorokina I grew up with weren't one for slowing down, no matter the twists in the road."

Baz slipped his hand around hers. His nearness and his touch was comforting, reassuring. "She's finding her way. These changes might slow her, but they aren't stopping her."

Being slowed by the difficulties of life but not stopped by them. There was shocking clarity in that. Not being loved by the man she adored, having her family hunting her, needing to wait weeks to make good her escape . . . it all *slowed* her. But she didn't mean to let it *stop* her.

The table in the kitchen was packed as tight as Newgate Street during a hanging, but this gathering weren't gruesome or solemn. Móirín was lighthearted, gabbing with her brother and sister-in-law. Vera lit up as well. She was happy, and Gemma was happy for her.

"I've been tossing the puzzle of that ash marking about in m'head all day," Móirín said between bites of stew, her gaze on Gemma. "I've not made heads nor tails of it."

"What mark?" Baz asked.

Everyone in the room knew Gemma's past; she'd explained to them the night before, so there was little point hemming over it. "We found one of my family's calling cards on the side of a building between here and Marylebone."

"They've calling cards?" Brogan blinked a few times.

"They leave marks," Gemma explained. "Telling others they've been there and which of them did the deed, whatever it were that time."

"Someone in your family was that far from Southwark?" Baz sounded as displeased with that as she was.

"Oi."

"Could be an old mark," Brogan said.

She shook her head. "Ash markings don't last long."

Brogan and Baz exchanged a glance, one that weren't anything like relief.

"What I can't sort," Móirín said, "is why they'd mark that building. There's no graveyard nearby. And, though 'tis a more well-to-do spot, nothing about it looked like a treasure trove."

"The Kincaids don't do nothing without reason," Gemma said. "And they don't lay crow about failures." If Uncle Silas marked that building, he was bragging, shouting to the London underworld that he'd accomplished something.

"What building was the mark on?" Brogan asked.

"Number 32 Welbeck Street." Móirín had apparently not only taken note of the address but committed it to memory.

The men both looked at Gemma. She shrugged; she hadn't the first idea what that building held. "Looked like a house to me."

"It is," Vera said, drawing everyone's attention. "Father

Popoff lives there. He's the priest attached to the Russian Embassy in London. The Russian Embassy chapel is at the back of that house."

"Is there a churchyard attached to this chapel?" Gemma asked.

"No."

"It weren't a resurrection, then." Gemma leaned back in her chair, mind spinning with questions.

"Maybe they was following a funeral from that chapel to a graveyard?" Vera suggested.

"They'd've marked the graveyard, not the chapel." She pushed out a breath. "They do more than resurrections, though. It could be they fenced something or gave someone a good ragging."

"Do they consider burglaries and beatings significant enough to leave their calling card?" Baz asked.

"Not usually. It'd need to be part of something bigger or aimed at someone important."

Móirín's levity had given way to concern. "I asked you this morning, but I'm asking again—are you in too much danger to be in that area?"

She didn't have a sure answer. Daylight hours were safer, generally. The right eyes on a place helped too. "Does that bobby chum of yours, Parkington, patrol that area every day, or was seeing him today an oddity?"

"I don't know where he usually patrols," Brogan said.

"I'm glad *I* don't," Móirín added.

In a whisper clearly meant to be overheard, Brogan said to the rest of the table, "Methinks she doth protest too much, yeah?"

Móirín shook her head firmly. "That constable's like a dog at a bone when he smells anything questionable. Some of us'd rather our particular bones be left in peace."

Weren't that the truth.

Baz took Gemma's hand, quite unexpectedly offering the comfort she desperately needed. But her heart couldn't survive breaking again.

She stood, knowing her anxiousness made her about as graceful as a cow in a field full of badger holes. "I'm needing just a few minutes to myself. I'll come back to help wash up, though."

She'd reached the sitting room door when the sound of footsteps stopped her. Baz had followed her.

"Tell me to take myself off if you want me to," he said, "but you've seemed upset since spotting me here. Have I done something to upset you, Gemma?"

"You ain't."

He closed the distance between them, standing directly in front of her. "Something has upset you."

"I've too many thoughts rattling around. I needed a bit of quiet to sort them out."

"Are any of those thoughts ones I could address?"

There were several, but she couldn't ask some of them. "Do you trust Parkington? You seemed to be keeping a distance between him and me at the CALL effort."

He leaned against the doorframe. "I wasn't certain if he would recognize you or what he'd say if he did. But if I didn't trust him at all, I'd either have found a means of sending him away or would've begged you to cry off that day." A tiny hint of East End flavor had snuck back into his words.

"If you told him the Kincaids had done something on Welbeck Street, and if you told him to keep his peepers peeled for ash markings on buildings, do you think he'd watch that area?"

"I'm certain he would."

Some of the worry on her heart eased. A blue-bottle stomping the street would make it safer.

"Tell him the marking for the Kincaids is two vertical lines and a letter *K*. The order varies, but it's always them three things and always right up next to each other. If the *K* is underlined, it means it's a family member working under orders from that brother."

Baz nodded.

"But if you get the feeling Parkington'll come looking for me, see if you cain't hold him off the scent, at least for two weeks. Three weeks at most."

Baz stepped closer, lowering his voice. "What happens in three weeks?"

Troubles might slow you down, but don't let them stop you. She could tell him some, take charge. Didn't mean she had to admit to everything. "I've a few irons in the fire. Once the sparks take, I can leave London, and my family won't be able to find me or hurt me again."

"You're leaving London entirely?" He didn't sound particularly pleased. "Where will you go?"

"Won't overly matter if it means being out of their reach."

He ran his hand lightly along her arm. "Gemma, what happens to you matters."

Oh, how tempted she was to simply drop herself into his

arms and forget for a time how much weight she bore. The silence between them stretched a little long, a little awkward.

A look of resignation spread over Baz's beloved face. "You're leaving in three weeks, then?"

She nodded. "At the most."

"And during those three weeks, will you keep working the job Stone found for you, even with the ash markings on your path?"

All her determination to remain stalwart and heart-whole dissolved. Her shoulders slumped. "I don't know what I ought to do, Baz."

He set his arms around her, just as she'd hoped he would. His embraces had always been tender and gentle. In a world that demanded she be hard, Baz's arms offered her softness.

"I'm cleaning in a wax museum," she said. "It's easy work, and I'm off the street, so it's safer. The sort of job I'd've given my eyeteeth for only a few weeks ago. But it's too far to come from Finsbury every day. And if the walk's riddled with Kincaid markings, I oughtn't be making the walk alone, but I ain't willing to ask Móirín and Stone to be m' nursemaids every day."

"Do you think there's more Kincaid marks than just the one you saw?"

She wrapped her arms around him, needing his strength. "I cain't be certain either way."

"If this job means that much to you, we'll sort a way for you to—to keep doing it. And if you're in danger, we'll formulate a plan for keeping you safe. But if—if you—" He was tripping over his words. "But if you'd like to come back to the house, Gemma, spend your remaining time in London there, I—You—"

She looked up into his face, expecting to find hesitancy in his expression to match his halting words. But it weren't what she saw at all. He looked . . . flustered.

Gemma reached up and lightly touched his face, her fingertips teasing over his long sideburns. Heat touched his cheeks. That was intriguing. Did he always blush when she touched him? If so, she hadn't noticed before.

"I want you to be happy, Gemma," he said quietly. "You tell me what you need for that to happen."

Happy *in the moment*? Or happy *in the long run*? The two, she knew, weren't always the same. Nothing would make her happier than being held by him, perhaps even kissed by him, and to accept his offer to return to Finsbury and pretend for a fortnight that things were different between them than they'd been before.

He liked her and cared about her. He held her and laughed with her. It weren't too far a leap from there to love, at least the beginnings of it.

But she'd debated this with herself before. For weeks, she'd told herself she just needed to give him time, give *them* time. She'd believed the argument enough to not merely confess to him that she loved him but to ask if he loved her.

The pain of his answer still sometimes kept her awake at night.

He wanted her to be happy. She wanted him to be free to marry someone he *could* love. And that couldn't happen until she had Mr. Sorokin's papers in hand and her plan set in motion.

"Perhaps the Donnellys would let me stay here for a fortnight or so," she said. "Móirín wouldn't be going out of her way to walk with me to Marylebone. I could keep my job, earn the coins I need."

Baz didn't answer right away. He also didn't drop his arms away from her. She stayed in his embrace, reassured for the moment but knowing the pain would come.

"I'd wager they'd be happy to let you stay."

Gemma closed her eyes. Kincaids didn't cry. It were one of the rules. Tears brought whippin's. She'd learned that long ago.

"Would you object if I came by and visited during the weeks you're here?" Baz asked quietly. "I likely can't every day, but if I came when I could?"

She hadn't the strength to resist that. "I would like that very much."

She thought she felt him kiss the top of her head.

"You were aiming for the sitting room in order to claim a bit of peace," he said. "Claim it. I'll tell Móirín that you'll have your supper when you're ready."

Gemma offered a quiet word of gratitude. He stepped back, and his arms fell away. He didn't quite meet her eye as he turned and made his way back toward the kitchen. How tempted she was to call him back, to say she would accept whatever affection he offered, that she didn't need him to fully love her.

But it hadn't been enough the first time.

She couldn't put herself through that torture again.

CHAPTER 14

Barnabus and Brogan had followed the Dread Master's instructions and organized a CALL effort in Shoreditch. The Donnellys were angels of mercy in the struggling areas of London and knew what was needed most; they'd easily learned that this corner of Shoreditch most needed help cleaning up the remains of a shop lost to fire so it could be rebuilt. A fire the DPS knew had been set by the Mastiff.

More Dreadfuls were there than had been at the previous CALL effort. Fortunately, that wasn't likely to raise suspicions, as it could be explained by the increased difficulty of undertaking such a physically demanding task.

Barnabus didn't know if Gemma would come as she had before. He hoped she would. He had no more than three weeks of her company remaining to him, and she'd chosen not to spend that time with him.

How many years would she be gone this time? *Years.* How could he endure that? He'd become so numb to her absence that, until she'd returned, he'd not realized how empty everything felt without her.

It always would now. Always.

"Tuck away the hangdog expression, Doc," Parkington said, handing Barnabus a bucket filled with ash and broken bricks. "I spy your wife coming this way with Móirín Donnelly."

Barnabus quickly handed the bucket off to Kumar, the next in line, then looked in the direction Parkington nodded.

Gemma.

He couldn't help a smile. She'd come after all.

"Last I saw her, she looked worried," Parkington said. "Stone and Móirín weren't subtle about keeping me from gabbing with her."

"Were you particularly interested in doing so?" Barnabus eyed him, trying to decide if he ought to warn Gemma off or not.

Parkington pulled him out of the bucket line and off to the side. He lowered his voice. "It ain't every day a fellow crosses paths with the daughter of Pacey Kincaid."

Panic set in. Parkington knew.

"People ain't responsible for who their parents are, Doc." Parkington set a soot-covered hand on his shoulder. "When I saw her on Welbeck Street, I only wanted to make certain she weren't in any danger. But Stone can certainly hold his own. And Móirín could scare a cat into skinning itself just by looking at it. I figured Mrs. Milligan was as safe as a stone in a peach."

"You know who she is, but you aren't going to—"

"To what? Arrest her?" Parkington shook his head. "She

cain't help the life she was born into. But I don't think that life is what she chooses to do now."

Relief swept over Barnabus. "On her behalf, I'll return your forbearance with a warning she asked me to tip into your ear. The home of the Russian Embassy priest was marked in ash with the calling card of the Kincaid family. That means the Kincaids did something there, something criminal. She thought that might help you piece together some puzzles."

"The Kincaids would bash her good if they knew she'd given me this information."

"I told her you could be trusted." Barnabus held his gaze. "Don't prove me wrong."

"I won't." He hooked his thumb to where Gemma and Móirín stood at the edge of the gathering. "Go save your wife from that she-cat."

"Móirín's a fine person," Barnabus said with a laugh.

Parkington held his hands up in a show of innocence before returning to the clean-up effort. The DPS trusted the man with a lot of information, though certainly not all of it.

The moment Barnabus moved toward Gemma, she moved toward him. They met in the middle.

"Móirín convinced me to come," she said. "But she didn't tell me Parkington would be here."

"She likely didn't know." He reached for her hand but pulled back immediately. His hands were filthy. "I'm glad you came."

She smiled a little. "So am I."

"I had a gab with Parkington. I don't think we need to worry that he'll cause you any grief."

After a glance in the policeman's direction, she asked,

"Did you tell him about the—" Concern tugged at her expression, and she didn't finish the question. But Barnabus knew what she was asking.

"I did, and he was grateful. He's also worried, though. If your family finds out . . ."

"Crossing the Kincaids has consequences," she whispered. "All the more reason to pike off and get myself away from London, i'n'it?"

Away from London. His heart dropped clear to his feet every time he thought about her leaving. "How long will you be gone this time, do you think?"

"So long as I'm here, I'm in danger, and so are the people I care about. I ain't willing to risk other people's lives."

Did that mean she didn't mean to ever come back? Surely not.

"You'll think I'm dancing around our topic"—Gemma lowered her voice even further—"but there's a man across the way who has been watching what's happening here. He was doing that when I first arrived, and he don't look the least pleased."

"It isn't someone you recognize?" He wanted to make certain it wasn't anyone in her family.

She shook her head.

Slowly, with as casual a demeanor as he could manage, he looked in the general direction Gemma had indicated. There was, indeed, a man across the way, watching. Not Mr. Snelling, the newspaper-carrying man who'd watched him once before and then dropped in at his surgery. Nor was it any of the London macks or rough-and-toughs Barnabus had encountered from his years of rescue work.

Brogan was nearby, so Barnabus subtly motioned him over. "Take a peek at that man across the street just over your right shoulder and tell me if you know him."

Brogan managed to look without appearing to be doing anything but chatting amicably with his friends.

"Manky huff," Brogan muttered. "That's him."

"Who?" Gemma and Barnabus asked in almost perfect unison.

"The Mastiff," Brogan whispered. "I saw him before the mangy bloke blew up the print shop. That's him and no mistaking."

Gemma had frozen on the spot.

Barnabus took her hand. She held fast to his in return.

"And he's not alone." Brogan subtly motioned Ana Darby over. "I'm not the expert you are, so I can't be certain. Tell me, the woman across the way, talking to that fierce-looking man. She's someone we know, yeah?"

Ana glanced, then sucked in a quick breath. It was testament to the years she had spent as London's most successful sneak thief that her expression didn't change at all. "That's Serena, the one the Mastiff has been holding against her will."

Under the pretense of checking the progress of the cleanup efforts, Barnabus watched the scene across the street.

The Mastiff said something to Serena. She shook her head, the movement jerking and tense. Her captor was still talking, anger in his eyes and expression. She watched him intently. The next instant, the Mastiff walked away. Serena remained behind, alone.

"We have to help her," Ana said. "If you'd seen the fear in

her eyes at the gambling den where Hollis and I first met her, you'd know how much danger she is in."

Barnabus had seen it more recently than that. "She's still terrified. And trapped. I saw her recently and tried to convince her to take the escape I offered her, but she was too afraid."

"Let's you and I see if we can talk her into coming with us," Barnabus said to Ana. "She might listen to you, or at least give it more thought."

Gemma set a hand on his arm. "Please, be careful."

Barnabus nodded. "We'll be *very* careful."

He caught Fletcher's and Hollis's eyes and motioned them over. Brogan slipped over to where Móirín was helping with the cleanup. He would most certainly whisper to his sister as much as he could without giving away DPS secrets. They would help Gemma stay safe while Barnabus attempted to help save Serena.

He and Ana moved to meet Fletcher and Hollis halfway.

"That's Serena," Ana said to her husband. "The woman we've been looking for."

Fletcher leaned a bit closer to Barnabus and talked out the side of his mouth. "Shall we catch up with her and try again?"

"That's the entirety of my plan at the moment."

"Spontaneity." Fletcher nodded. "I like this new version of you, Doc."

"You can gab later, boys," Hollis said. "Serena's walking away."

They moved toward her, but she spotted them and moved quicker.

"We need to work on our stealth, mates," Fletcher said. "She was flash to us in an instant."

They picked up their pace, following Serena down a narrower side street.

"Seems we've done this before." Fletcher motioned Hollis around the corner, likely hoping he'd catch up with Serena at the other end of the street.

But the street split into a *T*, and Serena went the opposite direction Hollis had. She looked back at them a few times, the briefest of glances. The winding streets often turned into labyrinths the farther one followed them. This path would likely prove no different.

Ana dropped from behind a wall directly in front of Serena. Barnabus hadn't even realized Ana had slipped away from the group. Having a sneak thief in their midst was a helpful thing indeed.

"Please, listen to us," Ana said. "We can get you out now. We can get you somewhere safe."

Serena shook her head over and over again. "He will find me."

"There are safe places we can take you," Barnabus said. "We can get you as far away from him as you need to be."

"I'll not abandon my children. He'd kill 'em in a rage."

Barnabus hadn't forgotten she had children tied up in this as well. "We've saved children too."

Still the terror in her eyes. Still the frantic shaking of her head. "Not from him."

"Yes, from him," Fletcher said. "We know who he is. He knows who we are, too, because we thwart him every chance we get."

She blinked a few times. The tiniest flicker of hope crossed her face, but she snuffed it out quickly. "If I went bridges with you, he'd nab my little ones before any of us could say Bob."

"Where are they?" Fletcher asked gently and with clear concern.

"They're at Trafalgar Square, earning their keep for the day. They're made to be bungnippers."

Forced to be pickpockets. That was more common than it ought to be.

"The children have to come back with a certain amount or . . ." She didn't finish; she didn't have to.

"We can send someone there right now, find them before he does," Fletcher said.

"You don't know them. *He* does." Serena was physically shaking. "Just me talking to you could've tipped him already."

"You tell us their names and what they look like, how we'll know them. We'll find them. We have eyes and ears all over the city."

Serena wrapped her arms around herself, doing little to still her trembling. "So does the Mastiff. He burns people." In a strangled whisper, she added, "Alive."

"We know," Barnabus said. "We will understand if you aren't willing to take the risk right now. But this may be your only chance. My mother was also trapped by someone cruel and exacting. I often wished when I was small that she'd taken the risk and tried to free us."

She was debating; he could see it in her eyes. "Would I have to be separated from them?"

Barnabus shook his head. "We can bring them to you."

"I've nothing to pay you with," she warned.

"We'd not accept it anyway," Fletcher said.

Serena's shoulders straightened, though she hadn't stopped shaking. "I'll go with *her*," she said, pointing to Ana.

It was quickly arranged. Hollis and Ana would hail a hackney and get Serena to one of the safe houses Barnabus had set up to help women escaping dangerous situations. Fletcher would go find her children.

"Do you promise me you'll find them?" Serena pressed, her voice breaking with emotion.

"I swear to it," Fletcher said.

She crumbled at that, though whether out of desperation, fear, or relief wasn't immediately apparent. Ana put an arm around her and, with Hollis, led her away.

Only Fletcher and Barnabus remained in the tiny, narrow street.

Barnabus sighed with relief.

"Wouldn't breathe too easily yet if I were you," Fletcher said. With a tip of his chin, he motioned to the walls on either side of them.

Barnabus had been so focused on Serena that he'd not taken time to study their surroundings. Scrawled on every wall multiple times, in everything from ash to mud to paint to what he feared might be blood, was a single phrase: "The Tempest is coming."

THE BACHELOR AND THE BRIDE

by Mr. King

Installment IV

in which an unexpected Danger places our Hero and Heroine in a most dire Situation

Sorcha felt as though hours had passed, though it had likely not been more than thirty minutes. She told herself to breathe, to remain calm, to not grow overly worried. But her mind returned rapidly and repeatedly to a similar wait undertaken in a dark cottage on a fear-filled night.

She tried to tell herself she had given Duncan ample warning about the dangers he faced, that his knowledge of it would protect him. But her father and mother had understood the threat of the *cù-sìth*. Her father, after all, had shouted for them to run for the cottage; it was the cottage, and the cottage *alone*, where they would have been safe. They had known what they faced; they simply hadn't had time to escape.

She alternated between pacing the road and sitting on a large rock nearby. She kept herself out of view of the path, not entirely certain how far one had to travel before seeing the *Bean-Nighe*. But, heavens, how she was tempted to look for Duncan!

Hers was more than merely the concern one human being ought to have for another. She liked Duncan. She knew him to be a good and kindhearted person. He was clever and caring. Handsome. Generous. How strange that he had never been married. Few in their village remained bachelors, but he had, despite his caring and generous heart.

She rose from her rock once more and began pacing. Duncan was undertaking the task, would be successful, and would return. Of course he would.

She hoped.

She turned back toward the rock on which she'd been sitting, but she didn't take a single step.

There, standing where she'd been, was Duncan. He had arrived silently. Granny's shoes were very effective. She hoped they had proven just as effective in his very dangerous task.

She remained rooted to the spot, watching him, unable to even speak.

"She was there," he said. "I never looked away. She didn't see me."

Sorcha began breathing a little more easily.

"I snatched her up off the ground, asked my required three questions, and answered hers. Then she let me go."

Sorcha pressed a hand to her pounding heart. "Then you're safe? The shroud will not be yours?" Her voice emerged a bit breathless. She'd been so very afraid for him!

"It will not. And, further, she told me how to heal Donella."

Most of the tension in Sorcha's body eased. She crossed to him. "What do we need to do?"

"We have to fetch water from the mouth of the gargoyle in the churchyard at Carrifran. If Donella drinks it, she will be healed."

"Then our journey is not yet complete." She hadn't anticipated that. They hadn't a great deal of time before they must return.

"I don't know where Carrifran is," he said.

"I do," Sorcha said. "It lies at least a day's walk from here."

"If we begin now, we should reach Carrifran tomorrow," he said, clearly thinking out loud. "That still leaves us three days before *Bealltainn*."

"Yes, but I have my suspicions that the Washing Woman is not the last creature we will encounter. You see, they are not solitary. They are not unconnected. That you had one interaction with a member of their race, and emerged triumphant, means others will be watching for you, determined to best you as the *Bean-Nighe* was unable to do."

"And what of your encounter with the *cù-sìth*? You emerged triumphant in that encounter," he said.

"The very reason Granny Winter has taught me so much of the ways of fairies and monsters. She is hopeful that the passage of so many years without significant interactions means they aren't particularly upset at my escape. Likely because they were successful in causing me so much pain."

"Are all creatures from that realm so vindictive and bloodthirsty?"

Sorcha shook her head. "Some are rather benevolent.

Some are neither good nor bad. But those that mean harm are more than capable of inflicting it."

"If you don't wish to continue," he said, "I will understand. You need only give me directions, and I will make the remainder of the journey on my own."

"I am not afraid."

"Neither am I," he said.

She'd long suspected he was quite brave. It was a wonderful thing to realize she was right.

"We had best begin," she said. "We have a long journey ahead."

They paused long enough for him to switch from the soft shoes to his sturdier boots. Granny's shoes were placed in the bag, and the bag slung over his shoulder. Sorcha pulled from her bag an apple for each of them, which they ate as they walked.

"What do you know of this town we are heading toward?" he asked.

"Not very much. I know where it is, but I've not been there myself. Granny Winter showed me a map a few weeks ago, talking about the various places and some of their history. She pointed out that town on the map, but she didn't tell me anything about it."

His face pulled in an expression of pondering. "I have my suspicions she knew you were going to be making this journey. Why else would she have a bag ready with things that were needed, and why else would she mention this town to you?"

Sorcha smiled to herself. Granny *had* likely known, or at least had had an inkling. There seemed very little that woman didn't know or couldn't predict. How she hoped Granny Winter had foreseen the possibility of success on this journey, even if success wasn't entirely promised.

They had been walking for nearly an hour, speaking of inconsequential things, sharing stories from their lives and their likes and dislikes, recounting things that had happened in their village and the people they knew there. It was one of the most pleasant conversations she'd ever had. The villagers were not unkind to her, neither did they ignore her existence. But they kept her at a distance, likely because she lived with Granny Winter, who was treated with respect but also with uncertainty.

The path Sorcha and Duncan walked took them into a meadow. Grass fluttered in the breeze. Wildflowers were abundant. No matter that the countryside held difficult memories for her, she still found it the most beautiful and inviting of places. Duncan hunched down a few steps into the meadow and plucked from the ground a beautiful purple flower. Not all men would notice such things, but she wasn't surprised he did. He had a gentle heart and a kind soul. She was surprised, however, when he offered the flower to her.

She accepted it. "No one has ever given me a flower." She spun it between her finger and her thumb, mesmerized by the whirl of purple hues.

"Not ever?" The revelation clearly surprised him.

"I know giving flowers to ladies is something men often do. I suppose I'm simply not the sort of lady they think of doing that for."

"I don't see why that would be." He stroked his pointed beard and mustache, his expression one of deep pondering.

"You're clever and kind. You're the very best of company. Beautiful and pleasant. You have a kind heart, and you care about people."

She felt herself blushing all the deeper. She was never paid such compliments. Granny Winter was not unkind to her, but hers was not a disposition which leant itself to saying flowery things. Sorcha breathed in the floral scent, then tucked the stem behind her ear.

They continued walking through the meadow. She couldn't imagine being more content with anyone than she was with him in that moment. They'd very nearly reached the other side, where the meadow gave way to a small copse of trees, and their path continued on. A niggling doubt tugged at her mind. They were going in the right direction, weren't they?

He was trusting her to get him to Carrifran. Was she certain they were indeed on the right path? She paused, still in the meadow, still within sight of the path through the trees. She turned and looked in the direction they'd come. Why was it she felt the need to go back? She couldn't ignore the very real pull she felt.

"What is it?" Duncan asked.

"I find myself wondering if we're proceeding in the correct direction. Something in my mind is telling me we should be going back."

"Back in the direction of Loch Dreva?" He clearly did not agree with her assessment.

"Perhaps not that far," she said. "We may have missed a break in the road or a turn we ought to have taken."

"I didn't see any," he said.

That he was doubtful of her settled frustratingly on her mind. Did he not feel this same insistence that they were going the wrong way?

She studied the meadow, hoping to discover some clue as to what was pulling at her. She spied a flash of blue light at a distance, dancing on the tips of the blades of wild grass. The light called to her. Beckoned to her.

"We need to go that way." Without hesitating or looking back at him, she rushed toward the spark, but it extinguished the moment she reached it.

Frantic, her eyes swept the area, searching.

The blue light appeared again, a bit farther ahead, back the way they'd come.

She chased it only to have it extinguish and reappear farther away. It moved faster, though she did too. The pull was undeniable, unmistakable. She couldn't have stopped chasing it if she tried.

Back it went, back along the trail. On and on she followed, not to the path they'd been on but into a nearby wood. There was no path, just flickering blue lights, tiny blue flames popping up everywhere, guiding her in the direction she knew she had to go.

Duncan caught up to her, running alongside her, digging in his bag. He pulled out the crock of butter and tossed it toward the blue flame. It stopped. Hovered.

She stopped.

Duncan set his arms around her, his embrace firm but gentle. "I know this creature," he said. "You mustn't follow it, Sorcha."

"I need to. It's taking me where I must follow."

"It's the will-o'-the-wisp. It is leading you astray, and it will lead you to your death if you allow it. You have to resist the urge to follow."

Something in his words penetrated the fog clouding her mind. The will-o'-the-wisp. It called to those who wandered, those who felt pulled toward something new and something different. It twisted around the mind, convincing people to run ever deeper into dangerous paths, away from the path they were meant to trod. It tugged at her wanderer's heart, tucked itself into her vagabond's mind, and pulled her almost beyond resisting.

She closed her eyes tightly and leaned against Duncan. She wrapped her arms around his middle and held fast to him, knowing her life depended on it. The mystical flame would eventually extinguish itself, searching for another unwary wanderer. She simply needed to resist its call until it did.

"I can still hear it," she whispered, afraid.

He stood steadfast, a lighthouse in a storm, holding her to him and whispering words of reassurance and promises to remain with her for as long as she needed him to.

"The flame has flickered out," he said after a time.

But its pull continued twisting around her mind. She held fast to Duncan, depending on him to keep her from following the lights again.

"There is a hollowed-out old tree nearby, one large enough for us to tuck ourselves inside," he said. "We'll be warm and safe there."

He kept hold of her as they walked, held her hand as

she set herself in the protective embrace of the tree, then sat beside her.

"We know now why Granny Winters included a crock of butter in her bag," Duncan said. "The will-o'-the-wisp is known to steal milk from cows to make into butter. Offering butter provided a needed distraction."

"I shudder to think what would have happened if you'd not helped me." Sorcha leaned against him.

He set his arms around her once more. "We make a fine team, Sorcha."

There was comfort in that. Comfort and hope.

CHAPTER 15

Móirín and Parkington both attempted to convince Gemma not to follow Baz into the shadows of the narrow street he'd gone down. The oddity of those two joining forces in anything at all might've been enough to stop her if not for the fact that the Mastiff was connected somehow to all of this. The Kincaids were dangerous, the Mastiff even more so. She needed to know that Baz was safe.

She passed Hollis and Ana walking with a woman she didn't know, likely the one they'd been trying to rescue. Seemed they'd managed the thing.

Gemma continued on and came upon Baz and Fletcher studying the walls on either side of them. She eyed the brick and stone as well. They were covered in writing, the same phrase scrawled over and over again. "The Tempest is coming."

"Who is the Tempest?" she asked.

Both men spun about.

"Gemma!" Baz moved swiftly to her. "You were supposed to stay with the others."

"Oi, but I don't always do what I'm told."

"Why is it you think the scrawls are a warning about a person?" Fletcher asked, his eyes darting from her to the walls and back.

"'Tempest' is always capitalized, i'n'it? Seems more likely it's a person than a thing."

Baz and Fletcher exchanged looks.

"Could be another cur in the Mastiff's network," Fletcher said. "The Protector. The Raven. Same type of name."

Baz shrugged. "Could be. Or this could be old writing, here for years, before the Mastiff arrived on the scene."

Gemma stepped closer to one of the walls, an oddity in the stone catching her eye.

"Some of this is in ash," Fletcher said. "Has to be recent."

One of the stones at her eye level had gouges in the surface, the sort made by a chisel rather than by time or accident.

"The words written in paint could've been there ages," Baz said. "It could be people making a point of rewriting it, a tradition or rite of passage or something."

Gemma ran her fingers over the grooves, tracing them. A portion of one "The Tempest is coming" in blue paint crossed over the etching, atop it. Touching the carving, she followed it with her finger.

KII

"The painted words ain't more than three years old," she said, her hand frozen against the wall.

"How'd you twig that?" Fletcher asked from somewhere behind her.

"The man who would've left this mark made his churchyard journey three years ago, and the words were painted over his mark."

Baz moved to stand beside her. "Your father's *K* came first."

She nodded. "I ain't never seen his mark left permanently, not on a building, leastwise. Something about this spot is significant."

"And that means it's likely also dangerous," Baz whispered.

She nodded.

He slipped his hand around hers, gently pulling it away from the wall. "Your father isn't here anymore, but we are. Fletch and me, Móirín, Brogan, Stone, Hollis, Parkington, Ana, Elizabeth, Vera—"

"An extensive list, Baz," she said with a smile. "But brown to this if you will: my uncles are still on this side of the grave. My cousins as well. They've people loyal to them who ain't exactly gentle kittens."

"You slipped from their grasp once before." Baz kept his hand around hers.

"Your home is the first place I ever felt safe." She took a deep breath, then stepped back, out of his arms. "But I won't *willingly* return that danger to your doorstep. Less than three weeks, Baz, and you'll be free of it."

"What if I don't want to be?"

He was being very gallant, insisting on yet another rescue. Dare she ask him if there was anything else underlying his question? In the moment, the fear of what she'd hear—*again*—overcame her hope of receiving a different answer.

Her hesitation was more than that now, though. The Kincaids were searching for her. She couldn't risk bringing them to his house. She couldn't put his life in further danger. The sooner she was no longer part of that life, the better for him.

"Parkington will be watching Welbeck Street. The Donnellys' flat is safe and tucked out of notice. We'll leave things as they are until I'm out of London," she said.

He looked disappointed. Did he have any idea how difficult he was making this?

"Are you still willing to let me come call on you?"

"Of course." Bless her, she weren't making it easier on *herself.* To both men, she said, "If a Kincaid marked this place permanently, it ain't a place you ought to knock about."

With that, she made good her escape, though she didn't rejoin the CALL effort. She needed to keep her wits about her, else she'd find herself the reason the Kincaid mark appeared on the walls of Baz's home.

"There's jobs to be had closer to Finsbury," Móirín said as she and Gemma made their way toward Marylebone. Gemma had been living with the Donnellys for nearly a week now. "Could be living with your husband if you wanted to be."

"It ain't that simple, as I've told you time and again."

"You're making it complicated, as *I've* told *you* time and again. You love Barnabus. Pining for him in that tiny cupboard of a room we have for you is a fine bit of nonsense when you could be with him."

"Being with him is too dangerous, Móirín."

"He's lived all his life facing dangers of one kind or another," Móirín said. "And he's faced your family before. But I don't suspect that's the danger you're most keen to avoid."

"What else could it be?"

"It'd be a fair dangerous thing loving someone you don't think will ever love you in return. But how is it you expect that to change if you're not ever with him?" Móirín gave her a look usually saved for the dullest of dullards.

"I *was* with him for half a year, waiting on that to change." Gemma stepped around a costermonger's cart. "I can't hold my breath that long again."

"So use that breath to tell him what's weighing on you."

"I have, more often than you know." Gemma tucked her hands in her pockets. "He's already done things for me he wouldn't've otherwise because he took pity on me."

"You truly think that's all there was to any of it?" Móirín shook her head. "Here I was thinking you were clever."

"You know he's a rescuer, going to any length to save anyone he can."

"And of all those he's rescued, you're the only one he's ever married. And the only one I've ever seen him hold in his arms. And the only one he's begged time and again to make her home with him." They'd reached the point where their paths divided. "This is more than a rescue to him, Gemma. Stop minimizing it."

"Minimizing what?" Stone spoke from behind them, not having given away his presence in any way.

Móirín didn't even jump. Gemma did.

"Our friend here is convinced the good doctor looks on her like a penniless waif in one of Fletcher's penny dreadfuls."

Móirín shook her head. "Thick as molasses in a cold snap, she is."

On that, Móirín made her way down the street leading to her job for the day. Stone motioned for Gemma to continue on.

"I didn't realize I'd be getting a full escort this morning," she said. "You'd think I were the daughter of a duke or some such thing."

"Doc'd kill the lot of us if anything happened to you. We're saving our own necks as much as yours."

"He's a little protective of me." Without a doubt, Móirín would insist that was reason enough for believing he was full in love with her. Gemma knew better. She also knew better than to let the topic linger. "Tell me about this woman."

"What woman would that be?"

She didn't think he was being coy. She doubted Stone ever was. "Your secret sweetheart."

"Ah." His eyes swept the area but not in a way that anyone would notice. He was keeping a weather eye out—and on her behalf, she'd wager. "Met her after I'd been living in London a few years. She sold secondhand clothes next to the tobacconist's shop where I worked at the time."

"Is she pretty?"

His smile was all the answer anyone needed.

"Is she from America, like you are?"

"How do you know I'm from America?"

"Well, you don't sound like any Londoner I've ever met. Took my next best guess."

Stone shook his head. "She ain't from America, but I am sure enough. She's lived all her life in London."

"Are you hoping to marry her?"

He nodded. "I'd have done so already, but life has complicated things lately."

"It does that."

This had to be the most she'd ever heard Stone say at one time. Was he always quiet, or only around people he didn't know well?

"Do you see her often?" Gemma asked.

"Whenever I can."

"And no one but Móirín and I are privy to any of it?"

He shrugged. "A fella's entitled to keep secrets."

"But you're digging into plenty of mine," she pointed out.

"Doc's a good man. And you seem a good sort as well." Stone looked at her with a solemn expression. "You ought to try making things right between you."

She'd not expected their discussion to take this turn. "Why should *I* be the one to close that gap?"

In a tone of voice too filled with compassion to be mistaken for anything but the concern of a true friend, he said, "Because he don't know how."

CHAPTER 16

Barnabus was confused.

He thought he'd been showing Gemma that he wanted her to return home, to at least spend the remainder of her time in London with him. He'd been careful not to press the matter, wanting her to make her own decision but knowing he hoped she would stay.

But she was, apparently, happier living in a tiny closet of a room, sleeping on a pallet on the floor, a guest in someone else's house, than returning home.

Confused frustration was likely not the best mindset for attending a DPS meeting. But timing was not on his side. Too much was happening in London's underworld for dithering.

Not every member of the organization would be present, but there was plenty to catch up on and business to attend to.

Nolan was sleeping lightly in the entryway, and Barnabus paused, listening to his slow and steady breathing, making certain he heard no rattling or wheezing. The man was like a favorite uncle to all of them: odd, yes, but beloved.

"I ain't dying, Doc," he said without opening his eyes.

"See to it that continues to be the case." Barnabus placed his penny on the small table alongside several others.

Nolan pressed the well-hidden button, and the wall slid open, affording Barnabus entry into the parliamentary room. It was far from empty.

Barnabus dropped himself into his usual chair and waited for things to begin. He was in no mood to talk and had no desire to exchange social niceties. He would, of course, help if someone were ill, but he wasn't looking to gab pointlessly.

"With me, gentlemen and lady," Fletcher called out to them all.

In near perfect unison, they rose, recited their oath, retook their seats, and waited for the meeting to begin. The mood was more somber than usual. The entire organization knew they were facing a bigger threat than they ever had before.

"I'll not belabor things," Fletcher said. "Serena, the housekeeper what was being held by the Mastiff, is at one of Doc's safe houses now, along with her children."

Fletcher had let Barnabus know this already, but it sent a surge of relief through him to hear it repeated. They had convinced Serena to trust them, even knowing she wasn't exaggerating the violent nature of the Mastiff's vengeance. They'd vowed they could keep her and her children safe, and they'd keep that vow.

"Stone and Brogan are keeping an eye on Gemma Milligan," Fletcher said. "Móirín is accidentally helping us there."

"Mighty good of her," Martin said with a chuckle.

Fletcher tossed out a smile but didn't stop his recounting. "The rotating guard we have near Doc's house ain't seen signs of danger, though there's been a starched bloke loafing about."

That brought their eyes to Barnabus.

"There's a fellow I saw on the street a couple of weeks ago," he said. "He came by later that day claiming illness but was perfectly healthy. He didn't tell me what it was he wanted. I'd wager that's the man you're seeing."

"Any hunches what he might be about?" Fletcher asked.

"None," Barnabus said.

Murmurs of confusion and worry rumbled through the room, though Fletcher didn't allow it to last.

"Brogan received a letter from his father-in-law, and it seems it ought to be shared with us." Fletcher motioned to Brogan.

Barnabus's ears perked up. Hearing from Mr. Sorokin might very well be the same as hearing from the Dread Master. That warranted all the attention he could give.

Their resident Irishman stood, unfolded a sheet of parchment, and read aloud.

Brogan,

I know of someone who works in Lord Chelmsford's home. It seems the efforts to do him harm have not ceased since the blackmail plot was foiled a couple of months ago. Whomever it was you worked with to untangle that scheme needs to know it has not ended. Chelmsford is part of this, somehow.

Whispers on the street connect the Mastiff to him, not as allies, not even as foes, but as predator and prey.
Keep Vera safe.
—Sorokin

The room sat in silence for a drawn-out moment. The DPS had recently extricated Lord Chelmsford from a blackmail scheme. The Mastiff, employing members of his criminal enterprise and forcing the hand of Mr. Sorokin himself had threatened the Russian ambassador into lying about Lord Chelmsford's career as a barrister, most specifically his work on the Radlett murder forty years earlier. They'd not managed to sort out why that particular case had been chosen.

"The Mastiff used the Russian ambassador to try to bring down Chelmsford, yeah?" Martin said. "And the resurrection men the Mastiff's using now left a mark on the walls of the Russian Embassy chapel, yeah?"

Nods around the room.

"Maybe he hasn't given up on blackmailing the ambassador either," Martin said.

"His blackmailing of the ambassador was entirely meant to bring down Lord Chelmsford," Elizabeth said. "But why? Lord Chelmsford isn't active in government right now. Had this happened six years ago, I might understand. He was Lord Chancellor then."

"If we knew what the Mastiff's end goal was in regard to Chelmsford," Stone said, "that'd tell us a lot about why he might be targeting the fella."

"It's something to do with the Radlett murder," Barnabus said. "That was the focus of the blackmail before."

"That case was important to Chelmsford's career," Hollis said, "but it's hardly the entirety of it. It's not even the bulk of it. He was granted his barony on account of many other things. That case, while well-known, is likely of very little importance to Chelmsford."

"Then," Fletcher said, "we need to sort out why it's important *to the Mastiff.*"

He was right, of course. Everyone—from Martin to Kumar, Stone to Hollis, Brogan to Elizabeth—looked as convinced as Barnabus felt. The Mastiff's connection to that murder and that trial was the key.

"How do we find that out?" Kumar asked. "We can't exactly ask the fellow directly."

"We could ask Serena," Brogan said. "She likely learned a great many things about the Mastiff."

"I'd not advise pressing the matter yet," Barnabus said. "In my experience, women who have only just escaped abusive and dangerous situations need time to feel safe and secure again. She'll not reveal secrets yet, and I can't blame her for that."

There were no arguments.

"While we wait and while we search, we need eyes on Chelmsford's house," Fletcher said. "I can have my urchins judge the weather from the outside. But we need one of *us* on the inside."

"I can do that," Martin said. "I've experience working in fine houses. Might be enough to get a position there."

Elizabeth looked to Brogan. "Have you the means of getting word to Mr. Sorokin? He apparently knows someone on

Chelmsford's staff. He might be able to get Martin a position."

Brogan shook his head. "We haven't the first idea where he is."

"Never fear," Fletcher said. "The Dread Master'll know how to get word to him."

Get word *to* Mr. Sorokin. Or the Dread Master *was* Mr. Sorokin. Though Barnabus's primary guess had always been Stone, the secretive Russian was quickly proving himself as likely a candidate.

"That leaves only one matter," Fletcher said. "Soon enough, the Mastiff'll begin killing people just so he can have them dug up. Might be doing it already. This fight is growing and swelling, and I don't know how we thwart 'im."

"The Tempest is coming," Stone said, arms folded across his chest. "It's a fight we're unlikely to win, and he knows it."

"There's some merit to Gemma's theory," Barnabus said. "The Tempest might be a person."

"Whatever or whoever it is," Fletcher said, "it's coming, and we are all that stands in its way."

"And we do not relent," Elizabeth said.

"And we do not forget," Hollis said.

"We are the Dread Penny Society," Fletcher said. "This is what we were made for."

Bodies of Light

being a Fictionalization of Reported and Corroborated Mysterious Phenomena

by Dr. Barnabus Milligan, physician

Chapter Three

The paper Dr. Palmer submitted to the College of Physicians on the luminescence he had observed was met mostly with silence. Though he was frustrated, he was not surprised. He'd filled the submission with details and theories but no data, no scientifically sound information. His next paper, he vowed, would be overrun with both.

It was in pursuit of this that he returned to Ireland, returned to the peat bogs where he'd first observed the cones of fire. He sat in the dark and the cold, watching and waiting for a return of that most extraordinary sight.

It did not return.

He did, however, experience something not entirely unrelated. The peat of those bogs, when cut, emitted an unmistakable, albeit brief, glow. It occurred when the peat was disturbed, and the light disappeared almost on the instant.

Could this, he wondered, be related to what he'd seen more than nine months earlier? Could there be a connection?

Determined to know more and return to London with answers, he made an examination of the peat himself. He cut a bit, causing the momentary glow to continue. As it disappeared, he immediately sliced off a bit more, and the glow to returned.

He guarded the slice of peat fiercely as he returned to the cottage he had let for a few weeks in pursuit of the answers he required. No one else was present; he could not permit the distraction. Palmer laid out his medical tools, quite as if he was about to undertake an examination of a patient or a dissection in a lab. He set his large cutting of peat on the table amidst his instruments. He lit a lamp and brought it near. Palmer set magnifying spectacles on his nose and bent over the peat block.

A bit of careful cutting and breaking revealed the presence of tiny white worms no more than half an inch in length. Palmer poked at them and nudged them and, in whatever way he could, caused the animals a bit of irritation, hoping to discover that they were the source of the soft glow he'd seen in the bog peat.

It did not seem to be enough.

Palmer refused to believe he was wrong yet again. The College of Physicians had dismissed his discoveries and hypotheses because he could not provide any evidence. He would have it this time. He swore he would. He would not rest without answers. *Could* not.

What else could irritate or cause excitation in the worms without causing them any harm? He looked around his cottage, searching for something, anything. His eyes fell upon a bottle of strong spirits. He could not place the worms in the alcohol as that might drown the creatures. The vapors, though, might prove sufficient.

He took careful hold of one worm with his smallest pair of tissue forceps. He filled a small, shallow dish with the alcohol, then held the worm over it, near enough for the vapors to envelop the creature. Mere moments later, it began to glow.

At last! At last he had succeeded in forcing a naturally occurring glow to appear!

The phosphorescence was a brilliant, beautiful, clear green that illuminated the entirety of the worm's body. But it lasted a mere instant.

He subjected several of the worms to the same treatment and achieved the same result. With enough of these tiny creatures in peat, agitation of that peat would cause dozens upon dozens to produce the green light at once, creating the twinkling glow he'd seen.

It did not, though, explain the columns of fiery light he'd seen at the beginning of the year.

It did not explain the lights that had illuminated Miss Lavinia's face.

And it did not explain the further phenomena of light he observed as the weeks and months continued to pass. For he'd committed himself to searching them out. Dedicated himself to the pursuit.

Palmer had attended the bedside of a woman dying of a pulmonary consumption not unlike that which had claimed Miss Lavinia Abbott. He had not tended to many patients since Miss Lavinia's passing. One could not pursue elusive answers and doctor at the same time. At least not often.

As he had in Miss Lavinia's home, he observed in this new location a moon-like light dancing upon the woman's face, with something of the look of lightning, something of the look of the glowing peat, but not precisely like either one.

He was not alone in observing the phosphorescent illumination of this particular patient's features. The unfortunate soul was attended also by her sisters and mother. The word of women was not generally considered by the medical establishment to be authoritative, but their corroboration of his observations might still have proven useful despite that prejudicial opinion—if only their recounting of the experience had matched his.

The light they had observed, the women insisted, had not been *upon* her face but hovering *above* it in the air she breathed out. It danced in diagonal glimmers, shimmering about near the head of the bed.

He did not think he had misjudged what he'd observed. He was too meticulous an observer. That this mystery held such weight in his mind made him even more aware of the details.

A fellow doctor in Ireland wrote to tell him of a similar experience occurring in a neighboring village. A man suffering with pulmonary tuberculosis was known to emit a glow as well. It was said, in fact, that these periods of body-produced light appeared nightly. It was described by the local people as a luminous fog or a sparkle of phosphorescence, but Palmer's colleague could not confirm this. He further indicated that all he had heard pointed toward the odd light existing, as the sisters previously mentioned had insisted, in the air rather than upon the person of the patient.

That, while intriguing, was not the phenomenon Palmer was chasing. It was not the mystery he grew more and more determined to solve. He would not—*could* not—rest until he did! It was no longer a matter of mere curiosity but of necessity.

Back in his own home once more, Palmer became all but consumed by the pursuit of answers. He attempted to coax a glow from every living thing he could get his hands on. None cooperated.

The question rested heavily on his thoughts as he went about his days and even as he attempted to sleep. He thought upon it as he ate his meals and as he dressed for the day and undressed for the night.

Early one morning as he brushed through his hair, now a bit overgrown and less well-kept than it had once been, a spark of light emitted, jumping about between the strands of hair. He'd seen such a thing happen before but had paid it little heed. Until now.

The same thing happened on occasion when pulling a nightshirt on or off. A bit of a crackling feeling would emerge. The spark would follow, only to disappear as quickly as it had appeared. Could not the various lights he'd seen on bogs and on faces be related to this?

And thus he spent weeks rubbing together various materials, pulling out strands of his own hair, applying various substances, attempting to determine what, precisely, could force the spark of light to return. Linen rubbed against skin sometimes worked. No matter the amount of hair he pulled, only that left upon his head ever showed any success, and that only rarely.

He might have continued his experiments indefinitely if not for the whisperings of two strangers he passed on the street as he returned from seeing a patient, something he did with less frequency. The two men were discussing the widely held belief amongst those of the lowest classes that human bodies could produce light . . . after death.

CHAPTER 17

Gemma had never imagined she'd one day find work cleaning a wax museum. But Madame Tussaud's displays were interesting, and the job paid a fair wage. Baker Street weren't in the rummest part of London, but it was a far-sight better than other places she'd worked and lived in. And it was reliable work. She'd soon have money enough for leaving London.

You ought to try making things right between you. She'd not managed to rid her mind of her discussion with Stone. He'd insisted Baz didn't know how to bridge the gap. And he'd implied that Baz wanted to. Móirín said it weren't such a lost cause as it seemed.

But what if they were wrong? What if she rebuilt that bridge only to have it crumble beneath her again? And if there was hope of building on their fondness, that'd make it all the harder to leave London when the time came. But if she didn't leave, her family would eventually find her. And if she was with Barnabus, finding her meant they would find him. Sometimes life didn't allow for any good options.

She left Madame Tussaud's that afternoon and made her way toward Welbeck Street. She could have gone back to the Donnellys' flat by a different route, but Parkington patrolled Welbeck. There was safety in that.

She passed by the cart of a fruit-and-veg monger, one she saw every day and who had shown himself to be friendly.

"What have you today, Peter?" she asked.

"Near about anything that strikes your fancy."

The Donnellys weren't exactly living in clover. They were also devilishly stubborn and wouldn't let her add to the household coffers while staying with them. She'd fetch a spot to eat on her walk home but also snatch a bit of veg to toss in the larder.

Peter had a fine selection of carrots, good size, still firm and fresh. She paid her coin and held out her hand for the carrots. But, along with them, Peter gave her a small envelope.

"From a mutual friend," he explained. "The papers you's waiting on."

Papers. From Mr. Sorokin, she'd wager.

"What do I owe you for these?" She lowered her voice but not so much that it would be suspicious.

"Our friend said he'd square with you."

She nodded. It was proper dangerous for the street mongers to carry extra chink around with them. It'd be best if Peter were left out of the money exchange.

Not wanting to risk revealing the contents of the papers to someone who might be passing by, she tucked them carefully into the pocket of her coat and continued on her way, joining up with Welbeck Street and heading south.

Behind her, someone else made the same turn—a man in a green hat pulled low. That in itself weren't unusual. The street was busy; people were about. But she'd seen that hat a few streets earlier. The man ought to have passed her while she was gabbing with Peter.

Gemma made an unplanned turn down Bentinck. It was nothing but homes of the working class. Only someone who lived in the area was likely to turn in that direction.

She didn't look back; she didn't need to. She heard his footfall. Another quick turn was mimicked by him. The roundabout route took her back to Welbeck, which was crowded with an absolute press of people.

Green Hat was still on her trail.

She could try losing her shadow in the crowd, but she might become stuck among them with no path out. If she ducked down a quieter alley, that might simply make her an easier target.

Gemma weaved around people and ducked behind carts. Now and then, she glanced back. Green Hat was always there. Every time.

She didn't dare go directly to the Donnellys' house. She'd not bring danger to Brogan, Vera, and Móirín. And Baz came by often enough; he might be there as well. But she couldn't keep wandering the streets forever, hoping to shake him. She slipped her hand in her pocket, comforted by the knife she had at the ready.

A few quick turns brought her to a narrow lane that ended at a churchyard. No passage. No escape. She'd been taught to fight. Seemed the time had come to do so again.

Gemma planted herself in the middle of the road, took

her knife from her pocket, then turned to face the man in the green hat.

He tipped his hat back. The late evening sun lit his face. She knew him: Uncle Silas.

"You know my father taught me to fight." She tightened her grip on her weapon. "I ain't opposed to a chivy duel even if you are family."

"I ain't interested in that bit of your education, girl. He taught you skills far more valuable to me."

She could hold her own against a lot of people in a fight, but not Uncle Silas. He was far bigger than she was. And he was as cold as an icehouse in December, too well acquainted with death to be bothered by the possibility causing it. Among the Kincaids, loyalty was demanded, but love didn't exist.

"You're wasting your breath," she said. "I want none of that life."

"You're a cleaning woman at a wax museum. You grunge up coins to buy carrots on the street. We can offer you far more."

She knew the Kincaids' purse was heavier than usual, but she didn't mean to tip her hand. "The resurrection game ain't never made a Kincaid wealthy."

"We're in fine feather, girl," he said, crowing a bit. "Could be in finer still iffen we had more skilled hands."

Gemma shifted her knife, keeping it fight-ready. "These hands won't never be put to that work again."

Far from intimidated, he pulled out his own knife, a sinister, self-assured smile tipping his mouth. "Think you're above us now, do you?" He spun the knife casually. "You ain't never been worth a groat without a shovel in your hand. You'll be taking it up again."

"Take yourself off, Silas. I ain't going nowhere."

"I can be very persuasive," he drawled.

From behind Gemma came a welcome and familiar voice filled with the sound of Ireland. "I think you'll be discovering, sir, that we can be quite persuasive ourselves." Móirín's presence would tip the balance.

But Móirín hadn't come alone. Parkington walked beside her, looking as menacing as she did. His focus was on Uncle Silas, and his expression held unwavering determination. Gemma had known a few bobbies in her time; this one still worried her a little. He seemed to have a good heart, but there was no doubt he could be fearsome.

Her uncle eyed the two of them, then looked back to Gemma. "We know where you work, mop, and we know the streets you frequent. You'll be seeing us again."

He pocketed his chiv once more, then tugged his oil-stained, mud-encrusted jacket and tipped his green hat. Rather than walking back in the direction he'd come, he stepped to the pavement and hopped over a wrought-iron fence into the churchyard. Quick as a flash, he was gone.

Móirín and Parkington reached her in the next moment.

"Did he hurt you?" the policeman asked.

"He hadn't had a chance to," Gemma said. "I suspect he would've in another minute or so."

Móirín was eyeing Gemma's knife. "You hold that like you know how to use it."

Gemma returned it to her pocket. With familiarity borne

of practice, she slipped it into its sheath sight unseen. "That were my uncle Silas. He'd kill a person soon as look at 'im."

"Never you fear, Gemma," Móirín said. "We've a high-and-mighty blue-bottle with us." She hooked her finger in Parkington's direction. "Never safer than when you're with a policeman."

"One of these days, Móirín Donnelly," Parkington said, "you'll confess I'm a fine person."

"Do you mean to make the same confession about me?"

He shook his head. "I've a strict policy against lying."

"And I've a strict policy against being too friendly with Peelers, so seems we're at an impasse."

Parkington dipped his head in her direction, then turned and left.

"Why is it you dislike him?" Gemma asked.

"I don't." Móirín tossed that out like it made perfect sense. "But 'tis a fun thing indeed watching him go red around the ears."

With a laugh, she nudged Gemma toward the open street. Together, they walked a roundabout way to Sackville Street and Piccadilly and then inside the flat.

Gemma made her way directly to her room. She sat on the low pallet and emptied her pockets of the knife she'd not had to use and the carrots she'd forgotten she had. Lastly, she pulled out the papers Peter had given her. She unfolded them, carefully, nervously.

The top was a letter of recommendation. It tossed out a heap of lukewarm praise like an employer often gave an adequate servant. The letter said she'd be a good pick for whatever position she applied for as she worked hard and didn't cause mischief. The letter identified her as Kate Mitchell. She'd need to call herself that after leaving London.

It was her new identity, her future.

She set the letter on the pallet beside her and studied the paper underneath it. It was a doctor's letter declaring that Gemma Kincaid Milligan had died of injuries from a carriage accident. It even contained a magistrate's signature, likely forged, which'd give it the authority she needed. The date of the "accident" was two weeks from that very day.

She could be declared dead. Her family, if they cared to look into things, would believe she was. Baz'd be a widow. He could marry again if he wanted. In two more weeks, they'd both be free.

And she would be utterly alone.

CHAPTER 18

Barnabus had spent more than enough time vacillating on the matter of Gemma's departure from London and his growing wish for her to remain. It was time he decided how to move forward.

He wished he could turn to his parents for advice in situations like this. But his mother had been dead for years, and neither of them had any idea who his father was. He was rather alone in the world.

But he had Mrs. Simms. She had a good head on her shoulders and, perhaps most significant of all, seemed to genuinely care about him.

"Would you mind terribly if I poured some worries in your ear while we clean up for the day?" he asked her. This was not one of those evenings where he was known to be at home to his patients. She would be leaving soon enough.

"Go on, then."

"I know you didn't care overly much for Gemma when she first arrived here." He set a jar of powders back on the shelf where it belonged.

Mrs. Simms gave him a stern look. "I never disliked her. I simply didn't know her or what to make of her."

"And what have you decided on that score?" he asked.

"I've seen the way you look when you talk about her. I've seen trust on your face when you look at her, which ain't a small thing. I don't know quite what it is that exists between the both of you, but I don't think it's a bad thing. And, seeing as you're married already, it's in both of your best interest to sort all this out."

"I *do* trust her." He, who trusted so few people, trusted Gemma. "I like her. And I like the person I am when I'm with her."

"And . . ." Mrs. Simms watched him expectantly.

"And I think she's happy when she's here and when we're together. I missed her while she was away, and she's said she missed me."

"And . . ."

"My mind is calmer when I hold her."

Her look shifted into one of almost maternal urging. "*And* . . ."

"And I think she feels that too."

"You're close as razors to the heart of the matter, Doc." She eyed him pointedly.

"And . . . I don't want to lose her again, because I . . . I love her."

On a whisper, Mrs. Simms said, "There you are."

"That's me betwattled, it is." He lowered himself onto a chair, mind spinning with surprise. "I love her. When did—when did that happen?"

"I'd wager a bit over three years ago," Mrs. Simms said.

He shook his head, but not really in disagreement. "She asked me—asked me directly—if I loved her. I told her I didn't. I didn't think I did. Heavens, I didn't think I *could.* It's not something I've . . ." He didn't even know how to finish the explanation. Too many thoughts spun in far too fast a swirl.

"Have you ever been in love before?" Mrs. Simms asked.

"I didn't know I was in love *now.*" He rubbed his temples with his fingers. "She left because of this. She asked me if I thought I could fall in love with her, and I told her that wasn't the person I was or the type of marriage we had."

"Oi, but she's here now. Seems to me you could clear that fog out right quick."

He stood and began pacing. "Except she isn't here. She's living with the Donnellys *instead* of living here. I even invited her back. *And* she hasn't asked me again if I loved her. She hasn't said she loves me. Only that she's leaving shortly and doesn't mean to come back."

"'Shortly' isn't 'immediately.'" Another very pointed and very wise look from Mrs. Simms set Barnabus's feet under him once more.

"There's still a possibility of making things right between us." It was almost a question.

"If you want my advice," she said, "you ought to do what should have been done to begin with. Court her. Give her a chance to decide if there's more between you than either of you believed."

"I've never courted anyone." He offered the warning as much to himself as to her.

Mrs. Simms shook her head. "Obviously."

He laughed a little. And fretted a little less than he had been. *Court her.* He could do that. He would enjoy doing that. Perhaps she'd discover the feelings she'd confessed to years ago weren't entirely gone. Perhaps she'd decide to stay. He didn't know how much of the three weeks of her time in London remained, but he'd do what he could with what time he had left.

A knock sounded at the door. His posted hours for the day had ended, but he never turned anyone away, no matter the time.

Mrs. Simms slipped out to see who had arrived while Barnabus finished up in the sitting room, his mind preoccupied with thoughts of Gemma, but his heart feeling more hopeful than it had in years.

Mrs. Simms returned in the next moment and announced simply, "Someone to see you."

He immediately recognized Mr. Snelling, the man who'd come to see him about a nonexistent illness. He was watching Barnabus with a look of curiosity, but not one that felt threatening.

"Is your throat giving you difficulty again?" Barnabus asked.

The man shook his head. "I thought it was time I told you why I really came by."

The unexpected candor was welcome, and Barnabus looked him over, studying him, searching for some sort of clue.

"I'm certain you didn't miss that I had taken note of . . . Well, I . . ." He grew more uncomfortable as he stood there, looking at Barnabus with drawn brows. "You look a terrible lot like my sister, and I can't get past it."

"The resemblance is likely a coincidence." Barnabus ignored the fact that he himself didn't believe in such things. "I haven't any family other than my mother, and she's been gone for a long time."

The man turned his hat around in his hands, spinning it by the brim. "I've not seen my sister in twenty-five years. We came to London to look for work, but the very first day, we were separated on a crowded street. I couldn't find her. I looked for days, months, years. Though I've little hope of finding her now, I still watch for her. Seeing you was . . . jarring. You look so like her."

Barnabus swallowed a lump of both emotion and apprehension. "What's your sister's name?"

"Agatha Snelling."

That wasn't very helpful. Barnabus had long suspected "Millie Milligan" was not his mother's actual name, but it was the only one he knew.

"She's only a year younger than I am," Mr. Snelling continued. "The right age for being your mother. And I wondered—" He shook his head. "I know there's little chance of it in a city this large, but . . . blimey, you look so much like her."

"As I said, my mother died several years ago. I can't tell you for certain if she and your sister are the same person," he told him.

"I realize this can't be proven," Mr. Snelling said, sadness touching his expression. "All you have is my word that you look very much like I remember her. But I don't know that I can ever fully believe there's no connection at all."

Barnabus couldn't argue with that. He felt the same way. There was no proving their connection, and yet the possibility pulled at him. And, if this man was, in fact, Barnabus's mother's brother, that made him . . . family.

Mrs. Simms was still in the room and had heard the entire exchange. She knew Barnabus's mother's history. She understood how it fueled his rescue efforts. He met her eye and silently asked the question she must've known was hanging his mind. She motioned him to join her on the side of the room, far enough away from Mr. Snelling to avoid being overheard if they kept their voices low.

"It obviously can't be proven," Barnabus said. "But it does feel possible."

"Did your mother look a great deal like you?"

Barnabus nodded. "Enough that people commented on it."

Mrs. Simms hummed in thought. "You'd do best to proceed with caution. Though I can't imagine what he would gain by lying about any of this."

"Life's taught me to be wary, I'll tell you that much."

"Take your time and get to know a bit more about him. If he's been your uncle these past years, he'll keep being your uncle moving forward. Rushing won't change that."

Mrs. Simms was wise. He'd long ago realized as much.

Just as he was making his way to where Mr. Snelling stood, another knock sounded at the door. Barnabus was seldom this busy late into the evening. Mrs. Simms gave a quick nod, indicating she would see to it. She was gone only long enough for Barnabus to invite Snelling to have a seat. She returned with a note in hand.

"This arrived for you, Doc. The one delivering it seemed to think it was urgent." She held it out to him.

He unfolded the note, then read silently.

We need to talk about Gemma. Come by as soon as you're able.

—Brogan

It was too vague for his peace of mind. Brogan wasn't one for brevity. There had to be a reason he wasn't saying anything specific. Was Gemma in trouble? Ill? Maybe she was ready to come home. Or maybe she was leaving London early. The idea clutched at his heart.

But here, in his house, was a man who might be family to him, who might embrace that role long after Gemma decided to move on.

Two people. Two shaky futures. Two uncertain paths.

"I told you all there was no point writing to Barnabus." Gemma pushed back her frustration and clung instead to the fact that she'd predicted his absence.

"Give the lad some time," Brogan said, sitting on the floor in front of the chair Vera sat in, wrapping her right foot in cold, wet cloths. Vera's injuries from the explosive fire at her shop included a regular swelling in her foot. "He has a bit of a journey to get here, after all."

She had made that journey. On foot, even. He could easily have arrived by now if he'd wanted to.

"He'll be here," Brogan said. "Reliable as the sun, he is."

"But for half the day, the sun's gone, i'n'it?"

Móirín pointed at her brother. "She has you there."

"The sun always returns just when it's meant to," Vera answered.

Brogan pointed at Móirín. "She has you there."

The room laughed. Gemma liked that there was always laughter about the Donnellys' home.

Vera's laugh turned into a cough, and it broke Gemma's heart knowing that her friend was always in some degree of pain. Her injuries were not simple, nor were they few.

Brogan was attentive but never suffocating, tender but never condescending. He and Vera treated each other as treasured equals, as sources of strength, as each other's beloved. What would that be like? Baz had never been unkind to her; she simply didn't have claim on his heart, and that stung.

He doesn't know how to bridge the gap. Could she?

"I think he'll be here," Móirín said.

"He is very busy." If she lowered all their expectations, she'd not be humiliated when she was proven correct.

"If you can't trust that he'll be concerned enough as your husband to come here," Brogan said, "trust him as Barnabus Milligan, the man who has almost single-handedly rescued, at last count, over two hundred women and girls from a horrible fate at the hands of London's macks and madams."

"I trust him as both," Gemma said. "But it ain't that simple."

A knock sounded.

Every eye in the room turned to her. Gemma's heart pounded a rhythm of anticipation even as her mind raked her over the coals for letting herself hope.

Móirín stood. "Place your bets, *fir agus mná*. We'll know soon enough who's knocking on our door."

"*Fir agus mná*?" Gemma did her best to recreate the unfamiliar words.

"Men and women," Móirín explained before slipping from the room.

"No bets needed," Brogan said. "It'll be Doc. No question."

Vera nodded. "You cain't convince me otherwise.

Oh, she wanted it to be Baz. Lying to herself didn't change what she knew to be true. She wanted it to be him.

Móirín returned in the next moment. "Anyone lose any money?" She twitched her head toward the front door as Baz appeared beside her.

Brogan, to his credit, didn't crow too loud about being correct.

Baz's attention settled immediately on Gemma. "Is anything the matter?"

Suddenly, she felt deuced embarrassed. He'd dragged himself all the way from Finsbury on account of her. "Everything is fine," she assured him.

"*Now*," Móirín said. "Nearly got herself knifed earlier today in the middle of the street by a man who looked a far-sight too familiar with his weapon."

"It was my uncle Silas," Gemma said. "He wanted me to join up in the trade again. I told him I weren't interested.

Móirín and Parkington sauntered onto the scene, and he scattered like the rodent he is."

Baz crossed to her. "I suspect your uncle Silas isn't one to be put off a scent so easily."

That was as true as steel. "He knows where I work. Told me all about my job and which costermonger carts I stop at. Said he could find me again in a heartbeat."

He took her hands in his, holding her gaze with his own. "He threatened you?"

"My family ain't known for asking nicely." She found his touch both calming and lovely.

"I don't imagine you can keep working for Madame Tussaud's, can you?"

She closed her eyes and simply let herself breathe. "It'd be too dangerous. I'll have to find something else."

"They'll likely find you there, too, though."

She sighed and leaned against him, tired to her core. "I've got an escape, though. A way to make certain they stop looking for me."

"You have?"

Did she dare tell him? Explain her plan? He'd provided other women in dire straits with what they needed to hop the twig out of Town. He'd understand. And he'd know she was offering him a chance to be free.

He deserved to know that.

She met his eyes. "I need to show you something."

CHAPTER 19

Barnabus walked with Gemma's hand in his up the stairs to her room. Once inside, she closed the door and leaned against it for a moment. Heavens, she looked beaten down.

He wasn't entirely certain what to do or say, so he crossed to stand beside her. "Are you certain you're fine? I can't imagine coming face-to-face with your uncle was a pleasant thing."

"It weren't. But Móirín got us home by a path I don't think I could retrace if I tried. Neither of us saw any sign we were followed."

That was a relief. "What's this plan you said you have for escaping?"

She stepped away from the door and crossed to the pallet she slept on. Reaching underneath, she pulled out two folded pieces of parchment. She held them carefully but with a white-knuckle grip. "I know even the dead ain't safe from the Kincaids, but they're nearabout as safe as anyone gets."

"The dead?"

She nodded. "I know someone who helps people in trouble, gives 'em a way out. I asked him to give me one."

She held the papers out to him.

He took them both, eyeing the top first. It was a letter of recommendation for a "Kate Mitchell." That made no sense. The second even less so. "Who's this doctor that's declaring you dead, Gemma?"

"He ain't real, I'd wager. Someone said to be away from London so folks here won't sniff out that he's about as real as the wax figures I've been looking after."

A forged declaration of death. "It even has a seal."

"Right and tight. No one'll question it."

"If your family sees you walking around London after hearing you're dead, that'll give away the—" In a flash, he understood. "That's why you're so set on leaving. You get away from London, have this sent to the right office, and, for all intents and purposes, Gemma Kincaid Milligan is dead."

"And Kate Mitchell gets to live a life free of resurrectionists and violent family members."

"And unwanted husbands?" he asked quietly.

"More you bein' rid of an unwanted wife. You'd be free, Baz. You could marry someone you wanted to be married to." Though her voice didn't waver, something in her eyes told him she wasn't as content with that outcome as she sounded.

He folded the papers and handed them back to her. "Why is it you're so certain I don't want to be married to you?"

She turned away, taking the two steps back to the pallet.

"Gemma?"

She knelt and put the papers back where they'd been.

He stepped over to her, sitting on the pallet she knelt beside. "Why do you think I don't want to be married to you?"

"I heard you talking to Fletcher and Elizabeth. You told them there weren't anyone else to help me, so you felt you had to. And that if there'd been any way to help me besides marrying me, that's what you would've done."

Blimey. He hadn't realized she'd overheard that. He couldn't even entirely remember what he'd said. "Marrying a stranger is a drastic thing, Gemma. For both people involved."

He heard her take a deep breath. "Now, you can get out of that drastic thing."

He set a free hand on her back, gently urging her to look up at him. She didn't.

"I wished there had been another way because your family had already forced you to live a life you didn't want. I felt like I was doing the same to you, taking away your ability to choose your own path. I have regretted that for three-and-a-half years, Gemma. Regretted *that*. Not *you*."

Without looking at him, she sat beside him on the pallet. He slipped his hand around her far shoulder, a one-armed side embrace.

"You never seemed happy being married to me," she said. "You was kind, and you cared how I were faring, but love never seemed part of the arrangement, and you said it weren't never meant to be."

"I—I don't—"

Gemma leaned against him, her head resting on his shoulder. "You sometimes have trouble talking with me."

"I stumble over myself with you," he said. "I've never had any deep connection to anyone aside from my mother. And she had no connections to anyone but me. I don't know how to be—how to make it work when . . . Marrying you meant we were connected, and I don't know how to not make that a disaster."

"My family life didn't teach me that either," she said. "The Kincaids are held together by greed and fear."

"So is this all we have to hope for?" he asked. "Two people looking for a connection but who can't possibly forge one themselves?"

"I don't know." Her tone sounded very near to exhaustion.

His first instinct was to shrug it off, to tell himself that if it couldn't work, he'd best not set his heart on it. But he'd come with the hope of courting her and the knowledge that he loved her. She didn't seem entirely opposed to the possibility.

"We weren't able to get to know each other much after we were first married," he said. "I should have tried harder so we wouldn't be such strangers to each other."

"The past often comes with regrets, don't it?" she asked softly.

He tentatively took hold of her hand. She didn't pull away. "I'm grateful you've let me come see you while you've been here. It's nice being with you, sitting beside you, talking with you."

She met his eye. "I like talking with you too. I ain't always been able to trust people enough for talking. I've needed to, though."

"I'm here now. I'm listening."

She shifted her position and tucked herself up against him, her legs bent and resting against his. He set his other arm around her and held her close. The arrangement felt like something a husband and wife would do at the end of a difficult day: quietly sitting, taking comfort in each other's nearness. He liked having her there, liked holding her this way.

"I was afraid it'd be one of my uncles what found me," she said. "My cousins ain't exactly doves, but my uncles are—" He felt her take a shaking breath. "Uncle Silas is a scorcher of the worst sort. People whisper when they talk about the Kincaids, but they scatter when they see him. He kills people, and they know it. Everyone knows it." Her voice had dropped to a strained whisper. "My uncle Arlo ain't much better."

"Do you think they'll give up on recruiting you back to the family business?"

He felt a shudder flow through her. "Never. No one questions Silas. No one thwarts him. My father could manage it now and then, but only by warning him that walloping and killing too many people would draw notice. It weren't my father's authority that won; it was my uncle not looking to get caught."

"I wish you had even just one person in your family you could think about with fondness."

"I know you think of your mother fondly," she said. "You don't talk about her much, but when you do, there is love in your voice." She looked up at him and smiled sadly. "I can tell you miss her."

"I do, and not just because she's the only family I have," he said. That spun his mind toward something else. "At least, I think she's the only family I have."

She turned her head to look directly at him, confusion in her eyes.

"There's a man that's come by the house a couple of times, and I saw him on the street at one point. He watched me very closely, enough that it caught my attention."

She held more tightly to him. "Are you in danger, Baz?"

He didn't know why it touched him so much that she worried for him. Perhaps because so few people had during his life. "I was wary of Mr. Snelling at first, but he came again today and explained his interest in me."

"What did he say?"

"That I look a great deal like his sister, and he wonders if maybe we're related."

"If you are, that'd mean you have family." She sounded as happy for him as he knew he would be if it proved true.

He nodded. "He lost touch with his sister twenty-five years ago. He's not heard from her since. I find myself wondering if his sister and my mother might be one and the same."

Gemma studied his face. Eager hopefulness sat in her eyes, something he didn't see often. She was so adept at hiding her thoughts that it was often difficult to know what she was feeling.

"That would make him your uncle," she said. "He would know where your mother came from and who her family were."

His mother had never shared those things with him. Life had torn her down enough that she'd kept so much about herself hidden, even from her son. He felt that gap keenly to this day.

"I would know my mother's actual given name," he said. "I'd know what county she hailed from, what brought her to

London. I'd know what other family she had—what other family *I* have."

"You deserve to have family, Baz." She set her hands on either side of his face, holding him gently. The soft, gentle touch warmed his heart even as it sped his pulse a bit. "You deserve to be happy. You have given so many people their lives back. You deserve to claim yours."

"Don't you deserve happiness as well?" he asked softly.

"It's difficult to feel something that don't even seem possible."

With her as close as she was, his arms wrapped tightly around her, the two of them pressed together with her hands gently caressing his jaw, he could actually believe there might be hope on the horizon. Hope. And family. And love.

"I don't mean to give up, Gemma."

"Give up on *what*?" she whispered.

"On us."

He kissed her. He'd meant for it to be a simple show of affection, of tenderness. But the moment his lips touched hers, all thoughts fled. There was warmth. Softness. And passion. He pulled her closer. She set her palms against his chest but not pushing him away. Touching him as if holding him there.

A sudden burst of laughter downstairs broke the magic of the moment. Gemma pulled back. She smiled the tiniest bit and, without a word, rose from the pallet and slipped from the room. There was no hurriedness in her step, no indication she had been affected by their kiss at all.

But he remained behind, trying to breathe, trying to make sense of a world that had, with that one tender, passionate moment, changed in an instant.

THE BACHELOR AND THE BRIDE

by Mr. King

Installment V
in which the Promise of a New Day turns to Fear!

Dawn broke, sending rays of soft morning light into the protective hollow of the tree where Duncan and Sorcha had sought refuge. The will-o'-the-wisp had not returned. Its call no longer seemed to pull at Sorcha, but Duncan could tell she was shaken by the experience. He was a little shaken himself.

Seeing her run, seeing her leave without so much as glancing back at him, had struck something more than fear into him. His heart had actually cracked, broken a little. Even before realizing what she was chasing, he'd been weighed down by the realization that she was leaving him behind. How had he come to care so deeply for someone he'd only just met? How was it his heart had grown so partial to her so quickly?

Waking up to the promise of the new day, the clear sky of a bright spring morning, with Sorcha sleeping soundly in his arms and Granny's miracle bag on the ground beside them, he felt strangely at peace. Just as Sorcha had said the day before, he was certain they would yet encounter more creatures before their journey ended. He didn't know what could possibly remain, what dangers awaited, but he wasn't afraid. And he wasn't alone.

"No one emerges whole from a harrowing journey when that journey is undertaken entirely alone." Was this what the *Bean-Nighe* meant? Was her answer not merely an avoidance of his question but also a useful piece of advice?

A moment passed, and Sorcha woke as well. Sleep remained heavy on her eyelids. Her movements were slow with lingering slumber.

"How are you feeling today?" he asked.

She smiled up at him. "Ever the doctor, aren't you?"

He laughed a little at that. "I suppose. I *am* asking as more than a man of medicine, though."

Color touched her cheeks. She blushed so beautifully, just as she had when he'd offered her the flower in the meadow yesterday. It was a joy to see her do so again.

"I am well," she said. "A little embarrassed to have been so quickly taken in by the will-o'-the-wisp. I do know better."

He took her hand in his. "The pull of that creature goes beyond logic and knowledge. You've nothing to be embarrassed about."

"I suppose I hadn't realized how much of a wanderer's heart I still have."

He pressed a light kiss to her hand. "Which is also nothing to be embarrassed about."

She sighed, the sound one of relief. "Thank you."

"We likely have a long day of walking ahead of us," he said. "I'm hopeful you still have some food in your bag."

She took it up and opened it. "I do."

"That is a relief," he said, turning his tone to one of absolute teasing. "I feared for a moment we were going to have to eat the vole."

She laughed, the sound of it settling like music on his ears. Had there ever been another person who brought him such easy and soul-warming delight?

He opened up his bag, intending to make a show of reaching inside for the vole. But he stopped, staring in confusion.

"What's the matter?" she asked.

"The soft slippers are gone."

"Did you leave them somewhere?" she asked.

He shook his head.

"Then they have disappeared?"

"So it would seem. I suppose there must be some sort of enchantment on them."

She shrugged. "I don't think Granny Winters would play us such a trick if we still needed the shoes."

"Then," he said, "perhaps they disappear when they are no longer needed."

Sorcha handed him a bit of bread and a slice of hard cheese. "What is left in your bag?"

"The spurs, the vole, and the stoppered vessel."

Her brows pulled together in thought as they ate their humble breakfast. Duncan hadn't any idea what the items could possibly be used for. But one thing felt quite certain:

they would be useful, *essential* even. And he meant to guard the bag closely.

Their morning meal completed and the sun fully above the horizon, they began their journey, walking as they had the day before, crossing miles, over hills, around rivers, through meadows.

Whenever they walked across the broad, open areas where flowers and wild grass grew, she took hold of his hand. He knew she was worrying that the will-o'-the-wisp would return and she would be unable to resist the siren call to wander. That she took comfort and strength in his touch was a fine thing indeed. After the third such meadow, she kept her hand in his, walking along quite as if it was the most natural thing in all the world. Truth be told, it felt natural.

The day was waxing long, though not entirely over. Sorcha said she felt certain they were going in the right direction, but the trek was taking longer than expected. Though she didn't say as much, he suspected she felt a bit guilty for having added to the length of their journey by running after the will-o'-the-wisp. But Granny had sent them with precisely the object needed to break that spell, which meant she had anticipated the need. And if their task was doomed to fail from the beginning, she would not have sent them. Duncan took great reassurance in that.

It didn't mean the outcome was guaranteed. But it meant there was a chance.

The road they were on grew more defined and easier to see. Trees grew on either side, and mountains loomed in the distance, but the path was clear.

Until it unexpectedly broke in two.

Sorcha kept back, clinging tightly to his hand and eyeing the area. "Crossroads are dangerous things," she said.

She had warned him about that before.

"Do you know which way we are meant to go?"

She shook her head. "Not entirely." She continued eyeing the area, but she didn't seem ready to run or abandon their mission. Hers was not an aura of fear but of vigilance.

"There must be some clue," he suggested. "Surely something will tell us which road to take."

She nodded and peeked down one road, then took a few steps, but not many, in that direction. He did the same down the other.

Just at the edge of the road, tucked among the trees, was a horse. It was calm and docile, dipping its head to take a mouthful of grass before looking around quite as if it hadn't a care in all the world. This was clearly not a wild horse, one inclined to bolt and jump at the slightest thing. It likely belonged to someone. And it likely could be ridden.

Ridden.

Granny Winter had placed spurs in his bag. She would not have done so if they weren't meant to be used. Being quite careful to not spook the horse, he removed the spurs from the bag and pulled them onto his boots, strapping them in place.

"I see a large outcropping of rock down the other road," Sorcha said, still at a distance. "I remember that was on the map of the road to Carrifran."

"How far from Carrifran?" He kept his eye on the horse as the sound of Sorcha's footsteps grew louder.

"A half-day's journey, likely." She was at his side. "Where did the horse come from, do you suppose?"

"I'm not certain."

"Granny did include spurs," she said. "That cannot be mere coincidence." Clever as she was, Sorcha had pieced together that bit of the puzzle almost instantly.

"I can only assume we are meant to ride it. A horse would get us to our destination more quickly."

She still looked uncertain. "Finding the horse at a crossroads does not feel like a *safe* discovery. The animal may very well be something other than it seems."

"Is there a creature belonging to that realm who appears in the form of a horse?"

She nodded. "Several."

"Are they all dangerous?"

She shook her head. "But at least one of them is: the kelpie. It is quite dangerous, in fact."

They approached the horse with caution. There must have been a body of water nearby; water dripped from its mane. Perhaps the animal was docile because it was tired. Perhaps it had been trapped for a time in a downpour. Except, it hadn't rained that day.

"What do you suppose we ought to do?" Sorcha eyed the horse with misgiving.

"Granny would not have given us the spurs if she didn't mean for us to use them."

Sorcha shook her head. "It's possible she included them on the chance that we did decide to ride the horse, even though doing so would be a mistake."

It might very well prove to be one. But could they truly

risk returning too late to save Donella? Their time was running worryingly short.

"I think we should ride it in the direction that we need to go," he said. "It will speed our journey and increase the chances we can return home by *Bealltainn*."

Sorcha agreed, though she seemed reluctant.

He climbed onto the horse's back, and Sorcha, using a fallen tree as a step, sat behind him, the rough fabric of her dress bunched up around her. Riding a horse very nearly atop its hind legs would not be terribly comfortable for her. He hoped, for her sake, this proved a gentle ride. She wrapped her arms around his middle. He took hold of the damp hair of the horse's mane, the only thing available to him. Not merely wet, the mane contained bits of seaweed.

Duncan pulled out a piece and, keeping hold of the mane with his other hand, held the seaweed up for Sorcha to see. "I've never known a horse to collect this in its mane."

"Seaweed!" she gasped. "It's the kelpie."

The kelpie. She'd said that was the most dangerous of the monsters appearing in the form of a horse.

Something about the feel of the creature beneath him began to change. It softened and grew more enveloping, almost as if he were sinking into it.

"Tell me what to do," he said.

"It will become sticky, making escape impossible. It will ride with us directly back to whatever loch it lives in and drown us in the depths."

The kelpie bolted.

Duncan needn't have held on to the mane; the kelpie had become so adhesive he couldn't have come loose if he'd tried. "What of the spurs? Why would Granny give us spurs?"

"The spurs are made of iron; they must be. Iron alone can control it."

Her grip on him tightened. She was holding so fast he could hardly breathe.

He dug his spurs into the flanks of the beast, which was twisting and shifting in shape. The harder he dug, the more solid it became beneath him despite feeling less and less like a horse. Using his legs and the spurs on his feet, he pushed and turned and nudged the creature in the direction they were meant to go. It bucked and jumped and made every attempt to loosen the grip of the iron spurs. Duncan held on for dear life, and not merely his. Sorcha's life depended on it as well.

From behind him, she called out directions, telling him which way to turn the kelpie, which way to direct it.

On and on they went, dodging trees, jumping over rocks and obstacles, moving faster than any horse ever could. Duncan's legs burned with the effort to keep control of the beast even as it made every attempt to dislodge him. The muscles in his legs were turning to gruel. He didn't know how much longer he could maintain control of the dangerous monster.

At last, the creature came to a jarring stop. Rearing up on its back legs, it slung them to the ground, then darted off on the instant.

Stunned, the air knocked entirely from him, Duncan lay on his back, hurting in every muscle of his body, his mind refusing to accept the reality that they might be safe.

He could summon only enough strength to turn his head and look for Sorcha.

She lay on the ground nearby, looking up at the moonlit sky. Her breath clouded above her in the chill of night.

Night. How was it that so much time had passed? Could they truly have been riding for hours?

Using what little strength remained in him, he pulled himself over to where she lay. He set an arm around her.

"Are you injured?" he asked.

"Exhausted. But whole."

He rested his head against hers, letting himself simply breathe. He closed his eyes, rested his body and mind, and silently prepared himself for whatever further dangers awaited them on this most perilous of journeys.

CHAPTER 20

If the Dread Penny Society didn't find a way to curtail the efforts of the Mastiff and his cronies, Barnabus was likely to lose his medical practice. He was, once again, away from his house and at headquarters for a meeting.

He didn't think the DPS was overreacting—he was well aware of the enormity of danger they were confronting—but, other than Elizabeth, he was the only one present who had a profession outside of writing penny dreadfuls. Stone took on laboring jobs here and there as needed, but he had the ability to take the time he needed. Brogan, Fletcher, Hollis, and Martin could come and go as they wished.

This was not a formal meeting, so they had gathered in the pub upstairs. Brogan spent a decent amount of time teasing those who did not choose Guinness as their beverage. Fletcher had eventually managed to rein them all in. Elizabeth was a good influence on him; she'd led him to be more focused than he had been before.

"What have you been able to sort out?" Fletcher asked Hollis.

He was the one who had known the most about the Radlett case when they had first come across the blackmail connected to it. They needed to know more than the cursory summary Hollis had offered then. There had to be a connection between this case and the Mastiff, or why would it be the focus of the blackmail?

"The murder in question occurred in 1823 in Radlett. There was no doubt the three men involved were guilty—one of murder and the other two of aiding in a murder. It was a particularly gruesome crime and captured the public's attention. Thurtell, the murderer, was convicted and hung. Probert, one of the conspirators, was offered the chance to turn King's evidence against the other two, and, in return for doing so, he received no sentence. Hunt, the third man, had been the most cooperative to the authorities, telling them where to find the body and other very significant details. He was convicted but spared execution, sentenced instead to transportation for life."

"Probert was given mercy and Hunt weren't?" Fletcher pressed. "Hunt was the more cooperative of the two, after all."

"An oddity, to be sure," Hollis said. "I have not found a good explanation for why that happened."

"Which one of the fellas did Chelmsford represent?" Stone asked.

"Hunt. And, though it is odd he was not offered the opportunity to avoid sentencing, he *was* spared hanging, which was a mercy in itself."

Other than this being a somewhat famous case, there

wasn't any obvious reason why Lord Chelmsford would be targeted for his role in it.

"And Lord Chelmsford was involved in only Hunt's defense?" Fletcher asked.

Hollis nodded. "It was one of his earliest cases. He's tried a great many more since then. The crime itself garnered a lot of attention, but the trials are not considered of significant note. Certainly not Hunt's. He was not actually the murderer, though he was involved in aspects of it, and the ghastly details of the crime certainly made him notorious."

"Why is the Mastiff using this case for his blackmail, then? Chelmsford's been Lord Chancellor. It seems there'd be more significant threats to level in that area of his life." Barnabus was trying to find some connection between it all. There must've been something personally significant to the Mastiff. "Do we have any idea what the Mastiff's actual name is?"

Fletcher shook his head. "I've even asked around over the last few months. Been trying to get a handle on the bloke. He's only known by that name."

"Any chance his name might actually be 'Hunt'?" It was all Barnabus could think of.

"He's not old enough to be John Hunt," Elizabeth said.

"Could be family to him, though," Brogan said. "Maybe he's upset at how Chelmsford handled the trial."

That was possible.

"If Hunt was going to hang but Lord Chelmsford got the bloke transportation instead, that'd be a mark in his favor with Hunt's family." Fletcher said. "Chelmsford kept him alive."

Maybe not a family member, then. Or not a family member *of Hunt's*. "Perhaps he's related to the victim, a son or nephew or something. Could be he's upset that Hunt didn't get a harsher sentence," Barnabus suggested.

"Or related to the murderer and is frustrated that he alone paid the ultimate price for the crime they were all part of," Martin added.

Both were entirely possible. "If the Mastiff is trying to discredit Chelmsford's legacy out of revenge for a family member, we have to assume he hasn't given up the plot yet. Family ties are complicated and not easily severed," Barnabus said.

Elizabeth looked to him. "Speaking of which, Stone has filled us in on Gemma's uncle."

"If it weren't so dangerous," Fletcher said, "and it weren't your Gemma in that danger, I'd give some thought to the possibility she might be able to learn from her family what the Mastiff's about and what he means to do, seeing as they're working with the cur."

Barnabus opened his mouth to object, but Fletcher continued before he could.

"We ain't actually going to run that line, so don't panic. It might not do any good anyway. The Mastiff's hold on the criminal element is so strong I suspect most of 'em do what he says without knowing anything of the whys."

That was likely true.

Fletcher turned to Martin. "The Dread Master managed to get you a position at Chelmsford's place," he said. "Have you learned anything there?"

Martin shrugged. "Chelmsford's jumpy. The staff's noticed, but no one seems to know why."

"Have *you* any inkling why?" Fletcher pressed.

"He's been thumbing through papers, whispering to himself about how he did the best he could, how he ought to have been appreciated by someone who, apparently, don't appreciate him." Martin shrugged. "And I heard him say, 'Who could still be angry about *this*?' So he's trying to sort who is angry about something or other."

"Sounds like Lord Chelmsford is thinking along the same lines we are," Barnabus said. "He's being blackmailed over the Radlett case because someone is still angry about how it played out."

"But who?" Elizabeth asked. "And why are they so upset with him that they'd go to these lengths?"

"I've crossed paths with Lord Chelmsford a couple of times," Martin said. "I'll see if I can't manage to talk a bit with him. Protocol among the staff makes that sort of thing difficult, but maybe not impossible. Another one of the footmen had a quick exchange with him: offering a good morning and asking if there were anything he could do for Chelmsford. I may be able to build on that approach."

They all nodded but without the firmness that came with conviction. The situation was tough to sort. It was frustrating to not have a clear way forward.

Brogan rose from his seat to top off his glass, and Stone walked with him. Hollis, Martin, and Fletcher put their heads together, trying to devise a plan for getting more information.

Elizabeth, who sat beside Barnabus, turned her attention to him. "How is Gemma holding up? It must have been an overwhelming thing for her to have her family find her, knowing who and what they are."

He nodded. "She's wary, but she's always been strong. Being with the Donnellys has helped."

"I suspect being with *you* would help more," she said.

"I did ask her if she'd come back to Finsbury, but she was not amenable to the idea."

That seemed to surprise Elizabeth.

"She doesn't want to bring this danger to my house on account of my patients and the women and girls I help to rescue."

"I can understand that," Elizabeth said. "But I suspect she is also protecting *you*."

"Like Sorcha does for Duncan?"

With a half smile that was one hundred percent mischievous, Elizabeth said, "I haven't the first idea why you're asking me. *Mr. King* is the author of that penny dreadful."

Elizabeth was, of course, Mr. King. But no one outside of the Dread Penny Society knew that.

"Well, Mr. King saw fit for his protective heroine to spend time *with* the not-entirely-incompetent hero rather than send him on his way 'for his own good.'"

"Mr. King's brave hero also isn't choosing to keep his distance," Elizabeth tossed back. "I can't imagine Duncan'd be making the least bit of progress otherwise."

"I have made a little progress," Barnabus said. "Gemma kissed me last night. Well, I kissed her, but she did too."

"Each other," Elizabeth said dryly. "The description you are searching for is 'each other.' 'We kissed *each other*.'"

He could smile at that. "Is it terribly obvious I don't have a great deal of experience with this?"

"What is terribly obvious is that you love her."

"I do. Took me a devilishly long time to put the right word to it."

"Has she told you how she feels?"

He shook his head. "Not recently, at least. She told me once, years ago, but I—"

"Broke her heart?" Elizabeth guessed with every indication she already knew the answer.

"I don't know how much of those tender feelings I crushed with my idiocy." He wanted to believe he could mend what he'd broken. "I'm hoping I can convince Gemma to stay in London through your wedding. That'd give me some time to court her as I ought to have done from the beginning."

Elizabeth's brow pulled a bit. "We aren't entirely certain when the wedding will be. With the Mastiff stepping up his efforts, things are growing chaotic. We've already had to wait longer than we wanted so Fletcher could establish himself in the circles that need to accept him for my school to stay open. The fact that he's been willing to wait, that he puts in the effort even though it frustrates him, means the world to me. Life is often a struggle. There's something beautiful about having someone who is willing to walk with you through it."

He wanted to walk through life's struggles with Gemma. If he had time, he might be able to show her that she could depend on him. If she grew to love him and trust him again, that was the future they could build together.

Chapter 21

The Charitable Authors League of London was staging another undertaking. Gemma would've liked to join in, but she knew it wouldn't be safe out in the open like that. She wouldn't invite trouble when CALL was trying so hard to do good. But staying hunkered down at the Donnellys' flat day after day was beginning to wear on her.

It did, at least, give her time to visit with Vera, which Gemma appreciated. Vera was not yet strong enough to spend hours on end standing and carrying things.

"Do you think," Vera said, "if we batted our eyes and looked a touch pathetic, Doc and Brogan'd take us to Richmond Park? It's enough outside London to be quiet and safe but not so far that we couldn't be there and back in the same day. And it'd be a deucedly welcome change to seeing only the walls of this house day and night."

"I don't know how you've endured it these past months." Gemma shook her head. "You must be going plum out of your mind."

She smiled. "A bit, oi. But I've been helping Brogan with his current penny dreadful, and that's been a lark."

"Has it?" Gemma wouldn't've guessed. "His stories aren't the light romps some of the other penny dreadfuls are."

"No, but they're a right riot to write."

Gemma laughed out loud. "Try saying that at a gallop."

"I'm not certain I could say it again at a crawl."

Vera had said that remaining behind during CALL events wasn't such a terrible thing. She was proving herself correct.

A knock at the door startled them both. They'd not been expecting anyone. Gemma met Vera's eye and received a shrug in return.

"Guess we'd best sort out who's disrupting our gab," Gemma said.

"Best let me. The Kincaids don't care a lick about me." That was true enough.

Gemma walked with Vera to the door but tucked herself out of sight. She took her knife in her hand, just in case, and held her breath as Vera reached for the handle.

She inched the door open, peeking around it.

"Papa!" On that single word, Vera pulled the door open fully.

Mr. Sorokin rushed inside, holding the young girl Gemma had seen with him in the hiding hole. The little boy kept close to his side.

"What's happened?" Gemma asked, eyeing the girl with concern. She was pale and listless.

His Russian accent more prominent than usual, Mr. Sorokin rushed through his explanation. "She's had a fever for a couple of days. No appetite. Today, she grew so weak that she's struggling to get about."

"Lie her on the sofa in the sitting room," Vera said.

"She needs a doctor." Gemma reached for her coat. "I'll go fetch Baz."

"I can do it," the boy said. "I can get word to him."

"You oughtn't put yourself in danger."

"I ain't meaning to. Doc Milligan, yeah? I know how to get word to him. No one'll even see me about."

"You're certain?" Gemma pressed.

"Full certain." He hopped out the door and was gone in a flash.

Gemma closed and locked the door. She took a deep breath to settle her pulse. Worrying that a Kincaid had found her had ratcheted up her anxiety. She needed a moment to regain her calm.

By the time she stepped into the sitting room, the girl had been situated on the sofa, and Vera sat in a chair next to her, tending to the patient.

Mr. Sorokin crossed to Gemma. "Did Olly go after the doctor?"

"Oi. Wouldn't hear a word against it."

"He'll be safe," Mr. Sorokin said. "He moves about as unseen and unheard as a mouse."

"And Dr. Milligan will come as soon as he hears he's needed," Gemma said. "He is as reliable as a lighthouse."

"Does he know yet that he is about to find himself a widower?"

Gemma nodded. "I got the papers from Peter. I explained

it all to Baz. A couple of days before I'm meant to have died, I'll pike out of London, make a life for Kate Mitchell."

"And what does the good doctor think of the plan?"

What did he think? He hadn't objected, but he'd also not declared the idea a rare bit of genius or an excellent escape.

The girl on the sofa moaned, which pulled Mr. Sorokin's attention back to her. "I wish I knew what to do for Licorice. She's been miserable."

"Bringing her here was the right first step," Gemma said. "The Donnellys'll keep her safe as an inside pocket. And Baz is here most every day. A person couldn't do better than to be here with them."

"Then why is it you're so set on leaving?" He gave her a pointed look.

Why? She knew why.

Her friends might've been able to keep her somewhat safe, but so long as she was in London and the Kincaids were determined to find her, Gemma couldn't keep the Donnellys or Baz safe.

She couldn't live with that.

Several months earlier, the Dread Penny Society had facilitated the escape of a particularly mischievous young orphan named Very Merry, who'd been forced by the Mastiff to undertake increasingly dangerous acts of thievery. She now made her home with Hollis and Ana Darby, safe from her one-time thief master but every bit as much of a troublemaker as she'd ever been.

She was well-known to all the Dreadfuls, yet all of them looked as shocked as Barnabus felt seeing her rushing toward their CALL effort.

Ana intercepted her. "Is something the matter?"

"Bob's Your Knuckle climbed in the window at the house sayin' Olly sent him to say Miss Vera needs to see Doc at her place."

"Did Bob's Your Knuckle say if Olly said the need was an urgent one?" Barnabus asked.

Very Merry nodded. "Seemed to think you oughta skip over straight off."

"Is someone ill or injured?"

"I ain't a newspaper, Doc. I ain't got all the gossip."

Ana didn't quite manage to hold back her amusement. "You had best make your way to Piccadilly, Barnabus. Vera wouldn't disrupt your efforts here if you weren't truly needed."

He couldn't argue with her on that. And knowing Gemma was at the flat, too, added a degree of concern. Was Gemma ill? Was Vera's back causing her more misery than usual? Had the Kincaids found them?

Barnabus pulled Brogan away from the cart where he and Fletcher were distributing vegetables. "I just got word that we need to go back to your flat."

Brogan paled. "Is something the matter with Vera?"

"I don't know."

Fletcher motioned for them both to go. "We've hands enough."

They were soon on their way, the journey made in silence.

Barnabus suspected Brogan's mind was as uneasy as his over what they'd find upon arrival.

At the flat, Brogan unlocked the door and let them both in. They followed the sound of voices to the sitting room.

A young girl, likely thirteen years old, lay on the sofa, pale and listless. Near her sat Vera with her arm around the shoulders of a boy likely five years the girl's junior, who was standing beside her chair. Gemma laid a cool cloth over the girl's forehead. Mr. Sorokin, of all people, knelt on the floor beside the sofa, holding the girl's hand and watching her with concern.

Mr. Sorokin looked up as they entered. "Do you have your doctoring bag?"

"I do."

That pulled all their eyes to him. His gaze lingered on Gemma. She looked weary but not afraid. With his mind at ease on that score, he moved toward his young patient. He took Mr. Sorokin's place, kneeling beside the sofa. He felt the girl's wrist, searching for a pulse. "Tell me what you can of her condition."

"She's been feverish a couple days," Mr. Sorokin said. "And today she's had no energy, no strength."

"Fever's been rising since arriving here," Gemma said. "The cool cloths ain't helping overly much."

Barnabus felt her face. She *was* quite warm. He checked her neck for swelling. "Has she mentioned pain in her throat?"

The little boy nodded, his expression heavy with worry. "Mentioned her throat, she did. I ain't seen her sick like this."

Barnabus pulled from his doctoring bag a vial of powders

and gave quick instructions to Vera on how to prepare them for the girl.

"A honey tea would soothe her throat," he added. "I suspect she's not been eating on account of her throat hurting. But not eating and drinking has left her weak. A weakened body struggles to fight off illness."

"We've been struggling to stay dry and warm lately," Mr. Sorokin said. "That likely hasn't helped."

Barnabus shook his head. "It likely hasn't. If you aren't opposed to the idea, you ought to stay here with her for a few days. She'd be warm and comfortable. The powders should break her fever, and the honey tea will alleviate her throat pain. Get her eating again, drinking water and weak tea, and she'll recover quickly."

"She can use the room I've been in," Gemma said. "The room stays warm, and the pallet's comfortable."

"I can take her upstairs," Brogan said. "We'll see her settled."

The girl opened her eyes enough to look at Barnabus. "Mr. Sorokin says you're the doctor who saves people from the bullyboys."

Barnabus nodded. "I do what I can to save people from whatever's troubling them, whether it's the sniffles or the snatchers."

She smiled weakly. "People talk about you. Most think you're a hero."

He could guess which ones didn't. Being despised by people who hurt the vulnerable was, in his estimation, a badge of honor.

Brogan carefully lifted the girl from the sofa and followed

Gemma out of the room and, no doubt, up the stairs. The little boy followed them. Vera had already left to see to the powders and tea Barnabus had prescribed.

He and Mr. Sorokin remained in the sitting room. He didn't know the man well—not at all, really—but he knew the vital role he had played in safeguarding these children. They were, without question, Licorice and Olly, the two urchins who needed protection from the Mastiff.

Mr. Sorokin had often provided Brogan with information about what was happening in the quiet corners of London, what was whispered about among the poor and struggling. No one was entirely certain how he managed to hear so much, but the DPS believed he'd built a network almost accidentally, having provided aid to so many who then remained loyal to him even years later. A network as vast as the one the Dread Master claimed. Barnabus couldn't shake from his mind the possibility that this man might very well be their mysterious leader.

"Have you heard any word of the Kincaids?" Barnabus asked. "Gemma is in danger from them."

Mr. Sorokin sat on the sofa. "They undertook a resurrection two nights ago, but it didn't go well. They were caught out and had to flee, though one of them was captured by the blue-bottles. They left behind some of their tools. They'd brought in some extra hands, seeing as they've more work than usual, but those hands have proven unreliable."

Which meant Gemma was likely in even more danger than she had been. Her hands knew the work. And the Kincaids knew it.

"Sometimes it seems the Mastiff has pulled so many into his web that we'll never untangle it all."

"That is the feeling in the dim corners of South London too," Mr. Sorokin said. "They feel his presence everywhere. And he isn't doing his work alone."

Barnabus nodded. The Mastiff had the Raven and the Protector, Mrs. Smith, countless others. And even with all that, they'd received repeated warnings that something bigger was coming, something even more dangerous.

"You were pulled into his schemes with the Russian ambassador." Barnabus kept his voice low but spoke fast, knowing there likely wasn't going to be much opportunity for discussing this once the others came downstairs.

"Escaping his clutches is nearly impossible once he sets his sights on a person." Mr. Sorokin sounded tired, and well he might be. Because of the Mastiff, he had been in hiding for months.

"You were asked to create forgeries regarding the Radlett murder as part of his blackmail scheme. That has come up again in connection with the Mastiff's efforts against Lord Chelmsford."

"That case occurred long before I came to England," Mr. Sorokin said. "Before being forced into the Mastiff's scheme, the only time I'd heard of that trial was not long after I arrived in London.

"A poor woman, destitute and desperate, came to me looking for letters of recommendation to help her get a respectable job. She had a little girl with her, and both appeared a breath away from starvation. She'd been forced into the kind of living you've dedicated your life to helping women escape.

"Her mother had worked at an inn for a time, until it closed on account of the tavern owner being implicated in a rather horrible crime. The woman didn't particularly want to talk about the case except to say that she wouldn't be opposed to finding a job in an inn like the one her mother had held all those years ago. I was curious enough to look into the matter of the long-ago crime and realized she was referring to the Radlett murder. That it came up again in the Mastiff's blackmail struck me as a little odd. But, then again, coincidences do happen."

"They do, yes, but they always make me wary," Barnabus said.

It was entirely possible there was no actual connection between the forged letters of reference Mr. Sorokin made so many years ago, the case that impacted that woman's mother in a roundabout way, and the blackmail now being perpetrated against Lord Chelmsford.

It was possible, but Barnabus didn't trust coincidences.

Bodies of Light

being a Fictionalization of Reported and Corroborated Mysterious Phenomena

by Dr. Barnabus Milligan, physician

Chapter Four

When Dr. Sefton Palmer arrived at the college where he had, a mere dozen years earlier, undertaken his medical education, he did so with an unmistakably frantic air. He would prove the existence of the lights he'd seen. He would discover their source, their cause, their nature.

He would, if it required pursuing the answers for the rest of his life.

Had his attention not been so entirely upon his pursuit, he might have noticed the odd looks he was receiving. He might have been concerned that people received him so quizzically. He was no more aware of these reactions than he was of his own haggard and unkempt appearance.

His steps took him to the office of the professor he'd most respected during his time at the college. Dr. Sherman would help him find the answers.

"Palmer." The good professor looked entirely taken

aback at seeing his former student upon the threshold of his office. "I had not expected you."

"What do you know of the presence of lights in the human body?" Palmer had no time for pointless niceties.

"I know that you submitted a paper on the subject not many months ago." Dr. Sherman did not seem pleased.

"I had hoped for help in solving these mysteries, but I have received nothing but silence or ridicule." Palmer held his hat in his hands, crushing the brim in his frustration. "You said, when I was a pupil of yours, 'The moment a doctor believes his learning to be complete, he ceases to be a good doctor.' It seems to me there are a great many poor doctors who have dismissed out of hand what I have actually seen. I pray you will prove an advocate of your own advice."

That seemed to soften the man. He waved Palmer farther inside his office. "The phenomena you described in your paper is not one that is recorded or known amongst your fellow men of medicine. It was met with skepticism, which is not unhealthy nor unheard of."

"Skepticism and dismissal are not the same thing." Palmer only just managed to keep himself from growling out the response.

"Not everyone has entirely dismissed it."

Palmer looked to Dr. Sherman once more. "Who is not dismissing it?" He wanted names. Locations. He needed others to pursue this with him.

"There have been a few whispers," Dr. Sherman said. "Some have seen twinkling lights on bogs or at sea. And the ability of some insects to glow is well known."

"I am not speaking of such things." He took to pacing, something he did with some regularity of late. "There is a connection to human beings. I know there is, and I've heard that some in the dissection room have seen corpses glow."

"When did you last sleep, Palmer?" Dr. Sherman asked. "You look exhausted."

"I don't need you to be my doctor. I need to know if you've heard of these postmortem glows."

"I have not," he said.

Dr. Palmer shook his head, speeding up his pacing. "But that does not mean that it has not happened, that it is not true."

Sherman stepped in the way of Palmer's pacing, necessitating he stop. "Take my advice, young man. Return to your flat. Rest. Alleviate this worry from your mind."

"It is not a 'worry.' It is a scientific mystery. I cannot merely abandon this pursuit."

"I fear if you continue, it will drive you mad," Dr. Sherman said.

"If I do not find the answers I need, it most certainly will."

Dr. Sherman watched him for a long moment, brows drawn in concern, as if Palmer was unaware of the dire nature of his own condition. Palmer did not flinch under the pointed gaze. He knew Sherman was mistaken; pursuing these answers was *not* an ill-conceived quest. It had become his life's mission.

A sigh emitted from the older doctor. "Blackstone still oversees the dissection room. Perhaps he will have some familiarity with the manifestation you speak of."

Realizing his one-time idol did not intend to offer much else in the way of help, Palmer left without a backward glance. The struggle for knowledge abides no sentimental loyalties.

He knew perfectly well how to find the dissecting room. He might have been struggling to find answers to difficult questions, but he was not struggling with his memory. Blackstone's office, located directly beside the room where the cadavers were kept, was empty, its usual living occupant apparently occupied elsewhere.

Irritated with the ceaseless obstacles he encountered, Palmer made his way into the dissecting room without waiting for its overseer to grant permission. The room was dark. No candles or lanterns were lit. The windows were covered in thick draperies. The odor of the room was not one any medical student ever forgot nor truly grew accustomed to. Palmer refused to be felled by olfactory discomfort.

He closed the door behind him, extinguishing every bit of light in the room, though there'd been precious little to begin with. Though he could see nothing, he knew what lay before him—a half-dozen tables with cadavers laid atop them, awaiting examination. Another encounter in this room that students struggled to not find disconcerting.

Palmer inched his way along the wall on which the door hung and placed himself in the corner, and waited. Waited for lights to appear. Waited for the rumors he'd heard to prove themselves true.

"Light up," he whispered in short bursts of breath. "Light up."

The room remained dark. Minutes ticked by. Perhaps

hours. Still, he remained in his corner, watching, whispering, waiting.

And then . . . the lights came.

The subjects upon the tables became quite unexpectedly lit by a remarkably luminous appearance, emanating, as it would seem, from the cadavers themselves. They were lit to such a degree that their forms and shapes and various parts were as clear to see as if every lantern in the school had been lit and brought into the dissecting room, as if the heavy curtains had been pulled back and sunlight allowed to stream inside.

Palmer made mental notes of all he saw, memorizing the details, taking in every possible aspect. The whispers he'd heard were showing themselves to be true.

He would be vindicated. He would be listened to at last.

He stepped out of the dissecting room, searching out someone to act as witness to the phenomenon. Dr. Sherman and Dr. Blackstone were emerging from the latter's office. Neither seemed overly surprised to see him, but they also did not look overly pleased.

"It is happening just as I said it would," Palmer announced. "They are glowing in precisely the way I've seen others. You doubted, but it is happening. It is happening now."

With looks of doubt, they followed him through the dissecting room doors once more. Soon enough, their disbelief would be turned to apology.

Again, the smell of the room rushed over Palmer. Again, he dismissed it. He pushed the door closed, plunging the room into the darkness necessary to see the glow.

But the glow was gone.

Utterly gone.

"It was happening," he growled out. "It was."

He could not see his colleagues, but he knew they would be considering him with equal parts pity and annoyance. He knew because that had become the near-constant response he received to his declarations.

"I am not lying, and I am not mad," he insisted. "I saw what I saw."

"Perhaps, Palmer, you should take a bit of time away," Dr. Sherman said. "Find a quiet corner of the country and rest your mind."

"I have not gone mad. And, somehow, I will prove it."

With that proclamation, he stormed out. He knew now that bodies could glow after death, and he knew of one other means of observing the recently deceased.

He needed to find a Resurrection Man.

CHAPTER 22

By the time Móirín returned from the CALL effort, Licorice was asleep, with Vera and Mr. Sorokin keeping watch in her room. Brogan was sitting with Olly, reading the boy one of Fletcher's penny dreadfuls. Móirín didn't linger but made her way to her own room. The house was calm and peaceful, and Barnabus had done all the things that he alone could do. He stood in the entryway, packing his doctoring bag once more, recounting in his mind any additional instructions he might want to give the Donnellys and Mr. Sorokin.

"Baz?"

He looked up. Gemma stood beside him, watching him uncertainly.

"Could I beg a favor?" she asked.

"No need to beg. You need only ask."

A quick smile flitted over her tired face. "Licorice is comfortably settled and resting. I'd not want to see her tossed off. And the Donnellys have three more houseguests now than they did this morning. The house'll be crowded, and the larder stretched thin."

Barnabus took slow breaths, waiting and hoping she was about to "beg the favor" he hoped for but not wanting to push her toward it.

"Furthermore, my family's searching for me, and the man they work for is searching for Mr. Sorokin and the children. All of us bein' here is a risk." She took a quick breath. "Does your offer still stand for me to return to Finsbury?"

His heart flipped over in his chest, and he didn't bother holding back his smile. "Always, Gemma. Not a moment goes by when I don't wish you were there."

"Truly?"

He'd told her before he wanted her at home and longed for her company. Clearly he needed to do a better job of showing her that. "I like the way your voice fills the house when you sing. I like having supper with you at night, talking about our days. I like that you make me laugh every day. The house is different with you there, in the best way."

Her eyes dropped. "Having me there'd be dangerous."

Barnabus cupped her cheek with his hand, bringing her eyes back up to his. "What will it take, Gemma, to convince you that no amount of danger will ever be enough for me to not want you with me?"

"If anything happened to you, Baz, I'd never forgive myself," she whispered.

"And if I didn't do all I could to convince you to stay, *I* would never forgive *myself*."

A tiny smile tugged at her mouth. "You truly like having me around?"

"I didn't realize how much until you were back in my life." He slipped his hand behind her neck and down her back, settling it at her waist. "Everything is better when you're here, Gemma. Everything."

She set her hand on his chest, her fingers fussing with his lapel. "Do you swear you'll be very careful while I'm there? Not take any extra risks?"

He brushed a kiss over her forehead. "I promise you."

She wrapped her arms around him. "And I'll leave off working at Madame Tussaud's. Then no one'll follow me back to Finsbury. That'll keep the both of us safer."

He embraced her in return. "You could help look after patients. I could use the extra help. It'd also give you a chance to get to know Mrs. Simms better."

"I'd like that."

Having her in his arms like she was, hearing her talk so easily of coming home, Barnabus couldn't imagine how he'd ever thought he could live without her. This was what he'd longed for these past three years. This was what he'd missed and mourned.

"Maybe you could teach me to waltz again," she said.

"Have you forgotten?"

"No. I just fancy dancing with you."

Looking past her shoulder, he spied Móirín watching them from the top of the stairs. Barnabus did not intend to let her ruin this rather perfect moment by teasing either of them.

To Gemma, he said, "Gather up your things. We'll head home as soon as you're ready."

She stepped back and out of his arms, offering a smile before hurrying up the stairs.

Móirín watched her go before returning her attention to Barnabus. "Convinced her to come home, did you?"

"She asked to," he said, "and I certainly had no objections."

"She's mentioned a few times that she's not meaning to stay in London much longer. Don't waste what time you have with her."

He not only didn't mean to squander the days ahead, but he also fully meant to do all he could to convince her to stay.

Supper that night was everything Barnabus could have hoped for, and it had nothing to do with the food. Gemma was there, and she was happy. They laughed and smiled, swapping tales from the past three years and even a few from their childhoods. They both had horrors in their pasts, but for that night, they kept to the lighter moments.

After they'd cleaned up their meal, they walked, hands clasped, toward the sitting room.

"If you haven't changed your mind," he said as they walked, "I would like having you help when we have patients."

Excitement filled her eyes. "When I first lived here after we were married, I thought so many times how I would enjoy being part of your doctoring."

They stepped into the room. "I wish you'd told me."

She smiled and shook her head. "We were strangers, Baz.

You were uncomfortable when I was around, and the last thing I wanted was to be a bother."

He lifted their still-clasped hands to his heart. "I suspect, Gemma, I made it deucedly difficult for you to know that you were never a bother or a burden. Having you here did, and *does*, me a world of good." He knew he was tiptoeing around the admission he needed to make, but sometimes courage took a little nudging.

She set her hand on the side of his face. "Being with you does my heart good too."

He slipped his hand around hers and turned his head, pressing a kiss to her fingers. A bit of color touched her cheeks; Gemma wasn't one for blushing easily. That provided a bit of a nudge.

"Why did you—" He stopped the question before it fully emerged. Apparently, his courage was lagging.

She pulled her hand from his but set it on his chest, keeping her eyes locked with his. "Why did I *what*?"

"Why did you leave? And why did you stay away for so long? And why are you so anxious to leave again?" It was as if, having asked one of the questions on his mind, he couldn't prevent the rest from following close on its heels.

"I need to leave London because if I don't, my family will find me. We both know what that would mean."

He knew all too well. The terror of what the Kincaids were and what they had done and would do never entirely left his mind. If not for the DPS keeping watch over Gemma, he'd have been driven mad with worry.

Barnabus set his hand atop hers on his chest, reminding himself that she was there and she was safe. And that he had courage enough to obtain the answers they needed. "The Kincaids aren't the reason you left before. Why did you leave three years ago?"

Her gaze studied him. "Do you not remember?"

"I remember you told me you loved me and that you needed to know if I loved you too."

The blush that had touched her cheeks a moment earlier slipped quickly into pallor. "That was one of the more frightening moments of my life. I was so afraid of what your answer would be."

Barnabus ran his thumb lightly along her jaw, praying she could forgive him for the pain he'd caused her. "I was wrong. I said then that love wasn't part of our arrangement, that I didn't think it ever would be. But, Gemma, I was wrong. Utterly wrong."

Hesitancy shadowed the hint of hope in her eyes. The time for courage had come.

"I liked having you here, and I certainly didn't want to you leave. But I was also worried you would remain here out of obligation. I didn't want to take away your autonomy the way your father had. I wanted you to have choices."

She watched him, silently and perfectly still.

Barnabus took a slow, lung-filling breath. "It tore me to pieces when you left. And though I didn't realize it then, I understand better now." He looked more deeply into her eyes, needing her to feel his sincerity. "I loved you. I told myself I didn't. Worse, still, I believed myself. But it was folly. I loved you, and I wish I had told you that."

"*Loved?*" She repeated, emphasizing the past tense of it.

He raised her hand once more to his lips and gently

kissed it. Somehow he would make right all he'd mangled these last three years. He wouldn't rest until he did. "I never stopped loving you. I never will. Not ever."

Tears started in her eyes. Gemma never cried. The pain he'd caused ran deep. He knew that. But now that they were being honest with each other, he could start to make things right. He could try.

"I will understand if you can't believe me yet," he said. "I know I broke your heart. But I will do whatever I can, give you whatever you need from me."

She pressed her fingertips to his lips, stopping his words—and nearly his heart with that personal touch. "I've waited so long to hear you say that."

Warmth filled Barnabus's chest, both from her touch and with relief that she was willing to forgive him for having been so thickheaded for so long.

"I love you, Gemma. I'll tell you that every day for the rest of our lives." He pressed his forehead to hers. "Stay with me, love. Let's build a life here. We'll look out for each other, work together, love each other." He slipped his arms around her. "I can introduce you to the man who might very well be my uncle, and we can have friends over for supper. We can waltz in the library as often as you'd like. We would be together. I can't imagine anything better than that."

"I love you, Baz," Gemma whispered.

She kissed his lips lightly, but he pulled her closer and deepened the kiss, reveling in the feel of her in his arms. Their marriage had begun on a difficult footing, but they were finding their way. They were finding reason to hope. They were finding love.

CHAPTER 23

Gemma straightened the antimacassar on the armchair nearest the fireplace. Baz's uncle would be popping in that evening, and she wanted everything to be perfect. Finding family meant the world to Baz. He'd talked about little else over the past two days.

And, over the past two days, she'd done her utmost not to think about the forged letter for "Kate" she kept with her at all times or the notification of death she'd left in Baz's desk for him to file when the time came. She had one week left before they had to be used. One week before she was supposed to be dead.

She could, she supposed, ask Mr. Sorokin to forge another death declaration, give her a bit more time. But the longer she waited, the more dangerous London became. Dying was her only escape. And her death was the only way Baz would be safe.

How could she possibly leave him now, when they finally had happiness within their grasp? But how could she even consider putting him in danger by remaining?

"Is he here yet?" Baz asked, stepping into the sitting room. He'd only just returned from looking in on Licorice at the Donnellys' flat.

"Not yet." She smoothed the front of her dress. It was the nicest one she had, but it weren't much to look at.

Baz crossed to her. He snaked an arm around her waist, then kissed her slowly and deeply. She hooked her arms around his neck and melted against him.

"You're beautiful, Gemma. Don't ever think otherwise."

She kept her arms snuggly where they were. "This dress ain't much."

"We'll get you a new one if you'd like. But for tonight, don't fret over it. My uncle will think the world of you; I'm certain of it."

We'll get you a new one. He fully expected her to stay. She'd not had the heart to remind him why that was such a bad idea. The last two days had been the happiest of her entire life. And he'd been bursting with excitement at introducing her to the man he hoped might be his uncle. She'd have to remind him of her plans, but she'd wait until the morning. Baz deserved a night surrounded by family he didn't think he'd have to give up.

"So you've twigged this Mr. Snelling really is your uncle?"

"We're both perfectly pleased to consider each other family, even if we can't ever prove it."

"I am so happy for you, Baz," she said, though a very real part of her wanted to simply cry. Baz had longed for family for even longer than she'd suspected.

He gave her another quick kiss, then spun her out of his

arms before crossing to his desk and setting down his doctoring bag.

"How is Licorice faring?" Gemma asked.

"Much better. Mr. Sorokin feels they can leave in another day or two. I suspect they don't particularly want to, but they know it's dangerous to remain."

He might've been gabbing about her instead of the children and their protector. Was she selfish to have stayed even as long as she had? These past days with Baz had been brilliant. He held her and kissed her, told her he loved her. But staying put him in harm's way.

One week before her only opportunity to free him came due. But she had to already be gone by then. That took planning. And time—something she was quickly running out of.

Baz peered out the front window, no doubt watching for his uncle. She joined him, and without hesitating, he set his arm around her again. She leaned against him. She closed her eyes, shutting out all the questions she had, all the uncertainty.

"I think I hear a carriage." Baz narrowed his eyes on the street outside. "That's likely my uncle. I'll let him in."

He moved with enthusiasm and excitement. This new family member was important to Baz. His patients were important. The rescue work he did was too. His writing. All those things tied him to London. The only thing tying her there was *him*.

In the dark quiet of night, she had contemplated suggesting he relocate to wherever she ran to. They could pretend to be strangers, fall in love, marry. This time it'd be because they wanted to. They could build a life they'd chosen together.

Except he wouldn't've truly chosen it. He'd have given up everything because she needed him to. Again.

And, just as he'd been forcibly separated from his mother when he was a boy, he'd be forced to sever ties with his uncle, the only connection he had to the mother he still mourned.

Why was it life rarely offered anything but terrible choices?

She tucked some loose hair behind her ear. He'd almost certainly be telling his uncle she was his wife. The only people they were keeping this marriage a secret from were her family. Baz's newly discovered family were welcome to know. That'd make pretending she were a newfound love down the road impossible without cutting his uncle out of his life.

She could hear their voices in the entryway, though she couldn't make out what they were saying. She swallowed the lump of worry building in her throat, telling her heart to slow down. There was an answer to all this somewhere. There had to be.

Baz entered the room first, a broad smile on his face. "Gemma, I'd like you to meet Mr. Snelling." He stepped to the side, allowing his uncle to enter.

Gemma froze. Ice wrapped around her heart and lungs.

Mr. Snelling was not Baz's uncle. He was *hers*.

"Uncle Arlo." The name pulled painfully from her. She took an involuntary step backward, searching for a means of escape he weren't already blocking.

A sinister smile spread across his despised face. He sauntered closer, leaving Barnabus behind him and unable to see the look he was giving her. He did not, however, lower his voice when he spoke. "I wondered how long it'd take you to show your face here, Gemma girl. You cain't run from this family. We'll always sniff you out."

Gemma didn't hesitate. Silas was more dangerous, but Arlo was no one to be trifled with. She reached for the window next to her, threw it open, and scrambled out. Her feet hit the soft soil, and, without a moment's pause, she ran for her life.

Gemma had practically jumped out the window, and Mr. Snelling had followed her. It all happened in an instant, and Barnabus's mind hadn't time to catch up.

Uncle Arlo. Gemma's strangled declaration echoed in his mind. His "uncle" was *her* uncle. He'd tracked her to Barnabus and used him to pull her out of hiding.

Barnabus flew out the door, being closer to it than the window. He had to catch the imposter and help Gemma get away. There was no sign of either of them. He could hear no footfalls and saw no shadows lurking about. He didn't even know which direction they had gone. How could he find her if he didn't know which way to go?

The Donnellys, maybe? No. She wouldn't risk leading her family to them, especially with Mr. Sorokin and the children there.

Gemma knew people in Southwark, but that was her family's stronghold. She wouldn't go there. Not being a member of the Dread Penny Society, she wasn't aware of the existence of their headquarters. She knew Barnabus had safe houses around London, but as far as he knew, she didn't know how to find any of them.

She had nowhere to go and therefore could be anywhere.

He refused to believe Arlo Kincaid had caught her.

Barnabus could hardly scour London on his own. He needed help, and he knew where to find it. He made his way directly to Fletcher Walker's flat. It was early enough yet that the man wouldn't be asleep, but he couldn't guarantee Fletcher would even be at home; he called on Elizabeth almost every evening. If Barnabus didn't find him at home, he would go to Elizabeth's school and ask for him there.

He hopped out of the hired hackney and rushed to the door. His frantic knock, bless the heavens, was answered quickly by Fletcher himself.

"We have a problem," Barnabus said, pushing his way into the dim entryway. "The man I told you was probably my uncle came by tonight to meet Gemma."

Fletcher watched him closely and silently. He must've sensed Barnabus had not come on a small thing.

"Except, turns out he ain't *my* uncle; he's *hers.* She caught sight of him and climbed out the window and ran like the blazes, with him right behind. I wasn't fast enough to catch them. She's gone, and I don't know where."

Fletcher's brows pulled together in concentration. "So his story about being your uncle was a ruse?"

Barnabus was inwardly kicking himself. "It was. And I swallowed the entire thing without even thinking."

"You can chew your leg over that later. We need to find her."

Barnabus nodded. "I need more eyes than just mine."

"You'll hate this, but it'd be best if you return home in case she doubles back. And we need to know where you are so we can get you word of anything we sort out."

He was going to be left out of the search? "No. I cain't sit there knowing she's in trouble and not doing a blasted thing."

"You *will* be doing a blasted thing. Your house is the one place she might come back to. But there's every possibility your false uncle will as well. I'll have someone watching your place. You make sure you're always armed. And, maybe, don't see patients for a while."

Barnabus wanted to object more, but Fletcher had a knack for these things. And he felt certain Fletcher would consult with the Dread Master, whoever that might be.

"I'll head first to the Donnellys on the off chance she goes there," Fletcher said. "And I can send Brogan out to start getting word to the Dreadfuls. We won't give up, Doc. I swear to you."

He still wasn't entirely convinced that he shouldn't be out pleading for the support of the Dreadfuls himself. But there was some wisdom in Fletcher's strategy.

Barnabus reluctantly took another hackney back home and let himself in. The empty silence didn't usually bother him, but it struck him forcefully just then. There was a heaviness to the stillness.

He walked into the sitting room. The table near the window was still in disarray. The memory of the terror in Gemma's eyes remained fresh in his mind. He had brought this danger here. He had led her family right to her. He didn't know when he would have a chance to apologize for that.

If they could only find her, if he could only be certain she was safe, some of the pain in his heart might ease.

He sat at his desk, leaned his elbows on the top, and rested his head against his hands. Maybe if he made a list of the places she'd lived that might help them find her. He pulled open the drawer, meaning to snatch out a piece of parchment. An envelope sat inside; one he didn't recognize.

He broke the seal and opened it. Inside was a single sheet of paper—the forged letter declaring that Gemma had died. Had she left it here for him? Likely. She couldn't, after all, file the letter of death herself.

Did she have the other paper with her, the letter of recommendation identifying her as Kate Mitchell?

If she managed to escape Arlo—No. Since she *had* managed to escape Arlo, she might simply flee London altogether. A few days remained yet before this letter was supposed to have been written.

If he didn't find her by then, he'd have to make an impossible decision: keep looking for her for the rest of his life or grant her this escape.

THE BACHELOR AND THE BRIDE

by Mr. King

Installment VI
in which our brave Duo's destination
proves quite unexpected!

Aching and sore after the terrifying ride they'd had on the back of the kelpie, Duncan and Sorcha pulled themselves up off the ground. Night had, indeed, fallen. They were at the end of their second day of traveling, and they had only two days to make the journey back home. There was no time for setbacks.

They kept their hands clasped as they walked along the road toward Carrifran. Only the moon in the clear evening sky lit the scene. No lights emanated from inside any home or building. No fires appeared to be burning in any hearths. The town was completely and utterly quiet.

Their steps took them down a street to the remains of a market cross. All was still. The buildings were in disrepair.

"Carrifran appears to be abandoned," Duncan said, unsure what that meant for their current endeavor.

In the distance, he could see the spire of the church. The road they were on would take them directly there. Sorcha kept near his side, but her steps were slow. He didn't know if she was weary from the journey or wary about what they might encounter next. He himself felt a great deal of both.

They arrived at the outer gate of the churchyard. It too appeared abandoned.

There was no way to tell how long it had been since anyone had lived in this town or worshiped in this chapel, but the eerie emptiness of it filled him with misgivings. And, yet, he could clearly see on the corner of the dilapidated chapel a stone rainspout carved to look like a gargoyle. This was their destination. This was where they needed to be.

"I do not imagine it will be as easy as it appears," Sorcha said. "More needs to be done, I'm certain. Something else must be waiting for us here."

He wished he didn't agree with her assessment. After all they had encountered, this seemingly clear path proved terribly unsettling.

Holding tight to Sorcha's hand, he took a single step forward. She did as well. The moment their feet touched the churchyard soil, a flash of lightning cracked the cloudless sky.

Without warning, without sound, without pause, a woman appeared before them. A ghost.

She hovered in the air, her feet not touching the ground, her green dress wafting as if in a breeze. She was impossible to miss, and yet her form was not entirely solid. Duncan could still see the church behind her, through her, obscured by her.

She stared at them, watching them with a look that clearly foretold danger. But she said not a word.

"What is your assessment?" he asked Sorcha.

"If I had to guess, I would say she's a Lady Grim."

"I had heard churchyard grims were animals—usually dogs."

Sorcha nodded. "Traditionally, the first living thing buried in a churchyard is an animal whose spirit guards the resting places of all who follow. But if that is not done, then the duty to protect the spot lies with whomever was buried there most recently. That person's spirit remains until someone else is buried, who then takes up the role, which is later inherited by the next to be laid to rest."

To the still silent and still watchful Lady Grim, he said, "We mean no harm. We have come only to fetch water from the mouth of the gargoyle. We need it to cure a very ill young girl in our village."

The Lady Grim said nothing. She watched him, but her expression changed from anger to something very nearly pleading.

"Is there something you need from us?" Sorcha asked.

The Lady Grim motioned with her ghostly hand toward a nearby grave. Duncan hunched down low enough to face the stone. He wiped the dirt from its face, making the inscription clear. The grave belonged to a woman buried more than one hundred years earlier on what, according to the inscriptions, was to have been her wedding day. She had been merely twenty-five years of age.

From his position, he looked up at the ghostly guardian. "Is this you?" he asked gently.

She nodded.

"No one has been buried here since?" Sorcha asked.

The Lady Grim shook her head.

Duncan stood once more, looking at the dilapidated

church and thinking about the crumbling village they'd walked through. She was the last person to have been buried here. And no one lived here any longer. No one else would ever be buried in this churchyard. She was trapped as the guardian of this place, held here for more than a century, unable to obtain her eternal rest.

"She is a prisoner here," Sorcha said, following his thoughts. "There must be a way to free her."

"I've never freed a grim," he said. "Is it even possible?"

Sorcha shook her head. "Grims aren't freed; they are exchanged."

They stood in silence for a time. Surely neither of them was meant to die and be buried here for this journey to be completed. Granny Winter would never have subjected Sorcha to such a fate.

He looked to the Lady Grim, who watched him with a sad, silent countenance. How desperately she must have wanted to leave, but it was not in her power to do so. He felt called to be a doctor, a healer. He did all he could for those amongst the living, but he had no ability to heal the dead.

"I am sorry," he said to her. "I don't know how to right this wrong."

She still didn't speak, didn't move.

Duncan tried to take a step toward the church. He was immediately flung back by an unseen hand. He landed on the ground, painfully but not injuriously.

Sorcha helped him to his feet. "It seems the only way to reach the church is to release her."

"Exchanging a life is out of the question," Duncan said.

"Whoever began this churchyard did not spare her this

fate. There is no means of freeing her other than finding someone to take her place."

"I will not sacrifice either of our lives for this." He could not. He *would* not. "The past two days have been life-altering despite the danger. I could never again imagine my life without you in it. I refuse to believe Granny Winter would send us on a journey that would bring us together only to tear us apart again."

She set her hand lightly on his arm. "I cannot imagine my life without you either."

There had to be another way to free the grim and save Donella. This could not be the end of their perilous journey.

"If only a true grim had been buried first," Sorcha said. "Animal spirits do not require an exchange."

Animal. "Does that hold true only if the animal is the *first* to be buried?"

She shook her head, her expression turning to one of deep consideration. "An animal could take over the duties of a grim even now."

And they had an animal. He pulled Granny's bag off his back and opened it. All that remained was the stuffed vole and the bottle. The small animal had seemed such an odd thing, but it now made perfect sense.

"Are there any rules about grims that say the thing buried must be newly dead?" he asked.

"I do not know." She met his gaze, hope shining in her eyes. "It *is* possible the vole can serve this purpose."

"It is worth trying," he said. "It is worth seeing if Granny Winter knew of our plight in such detail."

He turned his attention to the Lady Grim. "We are going

to try to free you," he said. "If we succeed, will you allow us passage to the gargoyle?"

She dipped her head in agreement. This was their chance, then.

In a bit of dirt under a nearby tree, Duncan began to dig. He'd no implements, only his fingers. He clawed at the soft dirt. Sorcha soon joined him. They didn't dig a large hole, nor a deep one. Simply enough to bury the animal sent with him.

As they dug, the wind picked up and swirled the tree branches. The smell of rain filled the air. He glanced at the Lady Grim as he continued his effort. Her hair and dress whipped with greater vigor, greater motion. She, he did not doubt, was creating this storm, but whether out of excitement or nervousness, he couldn't say.

At last, the hole was of sufficient size. He placed the vole in it, and he and Sorcha pushed the dirt back in to cover its resting place. They packed it down, making certain the remains were hidden, held fast, and safe. Sorcha placed a rock at the grave site, allowing it to act as a headstone.

They both stood and stepped back, looking from the tiny, makeshift grave to the Lady Grim. Was it enough? Would it work?

Lightning once more cracked, sending flashes of light across the sky. It disappeared quickly and with it the guardian of the graveyard. She'd come without a word, left without a warning. In the next instant, the sky opened, and rain began to fall.

Duncan and Sorcha rushed across the churchyard, crossing as quickly as they could over the rough, unkempt land, directly to the corner of the church where the gargoyle stood sentinel.

All that remained in Duncan's bag was the bottle. He pulled it out, realizing what its purpose was. In it, they would collect the water that would save Donella's life. He pulled off the stopper and held the vessel directly beneath the grotesque stone face. As rain filled the gutters of the church, water began to pour over the teeth and snarled lips of the carving. It splashed off Duncan's hands, off the sides of the vessel, soaking him and Sorcha but also filling the vessel.

Once the water reached the very brim, he plunged the stopper in place once more, then returned it to his bag and pulled the bag onto his back. He hoped it would be enough to heal young Donella.

He and Sorcha huddled beneath the archway of what had once likely held the church doors. It offered minimal protection from the elements, but it was enough. He wrapped his arms around her, holding her to him as the rain fell.

"We've managed it," he said. "We've managed it together."

"We still need to return home safely," Sorcha said. "I shudder to think what awaits us on that journey. And we've only two days remaining. I'm not certain it can be done."

From behind them, in the ruined remains of the church, he heard voices. They both turned, keeping hold of one another.

The church was filled with ghostly apparitions, people dressed in clothing of eras gone by, reaching back centuries. At the front of the chapel, in the chancel near the altar, was the Lady Grim, though now she wore a crown of ghostly flowers and held a matching bouquet. A man clothed in the garb of the same era as she gazed lovingly at her face.

Hers was the appearance of a bride, and the man was, no doubt, the one she would have married had she lived.

The ghostly bride gave her faded bouquet to a woman standing near her. She set her hands in her groom's. A ghost in priestly raiment stood before them.

"Their wedding," Sorcha whispered. "How long they must have waited for this day!"

Duncan pulled her closer. "It's a sight that could melt the heart of even a resolute bachelor like myself."

From within his arms, she asked, "Are you resolutely a bachelor or a bachelor who happens to be a resolute sort of person?"

"Bachelorhood has, of late, lost its appeal."

At the front of the church, the ceremony reached its joyous conclusion. The husband and wife embraced to the silent cheers of generations of their families. The sight, indeed, touched the heart.

With her groom's arm tenderly around her, the Lady Grim smiled at Duncan and Sorcha, then motioned back in the direction of the churchyard.

They looked that way. A bright doorway of light appeared. It emanated warmth and a sense of safety. Duncan could not express exactly why he felt secure in doing so, but he knew they needed to step through this bright passageway.

"I suspect that is a doorway home," Sorcha said. "They are offering us a safe return."

She felt as he did. That was reassurance enough.

Hand in hand, they moved from beneath the stone arch to the doorway of light and stepped through.

CHAPTER 24

Two days passed without a glimpse of Gemma. Barnabus had hardly slept, had hardly eaten. He didn't see any patients. All he did was look for her. Look for her and castigate himself.

On the third day, Mrs. Simms looked in on him despite his objections over her safety. She had countered with her objections to him being alone while he was worried. They'd compromised by agreeing to a very brief look-in. While she was in the kitchen, having insisted on making him a spot of tea and a bit of toast, an envelope dropped in through the letter slot in the front door.

Barnabus took it up like a starving man, not knowing if it contained anything of substance. He tore it open and read ravenously.

Doc,

I didn't know who else to send word to. The man you helped me escape—there's whispers he's meaning to do something soon. He's found someone that's giving him grief, and he's snuffing out whoever it is. I'm worried it might be you or one of 'em that helped me. Or it might be me.

The woman here says I can move to a different safe house since my little'ns and I don't feel safe. No one should feel safe. He smells blood, Doc. He has to be stopped.

Please don't let him find out I know. Please. He'll kill me and my children. I know he will.

—S

He didn't have to think long to piece it all together. Serena had heard the Mastiff was on the hunt. She was afraid, just as she should be. But was the person the Mastiff meant to "snuff" Serena herself? One of her children? Someone unknown to Barnabus?

Gemma?

Not willing to risk the letter being seen and read by someone who ought not to, he tore it in pieces, then tossed them into the low-burning embers of the sitting room's fireplace and watched the fragments turn to ash.

Mrs. Simms approached with a single piece of toast and a teacup. "You need rest Doc. You need to eat."

He shook his head. "Gemma's in danger. I can't stop looking."

"And how do you mean to look if you're collapsed in a heap on account of having exhausted yourself?"

A wave of defeat rushed over him. "I can't bear to lose her again. I can't."

She patted his cheek, though the gesture felt motherly

rather than condescending. "I'll lock up here. You go search a bit, see if you can't discover something."

"Thank you." He snatched up his hat and his bag—he never went anywhere without it—and reached for the door. "Promise me you'll take every precaution. Don't answer the door to anyone."

"If you make me a promise," Mrs. Simms said. "Swear to me you'll have a full and filling meal and then sleep tonight."

He smiled, though he knew the weakness of his expression gave away just how much he'd been neglecting himself. "I will."

She motioned him out the door. He slipped out. Before stepping away, he checked the fastness of the sign he'd hung directing patients to another man of medicine in the area, then the security of the bolt he'd slid into place with his key. Satisfied, he set his feet onto the pavement.

There was no point checking Southwark; Gemma wouldn't have gone where her family lived. Beyond that, he knew the Kincaids had connected him to her. Going to their safehold would simply invite trouble.

He smells blood, Doc. He has to be stopped.

He'd made quiet inquiries all around Finsbury. The Dreadfuls had done the same in every corner of London where they knew people.

He smells blood.

The search felt futile, but he couldn't give it up. He wouldn't.

Where could she possibly be?

His feet had taken him far afield when he spotted Fletcher

and Brogan walking together. He called out to them, then hurried to join them.

"Any luck?" Fletcher asked.

Barnabus shook his head. "None. Not even a hint of her."

"She's powerful good at hiding," Brogan said. "Kept herself tucked away for years after you were married. I suspect that's what's happening now."

Barnabus had repeatedly told himself that very thing. She wasn't being held captive by her family. She hadn't been killed by them or the Mastiff. She was simply hiding.

"None of the Dreadfuls have reported anything?" Barnabus asked.

Fletcher shook his head.

Where are you, Gemma?

A commotion nearby pulled all their attention.

"That's Lord Chelmsford's home," Brogan said.

"Maybe we oughta have a quick gab with Martin," Fletcher said, motioning them both toward the servants' entrance at the back, where chaos and shouts were spilling from the house.

A maid was screaming, tears streaming down her face. An older man—the butler, Barnabus guessed—was barking out orders, his ruddy cheeks a sharp contrast to his pale countenance.

Fletcher never had been one to wait around for people to talk with him at their convenience. He pulled aside one of the maids and spoke firmly but gently. "What's happened?"

"Claud stabbed him. Took a knife from the kitchen and just stabbed 'im."

"Who's Claud?" Fletcher asked.

"Footman here," the maid said. "Weren't no reason. No argument between 'em. Just stabbed him."

Merciful heavens.

"I'm a doctor," Barnabus said. "Take me to the injured man."

The maid rushed back inside. Barnabus struggled to keep pace with her in the press of people. They didn't need to go far, though. The violent scene had played out in the servants' dining hall.

And the victim was . . . Martin.

Barnabus dropped to the floor beside him. Years of training kept him calm as he checked his friend for signs of life. The wound in his back was high enough to have missed his heart and enough to one side to have avoided the major arteries. Barnabus's next biggest worries were whether the wound had compromised his lungs and whether the blood loss had already proven too much.

He pulled his stethoscope from his bag and popped the earpieces in his ears. He set the bell on Martin's neck. The man was lying on his chest; his neck was the likeliest place to find a pulse without turning him over.

Fletcher and Brogan were there in the very next moment.

"What can we do?" Fletcher asked.

"Shut up." Barnabus needed to focus. He was searching desperately for a pulse, knowing if there were one, it'd be weak.

"Stay with us, Martin," Brogan whispered.

A faint heartbeat. "Found it." He looked up at the gathered staff. "All the towels or rags you can find. Get his shirt off. Cut it if you have to. We need to put pressure on the wound and stop the bleeding."

Fletcher and Brogan got Martin on his side, working carefully but quickly to cut him free of his shirt. Barnabus pressed his stethoscope to Martin's chest, listening to him breathe. No gurgling, which was a good sign. But his breathing was shallow.

He tugged at Martin's eyelid, wanting to see if there was life in his eyes. "Look at me, friend. Show me you're still in there."

His eyes made an attempt at focusing. That was enough.

"He's still with us." Barnabus looked up at the butler hovering nearby. "Send someone to the mews to prepare a cart. This man needs to be taken to a doctor's surgery without delay, but he'll need to be laid flat to do it. A cart with an empty back."

The butler rushed off.

Fletcher motioned a footman over. "Where's the blackguard who did this? Claud, I'm told is his name."

"He run off. Out of the house."

"Go make certain Lord Chelmsford is safe."

Martin's shirt was off entirely, giving Barnabus his first look at the wound. It was a clean cut, deep but manageable.

"Towels," he called out to the staff. They brought plenty to the scene. To Brogan, he said, "Press a towel to the wound. Don't break the man's bones but press hard. We must get the bleeding stopped. If you soak through a towel, snatch up another one."

Martin's eyes fluttered open, though barely.

"Stay with us, Martin." Barnabus listened to his heart again, reassured by the steady pulse.

"Claud." Martin groaned out the name.

"He's flown," Fletcher said. "But we'll find him."

"He's a . . . plant."

Another man arrived on the scene, one Barnabus knew: Dr. Lowry. "The staff sent for me. How'd you arrive first?"

"I was nearby." Barnabus quickly caught him up on the situation.

"I can take him to my surgery. It isn't far."

"He is a friend of mine." Barnabus held Dr. Lowry's gaze. "Do all you can for him."

"I will."

The staff had procured a plank for transporting Martin. Moving him a little at a time, Barnabus, Fletcher, Brogan, and Dr. Lowry shifted him onto it. Brogan kept pressure on the wound.

"Go with Dr. Lowry," Fletcher said to Brogan. "Keep us informed."

"Aye."

A cart was waiting at the back of the house. The stable staff helped Dr. Lowry and Brogan get Martin settled, then sat on either side of him.

As the cart rolled away, one of the maids stepped up even with Barnabus. "Is Martin going to die?"

"I don't know. But Dr. Lowry can be depended on. And Martin managed to say a few words, which is a good sign."

"Everyone likes Martin. If any of us gets our hands on Claud, you'd best believe we'll thrash him."

"So will I." Barnabus's jaw set, anger bubbling now that he wasn't actively doctoring. "So will I."

He paced away, unable to keep still. Gemma was still missing. Martin had been stabbed. The Kincaids were terrorizing London. The Mastiff remained out of reach and was on the prowl. It was too much.

Fletcher walked alongside him. "Martin said Claud was a plant—a spy."

Barnabus forced himself to breathe and think. "If Martin knew that about Claud, it's possible Claud knew that about Martin."

Fletcher nodded. Strain pulled at his usually jovial features. "Claud discovering that would only have led to an attack if Claud was placed here by the Mastiff."

"Martin wouldn't have been careless about that information," Barnabus said.

Fletcher picked up his pace. "I doubt Claud sorted it out; he was likely told."

"You don't think one of us—?"

Fletcher shook his head. "I'd guess the Mastiff figured it out, or at least guessed that we'd have someone watching from the inside and set his informant on alert."

They'd passed through the servants' entrance. Lowering his voice, Barnabus said, "I received a letter from Serena. She's heard that the Mastiff discovered someone who's been causing him 'grief' and that he was going to be 'snuffing out' that person."

Fletcher glanced back at the house. "That person being Martin, it seems."

"If I'd suspected that Martin was the target, I would have come directly here. Might have prevented it."

Fletcher shook his head. "That she even tried is . . . well, that were a mountain of a risk, that. Right bricky, she is."

She *was* brave, there was no denying that. Barnabus would have to make certain she had been moved to another house, somewhere she felt safe. He likely ought to be seeing what could be done to get her out of London entirely. Perhaps Mr. Sorokin could create another death declaration and forged letter of reference.

Fletcher eyed the area around them with a narrowed gaze. "What do you suppose the chances are that murdering bloke is somewhere nearby, watching to see if he managed the thing?"

"I think it's possible, especially if he's meant to report back that he was successful and what Chelmsford's response to it is."

Without needing to coordinate, they began looking around the grounds, behind hedgerows and buildings. They didn't have to look long. Behind an outbuilding, tucked into a shrubbery, they found a man dressed in the livery of a footman, his right sleeve blood-soaked.

Fletcher yanked him none-too-gently out of the hedge. "Wanted to see your handiwork, did you? Feeling satisfied with the pain you've caused?" He held fast to the man, looking at him with a degree of cold anger Barnabus had never before seen on Fletcher's face.

"I did what I were told to do." Though Claud seemed unpleasantly surprised to have been found, he didn't look remorseful or afraid. "And I'll be rewarded for it."

"Rewarded with a swing on the gallows," Fletcher growled.

"The Mastiff'll spring me."

"I'd not waste my breath making that wager," Fletcher said. "The likes of the Mastiff'd sooner cannibalize his own than rescue 'em."

"Come now," a voice drawled from behind them. "That's a horrid thing to say."

Barnabus spun about. Fletcher turned enough to look without losing his grip on the murderer.

There, no more than a few strides away, was the man they'd been chasing for months. The infamous Mastiff, who had ended and upended so many lives. He and Claud made two. Barnabus and Fletcher evened those odds. This was their chance. If Gemma had eluded the Mastiff, here was the moment to make that permanent.

Barnabus took a single step toward the man.

"Don't be a cod," the Mastiff growled. "Just because I'm the only one you can see don't mean I'm the only one here. The odds ain't at all leaning your way, Doc."

"Deed is done," Claud said quickly, proudly. "Did exactly what you told me to. But these blokes mean to see me swing."

The Mastiff looked at him like he was a simpleton. "It ain't such a bad way to go."

For the first time, Claud looked nervous. "But it ain't how *I'm* gonna go."

The Mastiff gave him a look of pity.

"You're tossing me to the wolves?" Claud sounded frantic.

"It ain't the wolves you should be worried about," the Mastiff said. "The Tempest is coming."

In a tense and terrified whisper, Claud repeated that all-too-familiar warning, "The Tempest is coming."

The coming storm, be it a person or a criminal enterprise, brought fear even to a cold-blooded murderer. How much worse was this going to get? What more could the Mastiff and his comrades possibly have planned?

He smells blood. He has to be stopped.

The Mastiff turned a steel-hard gaze on Barnabus. "There's a family looking for you. I suggest you take care when returning to Finsbury. It i'n't exactly a safe place lately."

There was no mistaking the message. Gemma's family was coming for Barnabus.

Fletcher hadn't loosened his grip on Claud. Barnabus was tempted to make a leap for the Mastiff, but it was best to keep his head. Getting himself killed now wouldn't help Gemma.

"You're gonna let 'em nib me?" Claud said to the Mastiff, panic clearly setting in. "I'll be making the morning drop at Newgate for certain."

"He ain't any more loyal to his own people than he is to ours," Fletcher said.

A skin-crawling smirk pulled at the Mastiff's lips. "Do you have any idea the way those two groups overlap?" He laughed humorlessly. "Best clear your house, man. It's dirtier than you know."

On that declaration, he turned and walked away, casual as anything, as though absolutely nothing in the world bothered him.

"The blue-bottles'll be here soon," Claud said. "Hand me over to 'em, please. Let 'em haul me off."

"You're looking to be gallows' bait?" Fletcher asked.

"The Tempest is coming," he said, voice quivering.

"We've been hearing that all over London." Fletcher shook him a bit. "What does it mean?"

All the color drained from Claud's face. "The Tempest is coming."

"What is the Tempest?" Fletcher demanded.

"Or who?" Barnabus added.

Claud shook his head quickly, repeatedly, as if too terrified to think, let alone speak.

Fletcher dragged him back to the courtyard beside the servants' entrance. The police had arrived. The entire staff gasped and cried out and shouted when they saw Claud, identifying him as the murderer.

Among the arrived constables was Parkington. He gave his associates orders to secure the prisoner.

Claud stared down Barnabus as he was dragged away, mouthing, "The Tempest is coming."

"Coincidence that you're here?" Parkington asked Fletcher under his breath.

"Yes and no. We happened to be nearby, but we've taken more of an interest because the one what got stabbed was Martin Afola."

"Blimey."

"Dr. Lowry took him to his surgery," Barnabus said. "There's some hope he'll survive."

"The Mastiff was here," Fletcher said, lowering his voice. "Piked off just now but admitted straight-out that the attack was on his orders."

Parkington motioned with his head toward the corner of

the house. Smudged in ash was the letter *K*, flanked by two vertical lines. And the *K* was underlined. "This Claud ain't one of the brothers, but he is family, likely a child of one of 'em or a cousin or some such."

Gemma had told Barnabus time and again that the Kincaids had no qualms about murder. A cold pain spread through his chest. Murder. And one of them had been chasing her, determined to catch her.

"Have you had any success finding your wife?" Parkington apparently knew where Barnabus's thoughts had gone.

He shook his head. "There's not a trace of her."

"If I could guarantee you my fellow policemen would all overlook the fact that she's a Kincaid with a criminal past, I'd urge you to let the Metropolitan Police aid in your search." Parkington offered an apologetic look. "You've brought Stone in on the effort? And Móirín and Vera?"

Barnabus nodded.

"And Sorokin?" Parkington added.

Barnabus turned to Fletcher. "Could we get word of this to him?"

"I am certain he already knows," Fletcher said.

Parkington set his hand on Barnabus's shoulder. "I took on a few extra patrol assignments. That's letting me poke around more. We'll find her. I know we will."

Fletcher had often said that if Parkington would start writing penny dreadfuls, he'd stand him for membership in the DPS in a heartbeat. The man was fearsome and focused. He was also dedicated to the cause of the vulnerable. A good person in every sense.

"Thank you," Barnabus said.

The other constables had Claud locked into the transport wagon they'd brought. Parkington hopped up on back, riding there as they drove off.

"The Mastiff said the Kincaids are looking for you specifically," Fletcher said. "Either they're holding a grudge, trying to stretch us too thin to keep up with their efforts, or looking to get to Gemma through you."

"Or they've simply gained a liking for 'snuffing out' people," Barnabus said.

"It's time for you to go invisible," Fletcher said.

Barnabus shook his head. "I need to keep looking for Gemma. I can't simply hide away, twiddling my thumbs while—"

"The Dread Master gave me instructions that if your life were in danger, you needed to go invisible."

The Dreadfuls didn't often send someone into such complete hiding—going invisible, as they termed it. If the Dread Master was insisting he do precisely that, the situation must be more dire than he realized.

"To headquarters, then?" he asked in a whisper.

"No. To a safe house."

"I won't risk bringing the Mastiff's people to any of the places where I'm hiding the women and girls we've rescued. Especially with Serena hidden in one of them. She risked her neck trying to warn us. I—"

"Not one of *your* safe houses," Fletcher said. "The Dread Master's."

CHAPTER 25

Barnabus wasn't overly happy with going invisible, but he understood. Everything was in chaos and disarray. Word of the attack on Martin would reach the rest of the DPS soon enough, and they'd all be both more afraid and more determined. They would rally to the effort of safeguarding the rest. Until they could bring down the Mastiff, until they could remove that danger, they needed to focus on their enemy, not on protecting Barnabus.

So he went along with Fletcher, following him through roundabout ways, back alleys, under arches, behind buildings. He knew they were taking a circuitous path in order to reduce the chances of being followed. Indeed, Fletcher continually checked for exactly that. So did Barnabus. Through the long journey, neither of them said a word. Fletcher didn't waste a single bit of energy with his usual strutting and sauntering. He was focused and solemn.

Fletcher entered a small dwelling at the back of an alleyway, closing the door behind them both. Barnabus knew London well, yet even he was lost, having taken so many turns. Down a narrow corridor they went, and through another door made to blend in perfectly with the weather-beaten wall it sat in. This safe house was better hidden than any of the ones Barnabus had.

The door closed heavily behind them. Fletcher lit a candle, having known precisely where to find both it and a match. They walked down the narrow corridor to a third door. Fletcher unlocked it and pushed it slowly open.

Lantern light burned inside.

"Is someone else here?" Barnabus asked.

"Apparently." Fletcher met his eye. "Whoever it is had to've been sent by the Dread Master and had to've been given a key."

They stepped inside.

Stone sat in a chair on the far side, watching as they entered. Stone. That made perfect sense. If he was indeed the Dread Master, he could easily enter a hiding place known only to that man.

Stone spoke to Fletcher. "Is Doc needing to go invisible?"

Fletcher nodded. "The Mastiff's called for his head. Best we know where he is and that he's safe."

"There's certainly room enough," Stone said. "We'll need food brought, though. The larder's nearly empty."

Fletcher's eyes darted to Barnabus, then quickly settled on Stone. "Why has the Dread Master plopped you here?"

A question meant to misdirect Barnabus's possible suspicions, perhaps?

"To act as guard," Stone said.

"Guard for what?" Fletcher asked.

"Not what. *Whom.*" Stone rose and crossed to a secretary desk pushed up against the far wall. He pulled open a drawer and removed a sealed letter, which he handed to Fletcher. "This has been waiting for you, should you arrive here."

"The Dread Master's stationery." He broke the seal and read silently.

Barnabus heard footsteps approaching and turned toward the sound, wondering who else was taking refuge here. A moment later, she stepped into the room.

"Gemma," he whispered, hearing his own voice emerge with the inflection of a prayer.

She rushed to him and threw her arms around his neck. He wrapped his around her waist and pulled her close to him.

"Oh, Gemma. Gemma."

She held tightly to him, as tightly as he held her.

"I've been looking everywhere for you," he said. "No one has seen you. No one knew where you were. I feared your uncle had caught up to you."

"Stone was keeping watch over your house that night. He saw me scramble out of the window and got me to his flat without my uncle catching up to us. He hid me there until we got directions for coming here."

Still holding Gemma, half afraid she might disappear again, he turned his head to look to Stone. "Thank you."

"I'd have told you she was safe, but the Dread Master insisted I keep mum."

Barnabus turned wide eyes on Fletcher. Stone had just mentioned the head of their secretive society in the presence of someone who wasn't meant to know anything about it.

"Calm your worries, Barnabus." Fletcher held up the letter he'd received. "Stone was given permission to explain things to Gemma. Desperate times and whatnot."

"You almost lost your membership on account of sharing just a bit of information with Elizabeth before she joined."

"I doubt anyone is going to suggest the Dread Master be tossed out," Fletcher said. "No one has that power."

"Stone don't know who this Dread Master is," Gemma said. "And though I'm beholden to the bloke, I'm put out with him just the same. He wouldn't let me send word to you that I was safe." She gently touched Barnabus's face. "You look like you've hardly slept in days."

"I didn't know what happened to you. I didn't know where to find you. Sleeping, eating, resting . . . none of that mattered so long as you were in danger."

"I knew you'd be worried and looking." She remained in Barnabus's arms but turned her gaze to Fletcher and Stone. "It was cruel not to tell him. He should've been told."

"I know now," Barnabus said. "And I'm staying here: Dread Master's orders."

He motioned to the sofa, hoping to sit there with her.

Gemma's eyes suddenly widened, staring at his hands. "Is that blood?"

He'd not had a chance to clean his hands, and his skin was a horrifying rust color. "It's not my blood. It's Martin Afola's."

"Martin?" Stone looked from Fletcher to Barnabus, worry heavy in his eyes.

"The Mastiff sent one of his men to snuff Martin," Fletcher said. "Stabbed him. He's at a doctor's surgery now. We'll keep guard and hope for the best."

"The Mastiff?" Gemma swallowed audibly.

"And the house where it happened had your family's mark on it," Fletcher said. "With the *K* second."

"Uncle Silas," she said.

"The *K* was underlined," Barnabus added. "And the would-be murderer wasn't old enough to be your uncle."

She thought a moment. "Big fella? Bit of a dull swift?"

"Oi," Fletcher said with a nod.

"That'll be Silas's boy, Claud." She wrapped her arms around herself. "He were caught, then?"

"And the Mastiff doesn't mean to free him," Barnabus said. "He's going to let him hang."

"Could be that'll turn the Kincaids against him," Stone said. "Breaking that alliance would help our efforts."

But Gemma shook her head. "A Kincaid who's slapdash enough to get nabbed is left to the consequences. Silas himself has likely already declared Claud no son of his, agreeing entirely with the Mastiff for tossing him over."

"And if the Mastiff ordered them to kill you?" Fletcher asked her.

"He doesn't need to. I'd wager my last groat they're already planning to."

"So we stay here until we have more information," Barnabus said. "Until we know how to keep you safe and sort out what the Mastiff and the Kincaids have planned."

"*We*? You're staying?"

Barnabus put an arm around her. "We'll both be safe here."

"And together," she added.

Fletcher held up the Dread Master's letter. "Stone's permitted to leave if another Dreadful takes up residence in the safe house. Assuming Gemma approves of the change in guards."

She smiled at Barnabus. "Gemma wholeheartedly approves."

THE BACHELOR AND THE BRIDE

by Mr. King

Installment VII
in which our Hero and Heroine discover
the Grandest Adventure of all!

Passing through the doorway of light set Duncan and Sorcha directly in front of his humble cottage in their home village. The return journey, one that would have, no doubt, been filled with terrifying creatures, was avoided entirely. They'd returned with ample time, several days remaining before *Bealltainn*. Duncan still held the vessel of water in his hand, Granny's now-empty bag on his back. And he still had Sorcha at his side. She kept hold of his hand, giving no indication she had any intention of letting go.

They rushed inside the cottage without having to discuss it. There, sitting beside the cot where Donella had laid ill and suffering for nearly a fortnight, was Granny Winter. She rocked slowly back and forth, watching them enter without the least bit of surprise.

"We've returned," Sorcha said.

"I knew you must have been close." Granny Winter motioned to the floor directly beside her. There, piled neatly, was everything that had disappeared from the sack she had given Duncan. All the items must have returned to her as they'd vanished.

To Sorcha, he said, "Help the little one sit up. I'm going to give her the water."

Sorcha rushed to do so, no hesitation, no uncertainty. She gently assisted the poor girl, weak with illness, to a seated position, holding her and speaking soothingly.

Duncan sat on the edge of her bed. "Sip this," he said. "It will make you whole."

She gave a weak nod of understanding. Slowly, one drop at a time, she began to drink the contents of the small vessel. Her strength returned quickly. Sips turned into full swallows. Sorcha no longer needed to hold Donella upright. The last remaining mouthful of water, Donella took on her own, having strength enough to do so. She handed the vessel back to Duncan, smiling brightly for the first time in weeks.

Duncan looked to Granny Winter. She nodded. And she rose. She held a hand out to the little girl. "We've come to an agreement, Donella and I. This little one has lost her family, and I have room in my cottage. She means to come stay with me."

"Just as I did when I was orphaned," Sorcha said.

"You are welcome to remain as long as you wish," Granny Winter said. "But I suspect you are ready to begin anew."

Sorcha nodded. "For so long, I have feared what the world held. But I have faced it again and have discovered I am equal to it."

Granny Winter dipped her head. She turned to Duncan. "Sorcha has a wanderer's heart. It will pull her away, seeking adventures and journeys. You must decide what pull *you* feel."

He hardly needed to think about it. His life would be unimaginable without her. A mere few days on the road, facing dangers they'd never expected and finding in each other the welcome rest and steadfast connection they both needed, had taught him to trust her more than he had anyone else. To cherish her. To love her.

"I may not have spent much time journeying, but I've no objection to wandering the lochs and hills and valleys, especially if I can do so with her."

Sorcha reached her hands out. He took them both and pulled her into his embrace.

To Granny Winter, he said, "I believe you have your answer."

"But heed my warning," Granny said. "You have caught the attention of the fairies and monsters. You will not be free of them now. They will search you out."

"Then we will face that difficulty head-on," Sorcha said. "And we will help people along the way."

"Perhaps you would consider making us a gift of your magical bag," Duncan said. "Just as you promised, all we needed was found inside."

Granny Winter smiled, deep wrinkles crinkling in an expression of amusement. "All that you needed was inside *of you*. Courage, determination, cleverness. Together, you have all you need."

Duncan turned his gaze back to Sorcha. "Together, we have all we need."

And they did, indeed. As they walked the paths of life, they found in each other everything they had ever dreamed of.

CHAPTER 26

Fletcher and Stone returned the next morning with food and news. Barnabus had hoped they would.

Everyone got the bread and veg and smoked meat put away, then gathered in the little sitting room. Gemma sat beside Barnabus, tucking herself into his arms. She'd kept close to him ever since he'd arrived the night before. If he had his way, he would never let go of her again.

"Martin survived the night," Fletcher said. "But he had to be moved from Dr. Lowry's surgery."

"Why?" Moving a person as badly injured as Martin would not be done for any small reason; Lowry wouldn't have allowed it.

"Because Dr. Lowry was killed." Fletcher rubbed at his face. "The Mastiff's men, we're certain. They stormed the surgery, coming for Martin most likely, wanting to finish the deed. There were enough Dreadfuls there, along with Parkington, to get Martin out, though not without injuries."

"Lowry's dead?" Barnabus had agreed to send Martin with him. He'd put Lowry in that danger.

"And his housekeeper nearly was," Fletcher said. "The Mastiff's crimes are growing bolder. This one would've been far deadlier if not for Parkington. And while Martin is safe, we're more worried about you than we were even yesterday."

"Was the Kincaid mark on the house?" Gemma asked quietly.

"Two of 'em," Stone said. "No underlining."

"Bung your eye," she whispered.

"They came for Martin," Fletcher said, "but I'd wager my last ha'penny they were looking for *you*."

She leaned forward, elbows on her knees, head resting in her upturned hands. "They are killing people trying to find me, Baz. What am I going to do?"

"If they find you, they'll kill you too."

She shook her head. "But I ain't willing to let them hurt people just to stay safe m'self."

"One thing's for certain," Fletcher said. "Neither of you can be safe anywhere in London."

"If you are suggesting we run away," Gemma said, "best think again. Just because the Kincaids cain't find me don't mean they'll stop trying. People'll be in danger and on account of me."

"Asking the Dreadfuls to keep the two of you safe and look after anyone the Kincaids might cut down in their search while still trying to bring down the Mastiff will stretch us too thin," Fletcher said.

"How do we get the Kincaids to stop looking for Gemma?" Stone asked.

"Even the dead ain't safe from them." Gemma rose and paced away.

Barnabus hated seeing her so overwhelmed, so worried. What could even be done? She was hidden from the Kincaids for now, but they were laying waste to everyone connected to her. She could no more endure that trail of destruction than he could.

"They can taunt the living with the dead," Stone said, "but they can't actually hurt 'em."

She turned back, looking at Stone and Fletcher. "That was m' plan before everything fell to bits. I've the document needed to have myself declared dead."

"It's at the house," Barnabus confirmed.

"If they were full certain I were dead, they'd give over looking for me."

"They'd likely still target Doc, though," Stone said.

She turned worried eyes on Barnabus. "I couldn't bear it if they hurt you."

He rose and crossed to her. "If they think we're both dead, they'll stop looking for either one of us." He took her hands in his. "We'll have a new letter forged, one saying the *two of us* died in a carriage accident while fleeing London. The Kincaids would have every reason to believe we were running from them and that sent us in haste from Town."

"Baz, you would lose your medical practice. You wouldn't be in London to do your rescuing work. You'd be leaving everything behind."

He kissed her softly. "I lost you once, Gemma, and that taught me that *you* are everything to me."

"I don't ever want you to resent me."

"I never could."

She didn't appear convinced. "Marrying me weren't your idea."

"And yet it proved the best thing that's ever happened to me. What a coincidence."

The smallest of smiles tipped her lips. "You don't believe in coincidences."

"No, I don't."

She rested her head against him. He let go of her hands and put his arms around her. *Marrying me weren't your idea.* She still didn't fully trust that he wanted to be married to her, wanted to be part of her life for the rest of their lives.

"Will starting rumors of your deaths be enough, though?" Stone asked. "The Kincaids don't seem the sort to shrug and believe whatever they're told."

"They ain't," Gemma said.

Fletcher didn't seem thrown off by that declaration. "We need your uncles to *know* you're both dead. The Mastiff has eyes and ears everywhere. He'll hear if you've been seen dead."

"If I didn't know you better, Fletch," Barnabus said, "I'd think you were plotting to kill us."

"I don't do anything halfway." Fletcher's trademark smirk returned.

Barnabus didn't realize how much he'd missed seeing it, how reassuring the sight of it was, until it made a reappearance.

"What if we have a wake for the both of them at Doc's house in Finsbury?" Stone suggested.

"They'd have to be laid out in their coffins," Fletcher said. "Has to be right-tight or the Kincaid's'll see through it."

"They still will if we climb out of them pine packages and

go on our merry way." Gemma turned in Barnabus's arms enough to face the others. "My father always said a corpse ain't fully dead until the last nail goes in the coffin."

"So we nail you in. Load you into hearses," Fletcher said.

She shook her head. "A hearse that don't go to a churchyard would rig the jig. They'd know it weren't real."

"Resurrectionists've been known to cut corners," Fletcher said. "Do they ever resurrect a body before it's in the ground?"

Gemma watched Fletcher with both interest and growing worry. "I've been on a few jobs where a corpse was pulled from the coffin while still in the hearse. Saves the trouble of digging later. Of course, the driver has to be in on the plot as it ain't a quiet undertaking."

"Does the hearse have to be equipped in a special way to resurrect in it while its moving?" Fletcher asked.

Gemma nodded. "It ain't a simple thing."

"But it can be done?" Fletcher pressed.

Barnabus was beginning to understand the idea tossing around in Fletcher's mind. "You want Gemma to sort out how to resurrect me after staging my death?"

"Close," Fletcher said. "Resurrect *both of you*. In moving hearses. Without being caught out. And all before arriving at the churchyard."

She'd gone pale. "The Kincaids know it's possible to resurrect in a hearse. It'd have to be done in a way that they'd think it were impossible."

"You'd have to plan a resurrection that even the Kincaid brothers themselves don't think can be done," Barnabus said.

"Is that all? Generations of resurrectionists' knowledge

spilled into those four ears, and I have to fool them? Simple as apples, that."

"If you decide it can't be done," Fletcher said, "we'll think of something else. But they ain't going to stop looking for you unless they're full certain there ain't no one to look for."

CHAPTER 27

Gemma'd been running from the resurrectionist trade for years. She'd sworn she'd never connect herself to it again. Yet there she were, trying to formulate a way to out-resurrect the most skilled grave robbers in all of London.

"It'd have to be something that'd seem entirely impossible." She picked at the humble meal she and Baz had made for themselves. Fletcher and Stone had left, leaving her to plan something that couldn't be done. "They can resurrect in a moving hearse. All they need's a long enough jaunt to the churchyard and room enough for moving about. Loading our coffins into hearses ain't enough to toss the Kincaids off the scent."

"Do we choose a shorter route, then?" Baz asked.

"Bustin' a coffin takes time. Even my uncles cain't do it in an instant. And unless you know a couple trustworthy resurrectionists, I'll be offering up rushed training to whoever'll be springing us."

"You are the only trustworthy resurrectionist I know," Baz said.

"I'm the only trustworthy resurrectionist *I* know." She sighed. "I don't fancy teaching others to do this. It's a trade I'd favor seeing die, which I realize is a terrible pun."

Baz nudged her plate closer to her.

"I know," she said. "I grumbled at you for not eating when you was worried. The least I can do is eat, myself."

He shook his head. "As a doctor, I would advise against eating yourself."

Oh, he was good for her heart, helping her laugh when life was painful. "It's a proper shame we can't ask Dr. Palmer to set his mind on this puzzle. That bloke don't let a mystery go unsolved, do he?"

"You've been reading 'Bodies of Light,'" he said.

"I always knew you'd be quality at writing tales."

"You were the only one who did at first."

"And you are the only one who thinks I can plan this never-been-done-before resurrection." She popped a steamed carrot in her mouth, reminding herself she *did* need to keep her strength up.

"If it can't be done, Gemma, we'll simply leave London. Under cover of night or in disguise."

She shook her head, swallowing quickly. "The Kincaids and the Mastiff will hurt people in their search for us." She knew he'd no sooner let that happen than she would. "We need to move forward with the wake, with being nailed into our coffins and being hauled into hearses. But it's what to do from that point on I cain't sort. I can resurrect in a hearse;

I've done it—" Her heart refused to let her mouth finish the admission.

He set his hand atop hers. "You didn't choose the life you lived, love, any more than my mother chose the life she did. I'm not one of those hoity-toity types that assumes every desperate person had all the choices in the world and intentionally picked the worst one."

"It's why you work so hard giving those desperate people a choice that's at least a tetch better."

The corner of his mouth twitched. "And did you consider me 'a tetch better' than the choices you'd had before meeting me?"

"A tetch or two," she said with a shrug.

Baz laughed. She'd missed that sound the past three years. She wouldn't have to be without it again. But claiming that for herself was going to cost him everything he'd worked for. She didn't doubt him when he said he was doing so willingly. But there weren't no point pretending he'd not need to make that sacrifice now if there'd been anyone else to help her three and a half years earlier, if he'd not had his arm twisted then.

He threaded his fingers through hers. "We'll sort it out. I know we will."

His thoughts, she felt certain, were on their pretended deaths. She hoped the reassurance could be applied more broadly. She didn't want him to resent her for any of this.

"Our biggest difficulty in this escape scheme is that I ain't the one doing the resurrecting. I could manage that with hardly a thought."

"Something your uncles know," Baz pointed out.

That was true. "I'd have to be in the hearse with you to

unbox you anyway. While wider hearses can carry two coffins, there ain't room enough for a third person to do the resurrecting."

"So a resurrection would be considered impossible in a hearse with two coffins abreast?" Baz asked with a pointed look.

"Not *considered* impossible. It *is* impossible. The false bottom allows for the hiding of two people. The one doing the resurrecting would either have to leave one of the bodies in its coffin and climb in the coffin 'imself or be caught out in the back of the hearse when the doors was opened."

Baz rubbed at his mustache as he sometimes did when pondering a difficult puzzle.

They'd stumbled on something her uncles would think impossible, but only because it actually was. Unless . . .

She stood, stepping away from the table as half-formed thoughts rushed in and out of her mind.

"Gemma?" Baz's voice only vaguely made itself known.

"Silas and Arlo know there'd have to be a third person to get two people out of two coffins in a single hearse." The idea was so close, but her mind wouldn't sort it out entirely. "But a third person'd be caught out. If the hearse was opened at the churchyard and only the two coffins was there with no person larking about, they'd figure the coffins weren't emptied, leastwise not both of them."

"And they know neither of us would leave behind the other," Baz said.

She nodded, thinking frantically. "No third person. But without that third person, there's no escaping." *Do something the Kincaids believe to be impossible.* "There *is* one thing my uncles ain't never done." She turned and met Baz's eye. "They ain't never resurrected themselves."

"Have you?"

"Of course not. Cain't be done." But she knew that was the answer. She knew. "So that's what we're going to do. I'll get myself out of my coffin, then I'll help get you out of yours. And we'll have the length of a single hearse ride to do it."

She abandoned her barely touched meal and made for the secretary desk, pulling out a sheet of parchment and the nub of a pencil.

"We'll need someone who knows the scheme to act as the driver of the hearse," she said.

"Kumar worked for a time as a hackney driver," Baz said. "He'd do it."

She began making a detailed sketch even as she kept talking. "And we'll need to find a hearse what's wide enough for holding two coffins. They aren't unheard of, but it'll take effort, effort that'll need to be kept quiet."

Even if they managed to get out of their coffins before the hearse reached the churchyard, they would be seen the moment the doors were opened if there wasn't a place to hide.

"We'll need someone who's a dab hand at carpentry to make a false bottom inside it, far enough above the actual bottom for the two of us to lay flat, side by side, inside of it but low enough that no one glancing would realize it were there. Flowers and such can help hide it."

"Dominique worked as a carpenter. He's one of us too."

She snatched up another sheet of paper. "He'll need to modify the coffins as well so we can get them open from the inside but so as nothing looks amiss from the outside." She began sketching what she had in mind." This was the most terrifying part. If they couldn't get out of their coffins, they might be buried alive.

So many things could go wrong. Even if they managed to get out of their coffins but didn't hide themselves in time, they would be caught and the whole thing would fall to bits. Anything amiss, anything deviating from what the Kincaids expected, would change everything.

She paused in her sketching, uncertainty undermining her determination. "What if something goes wrong?"

"We have to at least try," he said.

She shook her head. "Resurrectionists don't resurrect people who ain't dead. Tools slip. Delicate efforts turn destructive. But those things don't usually matter. Cain't kill someone who's already dead."

Baz pulled a chair up beside hers at the desk. He sat and put his arm around her, something he did naturally and regularly now.

"Let's at least talk this through before we abandon it," he said. "What else would we need?"

She took a slow breath. "There has to be a jemmy bar in the casket with each of us so we can pry open the lids. That, of course, only works if Dominique alters the coffins and whoever nails the lid shut uses the right kind of nails."

"We'd each pry open our coffins?" he asked.

She nodded. "I don't know how long it'll take to resurrect from the inside. I'll likely be a bit faster than you and can help if you're not out yet. But we have to be fast. We cain't just hop out and leave the coffins open. We have to weight 'em, so the pallbearers'll be seen having to work at carrying their load. The lids have to be nailed back down, and they cain't show any damage."

So many bits and pieces. So many chances for failure.

Baz kissed her cheek, her jaw, her neck beneath her ear. "I believe in you, Gemma," he whispered. "We can do this."

"You'll keep your arm around me while I sort through this?" she asked.

"With pleasure, love."

And he did exactly that. He kept his arm about her waist or rubbed circles on her back with his hand. At one point, he fetched a bit of tea, but he gave her a quick kiss before he left, and he returned his arm to its place of comfort upon returning. And with his strength buoying her, she created her list, her instructions, her only hope for saving them all.

CHAPTER 28

Gemma stood a bit to the side of the table in the safe house, biting her thumbnail as she watched Fletcher and Stone read over her plans. There were so many things that could go wrong, she knew her mind wouldn't rest easy about any of it unless someone else thought it could work.

"Every hearse I've ever seen had windows on either side," Fletcher said. "Glass is devilish bad at hiding things."

"We'd a damber bloke who drove the hearses when we did a spot of coffin fishing inside. He'd make certain the funeral flowers were placed against the windows." She emptied the air from her tight lungs. "Worked well enough."

"Two caskets, a heap of flowers, the two of you breaking your way out of coffins without leaving a mark, and then hiding elsewhere in the hearse." Fletcher said. "Is there room enough?"

"It'll be tight as teeth," she admitted.

"Making it even more likely that your uncles won't suspect what you're doing," Stone said.

They were gabbing over important problems. *A lot* of them. It ought to've reassured her. It didn't.

Baz came and stood beside her. "They are a couple of the cleverest people I know," he said. "Their minds spinning on this alongside yours will see this sorted."

She shook her head. Seemed that was about all she did lately. "So much could go wrong."

"I know it's risky," he said. "But it's a chance we have to take."

"I've had time and plenty to think on what it'll mean to be 'dead.' This was tossed at you like hail in a storm. You'll suffer for it."

He pressed a kiss to her cheek. "Once we get on the other side of this, it will be worth it."

"I hope so." But as time passed and he weren't able to do his doctoring or watch over his safe houses and continue his rescues, "the other side of this" might start to feel like a burden. *She* might start to feel like a burden.

"I know that expression, Gemma," he whispered. "And I know what you're worrying about. I won't resent or regret this. Being together is what I want, not what I'm being forced to accept."

"You'd not need to accept it if not for—" She tried so hard not to think about the reasons he'd married her three and a half years earlier. No matter what he might feel now, there was no escaping the fact that he had been forced into connecting himself with her.

"We can hold a wake for the two of you at your house," Fletcher said. "There'll be mourners, obviously, but we cannot risk any of them knowing that you're alive if they don't absolutely have to know. Secrets don't keep well when held by too many people."

Gemma nodded. "People being seen grieving over the two of us in open caskets will show my uncles and the Mastiff that we really are dead."

"The open caskets do give us spot of trouble," Stone said. "They have to be open so you'll be seen in them. But no one'll believe you're dead if they can see you breathing. Neither of you can hold your breath through the entire wake."

Gemma lowered her brow. She was so tired, so overwhelmed. "The best we can do is breathe as shallow as possible."

"Even shallow breaths raise the rib cage," Baz said. Hearing his uncertainty chipped away at hers.

"Could we hide you with flowers?" Fletcher asked. "Place blooms all around you two? No one'd see your chests move."

"The flowers would move," Stone said.

Gemma held her hands up in a gesture of helplessness. "I haven't the first idea how to prevent a person from breathing for an hour or two if that person's meant to still be alive at the end."

"Could we build something in the casket itself?" Baz asked. "Like the false bottom in the hearse, we would actually be lying underneath a wood plank or whatever it might be. Then we set the flowers on top of that. Then they would hold still, and we could still breathe."

All the men looked intrigued by the idea.

Gemma hated to knock the ladder out from under them just when their hopes were climbing to new heights. "We'd never get out of the coffins if we did that. There'd not be room enough to do what we have to do to escape."

Fletcher's mouth twisted in an expression of pondering. Stone's jaw was set, determination in every angle of his face.

"What if we took the plank the flowers are resting on out of the caskets before nailing them closed?" Fletcher suggested. "Then you'd be able to move."

Again, Gemma shook her head. "Shelves and planks and stuff ain't ever put inside coffins. If anything is odd at all, mark me, my uncles will notice. They'll notice, and they'll spin on it, and they'll sort it out."

"Two coffins in a single hearse is out of the ordinary, though," Fletcher said.

"Oi. It's uncommon, but it ain't unheard of. My uncles'll likely believe it's a heap of sentimental foolishness. And two coffins abreast in a hearse'll convince them there's no means of resurrecting during the journey to the churchyard."

Stone took up a lead pencil and began sketching something. Gemma very much wanted to know what it was, but she hadn't the energy for a single step.

Baz must've noticed her flagging spirits. He pulled her into a hug.

"I will say," she said in an exhausted whisper, "I'm grateful that, if this works, you'll hold me like this all the time."

"All the time." Baz kissed the top of her head.

"It'll be different now than when you first crossed paths with a desperate mot with no one to help her. There's something to be said for the path a person's on because he chose it and not because there was no other choice."

He continued to hold her, his embrace reassuring.

"I think Stone's onto something," Fletcher said. He motioned them over.

Baz kept an arm about Gemma's waist as he walked with her to stand behind the two men.

"That looks like a crinoline," Gemma said.

"That's the idea," Stone said. "They're strong enough to hold heavy dresses in whatever shape fashion demands, but they're moveable and ain't too heavy."

"They can also be collapsed," Gemma said. "If we can find a means of securing them in place during the wake, covering us to the shoulders or so, then it'd be easy to unfasten them from whatever's holding them in place. We could push them down to the foot of the casket once we're nailed inside. That'd get them out of the way."

"A blanket can be put over the crinoline and flowers on top of that," Stone said. "You can be breathing under it, and no one'll see."

"The flowers can then be put against the windows in the hearse," Fletcher said.

It was possible. Difficult and risky and dangerous . . . but possible.

"You think Kumar'll be able to find a double hearse?" Baz asked.

Stone nodded.

"And Dominique worked in carpentry," Fletcher said. "We can give him your specifications, and he'll make certain you've got a couple pine boxes suited to the task."

They were really going to do this. Gemma's heart pounded even as it dropped further and further into her stomach. She looked to Baz once more. "You don't have to do this, you know. You could just leave Town."

"The Mastiff and your uncles would still target people who know me, trying to sniff out where I went, believing I could lead them to you."

"Not if they are convinced *I'm* dead."

"Are you saying you don't want me to start new somewhere with you?"

"That ain't it at all. I—you—you didn't ask for any of this. You married a Kincaid to save me from a terrible fate. I feel like I'm dragging you into a rather terrible fate now. You'd be dying in a very real way. You couldn't be Doctor Barnabus Milligan anymore. You wouldn't be the Barnabus Milligan who runs safe houses in London and rescues people. There'd be no chance of maybe meeting your actual family after all."

"You *are* my actual family, Gemma."

"Because you didn't have a choice." She stepped away, trying to calm the storm of conflicting emotions swirling inside her. She wanted him to come with her. She wanted him to build this new life with her. But she couldn't bear to think of him giving up so much for a wife he'd not chosen to begin with.

Baz moved to stand behind her. "I never should have said I married you because no one else could help you."

"But it's true," she said.

"Sometimes the truth can be worded in such a way that it becomes a lie." His arms wrapped around her. He rested his cheek against hers. "Acknowledging that we were in a situation where choices were limited has given you the very false impression that I am not choosing this—choosing *us*—now."

She closed her eyes, letting the moment write itself on her mind and wrap itself around her heart.

"Though I'd love to stand here all day, holding you like this," Baz said, "our two friends over there are likely to grow impatient if we don't get back to the business of our untimely deaths."

"I cain't think of anyone I'd rather untimely die with," she said.

He laughed, then kissed her cheek once more.

Gemma felt a bit better. She was still overwhelmed, and they were still facing tremendous danger. But she felt a very little bit better.

CHAPTER 29

Mr. Sorokin had worked a miracle.

A new letter was forged in a shockingly short time, testifying that Dr. Barnabus Milligan and Mrs. Gemma Milligan, née Kincaid, had been killed in a tragic carriage accident caused by excessive speed on a lesser-traveled road leading away from London. But he'd done something far kinder even than that: he'd created a certificate of graduation from medical college for one Bernard Mitchell. In a quiet village at a distance from both London and the medical college in Scotland, Barnabus could work as a doctor.

"Bernard ain't so different a name to Barnabus that people'd raise a fuss if they heard me calling you Baz." Gemma had only just finished reading the documents Fletcher had brought by. "I'll do my best to remember not to, but habit and what."

"You could always invent a new pet name for me."

"I can think of a few." Her reply was as flirtatious as his suggestion had been.

Fletcher made a gagging sound deep in his throat.

"Take pity on him, love," Barnabus said to Gemma. "Elizabeth's not here, and that makes him grumpy."

"Are you grumpy when I'm not with you?" she asked.

"Yes, he is," Fletcher tossed back.

Gemma looked over the documents again. "I'm glad you'll still be a doctor. That'll answer a few worries."

He and Gemma wouldn't be destitute, and he wouldn't have to give up a career he'd felt called to do. And he fully suspected that would alleviate some of the guilt he saw lingering in Gemma's expression.

But it wouldn't be enough to wash away the doubts she had. He needed her to know that being with her was what he wanted, not something required of him.

So he'd hatched a plan of his own, one Fletcher meant to help him implement.

Gemma hummed a few bars of "She Moved Through the Fair" as she fetched her detailed list of preparations for their upcoming escape.

The three of them sat at the table, and Gemma spread her papers out, going over each item one at a time.

"Has the hearse Kumar procured been altered with the false bottom?"

"It has," Fletcher said.

Gemma marked that off. "And the coffins have been made?"

"Oi, and with the marks on the lid telling Stone and me where to pound in the coffin nails."

From what Gemma had explained, that part was crucial, as her design ensured not all the nails pounded through the lid connected with the wood beneath.

"And the nails you've got are the short ones I told you to get?"

"We measured five times," Fletcher said. "They're what you sent us out for."

Some of the nails would have to make contact with the frame, otherwise they risked the lids sliding off when they were carried into the hearse.

"And the notches carved on the inside?"

"Deep enough to feel but not so obvious they'll be seen," Fletcher said.

The notches, Gemma had explained, would indicate where the nails holding the lid down were at. Barnabus and Gemma would use jemmy bars to pry the lids open from the inside, but they would do so in utter darkness. They'd not only waste time prying the lids if they didn't know where they were secured, they also risked cracking the wood. Nothing could look amiss when the coffins were carried from the hearse to the chapel and then to the churchyard, or her family would spot it.

"And the jemmy bars?"

"Will be placed on your right side," Fletcher said.

Gemma nodded and breathed and gave every indication of reassuring herself. Without every adjustment she had specified, it would be impossible to get out of the coffins without help. Kumar would not be able to stop the hearse to assist them without giving away the entire thing.

"What else?" Fletcher asked.

What else? Barnabus had all but memorized the list himself. So much depended on getting every detail correct.

"The crinoline barriers for placing over us in the casket?" Barnabus asked.

"All right-tight." Fletcher nodded. "And the blanket to go atop them and the flowers for going atop that."

Gemma motioned with her chin toward the small posy in a cup of water that Fletcher had brought with him. "We'll need a far-sight more blooms than that."

"There'll be plenty," Fletcher said. "It's all arranged."

Gemma tapped her lead pencil on the table nervously. "When the hearse reaches the church, if all's not gone to bits, you and the other pallbearers will pull out coffins that look exactly like they did when you slid 'em inside. They'll feel heavy on account of the sandbags—" Her eyes pulled wide.

"Kumar'll have them waiting in the hearse for you," Fletcher assured her.

Gemma checked that off her list. "The coffins'll feel heavy as you carry them inside the church for the funeral. They'll be watched; no chance they won't." She had attended a lot of funerals, very few of which she had actually been invited to. Some of the stories she'd told Baz of her childhood would haunt him the rest of his days.

"By the time you come back out, we'll be out of the hearse and slipped off. Once Kumar signals it's safe to do so, 'course."

"Do you know where you'll pike off to?" Fletcher asked.

"The Dread Master suggested we come back here first," Barnabus said. "That'd give us time to fashion workable disguises and choose a final destination."

Fletcher gave them a look that could not be interpreted

as anything other than grief. "We'll miss you two when you've hopped the twig. But you'll be safe."

Gemma nodded. "And so will the rest of London. No one's candle will get snuffed because we're being looked for."

"I wish I could thank Brogan for taking charge of the safe houses when I went invisible," Barnabus said. Brogan wasn't one of the few being told that the wake and burial was a ruse. He felt bad about that.

"He'll look after 'em well," Fletcher said. "Already let me know Serena was safely moved to a different spot and she ain't worrying herself into the grave anymore."

Barnabus was relieved to hear that'd been managed. "She endured a lot at the Mastiff's hands and still helped Ana and Hollis last year when they were trapped. She even sent us word in time to save Martin. I hope Brogan can find a means of helping her get out of London. It's the only way she'll be safe from the Mastiff's revenge."

Gemma reached over and set her hand on his. "Fitting, i'n'it, that she's your final rescue? Saved her from the very person you're now escaping, who she worked to save others from."

He hadn't thought of it that way, but she was right. Since he had to leave behind his rescue efforts in London, this was a fine note to end his work on.

"Chelmsford's house has been shut and the staff sent off," Fletcher said. "The Mastiff's crowing about it, saying he drove the man from Town."

"Any idea where the baron might have retreated to?" Barnabus asked.

Fletcher shook his head. "Theory is he's rushing to his

country home in Stamford. But some think he's still in London somewhere."

"And the Mastiff's the reason this toff swell is in hiding?" Gemma asked.

"The Mastiff's working to undermine the role Lord Chelmsford played in a murder trial ages ago in Radlett," Barnabus said. "We aren't certain why."

"The murder of William Weare?" Gemma asked.

She'd pieced that together quickly. "Yes, Chelmsford represented one of the co-conspirators."

"There's a waxwork of the man what did the deed, John Thurtell, at Madame Tussaud's. I read the information there. A gruesome crime, that. Did Lord Chelmsford stand council for the one that walked away or the one that were sent to Botany Bay?"

"Botany Bay." Fletcher was watching her closely. "What all did you learn about the case?"

"People thought the punishments of them two should've been the other way 'round, that the one that sailed to Australia should've stayed in England a free man and kept his inn running."

His inn. Barnabus spoke up. "Sorokin told me he once forged a letter of recommendation for a woman who'd fallen on difficulties and was hoping to find dignified work at an inn like her mother had."

"Hunt's inn?" Fletcher asked.

Barnabus nodded. "We both thought that a rather remarkable coincidence since Hunt was connected to Chelmsford and the case the Mastiff was focused on."

In near-perfect unison, Fletcher and Gemma said, "You don't believe in coincidences."

No. He didn't.

Fletcher slouched in his chair. "Every time I think this puzzle cain't get more complicated, it goes and does just that."

"Is Martin still safe?" Barnabus asked.

"He is, and he's recovering. We're hopeful he'll pull through."

"And the others who were injured in the attack at Lowry's surgery?"

"Healing."

"Sorokin and the children?" Barnabus had a long list of people he was concerned about.

"Back in hiding now that the girl's well."

Gemma's gaze held unfocused worry.

He took her hand. "Is something worrying you, love?"

"What could possibly be gnawing at my mind?" The dryness in her tone was matched by the shake of her head. "The bloke I love more than anyone else is soon to be nailed into an eternity box under my instructions, and if the plan I've hatched for getting him out don't work perfect, he might be buried alive. And all this is happening in a city under siege by a merciless killer who has enlisted the help of my merciless family. What about that would worry a person?"

"Would you repeat the part about loving me more than anyone else?"

She leaned toward him and kissed his cheek. "I do, you know."

"I'm pleased to hear that because I have something extremely important to ask you."

"That's my cue," Fletcher said. He pulled a handkerchief from his pocket and the small bouquet of flowers from the cup. He tied the handkerchief around the wet stems, then plopped it into Barnabus's hand. "Do your worst, my friend."

"I think you mean 'my best.'"

Fletcher looked at him like he'd grown a second nose. "The last time you did this, I suspect you *were* doing your 'best.' I thought it wise to suggest you take a different approach this time 'round."

"The last time you did *what*?" Gemma asked, clearly confused.

Barnabus drew Gemma's attention to him. "I'd be the most fortunate man in all the world if you'd agree to marry me."

"Again?" She eyed his flowers, then him, then Fletcher.

He wasn't approaching this right. He'd wanted it to be romantic and poetic, but it was, instead, proving to be neither.

Barnabus took her hand in his free one. "I want to marry you, Gemma. Our own choice this time. Fully and completely because we want to. Because we love each other. Because neither of us can imagine living our lives without the other."

He placed the flowers in her hand. A lady ought to have flowers when being proposed to.

"In the eyes of the law and the church, everything's already right and tight. But it's not right in your eyes, and that's what matters to me. I want you to know that I married you because I chose to, that our wedding was something we chose together because we wanted it."

"We don't have a vicar here." She sounded uncertain but not opposed to the idea.

"I talked Fletcher around to filling that role."

Gemma lifted an eyebrow. "You were aiming for irony, were you?"

"Convenience, actually. Had to be him or Stone, and Stone's off making arrangements for a double funeral." He kissed her hand quickly, tenderly. "Will you marry me, Gemma? Again?"

"Could I change into my other dress first? It's nicer than this one."

Relief wrapped around his heart; she was accepting his proposal. "Of course."

She leapt from the table and hurried into the bedroom, the flowers still in her hand.

"She's a right'un, Doc," Fletcher said. "Sharp as shards and brave as arrows."

"And, by some miracle, she loves me," Barnabus added.

"It's a miracle the women we love don't think we're all a heap of rubbish."

Barnabus looked at his friend. "Thank you again for all you've done for us and all you'll be doing the day of the burial."

"It'll be the most incredible feat the DPS has managed to date, and those few of us who know won't ever be able to tell a soul." He shook his head. "We've managed some incredible things, ain't we?"

"We have at that. I'll miss being part of it."

Fletcher slapped a hand on his shoulder. "And we'll miss having you."

"Any chance you'd tell me the identity of the Dread Master before I pike off?" Barnabus asked. "I've whittled my guesses down to two, and I'll wonder the rest of my life which was correct."

"Afraid not, Doc. You'll simply have to decide for yourself which guess is correct and then live your life assuming you're right."

"Can't blame me for asking."

"You're certainly not the first."

Barnabus rose and crossed to a small, tin mirror on the mantelpiece. He smoothed his hair and mustache. It was about all he could do to neaten his appearance. Gemma would have to simply take him as he was.

The bride herself stepped into the room. She'd changed into a dark-gray gown, not overly fine and not boasting a single bit of lace or any unneeded ruffles. But she looked lovely.

It wasn't a dress he'd seen before. The Dread Master must have arranged for her to have it, likely on account of her having run from Finsbury entirely empty-handed. Their mysterious head had also provided Barnabus with clothes to replace the bloodstained ones he'd arrived in.

"This is also the dress I'll be 'buried' in." Gemma indicated it with a flourish of her hands, one of which held the bouquet of flowers. "I think I like today's use of it better."

"I wish this could be a grand wedding with friends and celebrations."

Gemma crossed to his side. She set her hand gently on his cheek. "I don't need all that, Baz. This wedding's about you and me. That's what matters."

He wrapped his hand around hers, shifting it to his lips and kissing it softly. "A shame we have to put up with Fletcher being here."

"I'd be happy to leave," he said dryly. "But there's this demanding doctor who's asking me to pretend I'm clergy in order to oversee a *very* small wedding."

Gemma didn't pull her hand away as she turned to look at Fletcher. "I'm sorry we'll miss you and Elizabeth getting churched."

"I was hoping to have married her by now, but the Mastiff would likely turn it into a bloodbath." Fletcher pushed out an audible breath. "But a quiet ceremony would undermine her reputation, and she'd lose her school."

"It's painful being pulled away from the person you love," Gemma said.

Barnabus held her hand even tighter. "We'll not have to be ever again."

Pulling a paper from his frock coat pocket, Fletcher said, "Shall we?"

They arranged themselves much the way they would've been if being married truly in an official ceremony. Barnabus and Gemma stood side by side; she held her flowers in one hand and his hand in the other. That was, perhaps, not fully proper for a wedding, but he certainly wasn't going to complain.

"I wrote down my own version of a right-tight wedding ceremony." Fletcher eyed them both with a smirk. "I think you'll find it an improvement."

"Oh, blimey," Barnabus whispered.

Gemma only grinned.

"Barnabus Milligan, are you marrying Gemma on account of you're wanting to and think it a bang-up idea?"

"I am."

"Do you love her, or are you dense as a log?"

On a whisper, Barnabus said, "The officiant doesn't usually insult the groom."

Fletcher shrugged. "You're obligated to answer the question, Doc."

"I do love her." He looked to Gemma. "I do love you. With all my heart."

"Are you choosing to spend all your life with her and marry her no matter the messiness that got you two churched the first time? Honestly *choosing* it?"

"Honestly, happily, willingly choosing it," he said.

"That'll do, 'suppose." Fletcher flipped his paper over, more questions written on the back. "Gemma Milligan, do you believe him, no matter that believing people ain't an easy thing for people who've lived their lives on the streets of this heartless city?"

"I do believe him," she said.

The ceremony could've ended there, and it would've been enough for Barnabus. Gemma knew he loved her and wanted to be married to her and was choosing this life with her. That had been lacking for so long, a heavy cloud hanging over their lives.

"And are you marrying him because you want to, no matter that he's sometimes a dull cove and writes penny dreadfuls that don't have a single monster and ain't about street urchins like the stories written by real authors?" Fletcher wrote about monsters and street urchins, something Gemma's laugh indicated she was well aware of.

"Again," Barnabus whispered, "you don't have to insult the groom."

"I'm marrying him because I want to," Gemma said. "And if the rest of what you're meaning to say ain't nice to him, I'll belt you."

Fletcher made a show of reading through the rest of his notes for the ceremony and dismissing it all as unusable.

"Guess all that leaves me to ask is—Gemma, do you love Barnabus?"

"I do." She looked at him once more, the tenderness in her eyes nearly stealing his breath.

"Are you choosing to spend all your life with him and marry him no matter the messiness that got you two churched the first time? Honestly *choosing* it?" Fletcher repeated the final question he'd posed to Barnabus.

"I am."

"Well, then. I think that makes you pretty well married." Fletcher stuffed the paper back in his pocket. "See you both at your funeral." He popped his hat on his head and slipped out.

Barnabus pulled Gemma into an embrace. She set her hands on either side of his face. He kissed her softly and tenderly. As dangerous as the coming days would be, as difficult as it would be to successfully manage their escape from the Kincaids and the Mastiff, it meant they would never be torn apart again.

And that would be worth all the danger and difficulty in the world.

BODIES OF LIGHT

being a Fictionalization of Reported and Corroborated Mysterious Phenomena

by the late Dr. Barnabus Milligan, physician, whom the publishers of this work grieve deeply

Chapter Five

Weeks had passed since Dr. Sefton Palmer had seen patients, attended bedsides, or interacted with any of the society he once had kept. Nothing was given place in his life but the question of lights. Nothing.

He stood in a graveyard at the very outskirts of London on a January night, one year to the day when he had first seen the columns of fire over a bog in Ireland. One year with more questions than answers. One year of replacing his doctoring with this pursuit. One year that had brought him to this place of death in the company of one who made his living disturbing the peace of the dearly departed.

Palmer had thrown his lot in with a resurrectionist.

They, a man who had once dedicated himself to healing people and a man who stole bodies from graves, stood in the dark, looking over the rolling mounds of dirt and the near-toppling headstones.

"You've seen corpse-lights?" Palmer asked his companion, not for the first time.

"All of us what ply our trade in these yards 'ave seen 'em." The man spoke in gravelly tones, with no indication he found the occurrence the least intriguing. "I've a mate who comes from Wales. He calls 'em *canhwyllan cyrph*. Another bloke what plies the trade quotes some Scottish poet, writing about dead knights and their graves glowing bright in the dark."

It was a poor summary of Sir Walter Scott's "Minstrelsy of the Scottish Border," but Scott was hardly the only writer to recount such a thing. Irish poet Thomas Moore spoke of them as well. Many accounts existed of such things. And if Palmer's theory that these lights were the result of decomposition were true, the sight of them in graveyards made perfect sense.

Then, where were they?

Palmer paced among the graves, making note of those headstones still standing, careful of those toppled over. The grass grew high and wild. Perhaps that was hiding the lights he'd come to see. Perhaps conditions weren't right. But he didn't know what the "right" conditions were.

"Have you seen corpse-lights in *this* churchyard?" Palmer asked the resurrection man.

"Oi."

"And was it on a night like tonight? Clear skies. Cold. The previous night was quite wet."

"Oi."

That, Palmer had decided, was part of the equation he

was attempting to discover. The air needed to be cold. The ground and therefore the body needed to be wet, though it need be not raining at the time when the lights were expected. That the pattern still held true was a promising thing.

He would find his answers tonight. He was determined to.

"Have you ever seen these lights when the ground was not wet?"

"This 'ere's London." The man spoke sardonically, a tone he'd struck from the moment Palmer had first approached him about this undertaking. "When is the dirt at our feet ever not wet?"

It was a fair enough question. "Have you seen these lights anywhere other than graveyards?"

"Oi. And I've heard tell of them appearing in odd spots. There were a man drowned at Ettrick. Couldn't find his body at first, but then the corpse-light gave him away. Found him straight off."

Bodies even glowed in the water. This was not a trick of his imagination. Palmer was right. He would be believed, and he would not rest until he was. If he had to hire the assistance of dozens of resurrection men and house breakers and criminals of every ilk, he would do so. No more would he be ignored and dismissed and pitied.

He paced the churchyard, eyes constantly surveying the expanse of it, the crumbled remains of the nearby church, the tall, flowing grass, the quiet of this all-but-abandoned corner of the world. The glow would come. It must.

"Can you not encourage the corpse-lights?" Palmer pressed. "Agitate the soil or some such thing."

"They don't come because you demand it." The resurrectionist picked at his fingernails with the point of a sinister blade. "It needs the right timing and a new body."

"So resurrect one," Palmer shot back. "It's why we're here, isn't it?"

"I'm here for a body, yes. The freshest ones fetch the best price."

The freshest ones also, it seemed, produced the most light. "Where is the body you've come to harvest?"

He could see no newly turned-over dirt, no grave newly dug and filled. Indeed, not a thing in this churchyard appeared to have changed in decades, perhaps centuries. Had he been duped? How dare the man!

Palmer bristled. "I cannot see these lights if you've not brought me to a place where you mean to ply your trade."

"I mean to ply it, never you fear." Moonlight played upon the man's ghastly features. "I'm not one for wasting m'time."

"Neither am I. So point me to this body you've come for."

With a look of pity not unlike the one Palmer had seen in the dissecting room but this time filled with a stomach-turning dose of amusement, the resurrectionist smiled at him. "The freshest ones fetch the best price."

It was long after whispered in the College of Physicians that a young doctor by the name of Palmer had driven himself mad in pursuit of an unanswerable question. He had abandoned his patients, his home, and his faculties. In the end, he had disappeared. That was offered as a warning to his fellow men of medicine not to allow the inexplicable to become inescapable.

Dear reader, remember: Though this tale be cautionary, at its heart are two truths. The first, that lights have indeed been known to appear in all the places where our Dr. Palmer pursued and encountered them. The second, and far more important is this: Some questions are best left unanswered.

CHAPTER 30

The smell of flowers was almost overwhelming. The coffin, though, was surprisingly comfortable. Gemma was able to lie perfectly still while breathing lightly and shallowly beneath the crinoline cage that was hidden by a light blanket and a layer of flowers.

As no one had yet cried out in shock or dropped dead with fright, she figured Baz was managing to keep still as well. Conversations bounced around. Words of remembrance were offered. Gemma didn't know how many of Baz's friends knew he weren't actually dead and how many believed they had lost someone they cared about. In the end, it didn't really matter. He'd be dead to them either way.

As unnerving as it was to lie in a coffin, knowing that somewhere someone was watching, ready to report back to her family and the man they answered to, it weren't nothing compared to the way her heart pounded with terror at the thought of the lid being nailed in place with her still inside.

She and Baz had practiced finding and pushing out a nail from a plank of wood in the dark, but it'd taken Dominique a few days to alter existing coffins for them to use, especially given he'd been altering a hearse as well. They'd run out of time for practicing escaping the coffins themselves.

That worried her.

She'd pried open coffins before, but always from the outside. And she was blasted good at doing it without leaving marks, without drawing attention. She hated that she was good at that. But it also meant she'd a head full of knowledge on coffins and how they worked. She prayed that'd be enough to get her out quickly, with time enough to free Baz.

Gemma forced herself to keep breathing shallowly as she heard Brogan tell the mourners it was time for removing the flowers and nailing the lids in place. Stone and Fletcher would be doing that as they'd been taught of the trick of it.

With her eyes closed, Gemma felt the darkness descend. Her heart drubbed a steady beat of worry. With the lid on, she could open her peepers at last. She immediately regretted it. Nothing but darkness and distant, echoing voices. Panic slithered over her like a snake in a garden.

The nails were pounded one by one. Heaven help her if they weren't doing it proper. The coffin was lifted. She slipped her hand beneath herself and felt around until her fingers found the steel pry bar. Her lifeline. Her means of escape.

The coffin wobbled a little as it was moved. After a time, it thudded hard underneath, likely against the floor in the back of the hearse. Then it were shoved forward, deeper inside the vehicle that was to be the scene of the most impossible resurrection ever undertaken.

She ran her fingers along the inner edge of the coffin near

the lid, following the notches Dominique had placed there. She heard the thud of Baz's coffin set next to hers. Muffled voices filled the space around her, and the coffin was jostled. They'd be placing the flowers on either side to block the view through the hearse's windows. She had to wait until all was quiet and the hearse was moving before she'd risk making a sound.

An eternity passed. There was air enough in the coffin, but her mind screamed that she was suffocating. It was the panic of being nailed in. Only a trick of the brain.

She felt the hearse jar into motion, bumping over the cobblestone street. Now was her chance. She jammed the jemmy bar in place, prying the coffin lid slowly and carefully; the smallest crack in the lid and they'd be sniffed out. Applying pressure only on the nails holding the lid shut, that was the safest way. Once those nails were pried out, the lids could be lifted and moved.

Gemma worked one side a little at a time. Blessed air began to leak inside. The lid wasn't free enough to let in much light. She worked at both sides, moving each a little at a time, keeping the lid from bowing. With those nearly free, she bent her arms over her head. She slid the point of her pry bar into the tiny crack between the lid and frame. There was one nail at the head that needed to be loosened. It was a harder angle to manage.

This was taking too long. Every minute was crucial.

The top finally gave. There were only two nails left, both at the foot.

She folded the crinoline cage on itself, giving her more room to move. Gemma shifted and adjusted, needing to get her jemmy bar into the back end of the coffin and begin prying the lid there.

But she couldn't.

There wasn't room enough to sit up or change the direction she was facing. She couldn't reach it.

No, no, no. This had to work. Hers weren't the only life on the line.

If she couldn't get the jemmy bar where she needed it, then she'd have to get something else wedged in that gap. The toe of her boots could work, but only if she created enough space. If she got the lid loose enough, she might be able to kick it the rest of the way. That *had* to happen while the hearse was still on the busy and noisy streets. But she'd risk damaging the lid.

One side, then the other, she worked the lid open farther and farther toward the foot, as far as she could reach. As a gap appeared at the bottom, she did her utmost to jam her foot inside it. Bit by tiny bit, she created space. A quick upward kick knocked it loose. With her hands and knees, she lifted and slid the lid to the side.

Light and air spilled in. She could hear the wheels on the cobblestone. And a knock from inside the coffin next to hers. Baz needed her help.

Gemma sat up. There was little room, the very reason her family'd think this escape couldn't be managed. The lid she'd removed was now on top of Baz's; there was nowhere else for it to go.

She balanced herself on the lip of the coffin and slid toward the front of the hearse where they'd stowed the sandbags. She hefted them, one at a time, into her coffin and spread them out. With all three in place, she slid the lid back on top of her coffin, giving her access to Baz's.

His lid was sticking at the feet, just as hers had. She crawled atop her coffin, its lid precariously in place. She had to lay there, as there weren't enough room overhead for anything else. She pushed her jemmy bar into the tiny gap Baz had managed to make on his own. Careful not to cause any obvious damage, she pried the last nail out, whispering, though he likely couldn't hear her, "I'm here Baz. I'm here."

After a moment, the lid popped free. She slid out of the way as Baz pushed it up and over onto her coffin. Two coffins in one hearse was tight, even in one designed to hold two.

In a low voice, she said, "Snatch the sandbags. Getting out took longer than it ought. I'd wager we're nearly to the churchyard."

He set to work without hesitation. When the bags were in place, he moved the lid back. Tied to a hook at the front of the hearse was a hammer and a small bag. They had to work quickly. Baz pounded nails in near him. Gemma pounded near her.

The hearse was slowing. They were approaching their destination. They both scrambled to the front of the hearse and the hinged flap that gave access to the false bottom. It wouldn't be easy to fit in the small space; the gap couldn't be made very large without leaking the entire scheme.

They wriggled and twisted and bent, trying to slide into their hiding place.

The hearse stopped.

No words passed between Gemma and Baz. They had to get out of sight, and they had to do it now.

Voices could be heard on all sides.

This was their final chance.

They managed to slide themselves in and pull the hinged door closed in the very instant the voices outside became clear. The doors at the back opened.

In the darkness, she felt Barnabus's hand brush against her arm, an unspoken reassurance that he was there and they were together.

The hearse jostled and shifted. Gemma held her breath. Only when she heard the hearse doors slamming shut did she dare take even the shallowest intake of air.

After a moment, all was still. Even the voices that had sounded on either side of the carriage could no longer be heard. The procession had gone into the chapel. She and Baz had only the length of a funeral before everyone would exit again and make their way to the graveside.

She still needed to wait for a signal from Kumar, though, before moving.

Footsteps sounded on the gravel around the carriage. Was someone examining the hearse? Was Kumar simply checking the area for someone suspicious?

Baz's hand found hers. He squeezed it.

The carriage shifted.

In a tone that indicated he was talking to himself but loud enough to be overheard, Kumar said, "Might as well have a bite to eat."

The hinged flap opened the tiniest bit.

Kumar kept his voice quiet. "Someone's watching. Don't get out."

Criminy.

Kumar had left the hinged door open a little. Blessed fresh air.

Gemma imagined him on his perch, nibbling on a meat pie he'd brought with him. He'd look to any curious eyes to be a driver biding his time with nothing at all in the world to be doing or fretting over.

Time crawled. The bit in the chapel would be done soon. The coffins'd be carried out and lowered into the ground. Kumar'd have to drive off. If any suspicion remained among the Kincaids, they'd follow him, watching for someone to climb out of the hearse who oughtn't've been there. This was their best chance for escaping, and they were running out of opportunity.

The hearse began to move. Kumar hadn't said anything or explained. She'd had a chance to come to know him a little during the CALL events, and she'd met his wife and oldest child. And Baz had assured her he was dependable. Whatever reason he had for moving the hearse, it must've been a prime one. They didn't move far or roll forward for very long.

Kumar leaned back into the hearse, barely visible in the small gap of the hinged door. In a low voice, he said, "The procession will be leaving the chapel in a moment. The couple of blokes who are watching me will be keeping an eye on that. If you are very careful, you can slip out of here and into the toolshed right next to where we are now. You'll have to hide yourself in there for a time. The churchyard is entirely walled. You'll not get out without being seen if the place ain't empty."

They'd not planned on this bit of bad loaf.

Kumar plopped a hat on his head and alighted from his

driver's perch. At a little bit of a distance, she could hear him say, "There you are, old girl. That'll get the sun out of your eyes." He was likely speaking to the horse. It would give an explanation to whoever was watching.

A moment later, muffled voices could be heard at a distance, then the shifting of gravel. The funeral procession had begun.

Slowly, carefully, she and Baz slipped out of the false bottom and into the interior of the hearse. Those who'd removed the coffins were smart and had left the flowers against the glass to either side. The view from the outside'd be obscured. They crawled slowly through the hearse, taking care not to jostle the flowers. At some point, Kumar had unlatched the door at the back.

Baz opened it a little at a time, likely hoping to avoid any squeaking from the hinges. Soon enough, it was open enough for them to slip out. The hearse sat very near the wall surrounding the churchyard, angled so the back end wasn't visible. Kumar had managed the positioning brilliantly. They were able to alight to the ground and carefully close the doors again.

Directly to the side of the hearse was a small shed. Moving slowly so they wouldn't draw attention, they made their way there. Gemma stepped in first, followed by Baz, who closed and latched the door.

A small, dingy window sat at the top of one wall, letting in a dim, brown-tinged light, enough to navigate by but not enough to see much. Anyone who managed to get to the high window wouldn't be able to see a deuced thing through it.

A perfect hiding place.

They sat on the dirt floor and leaned their backs against the wall. For the first time since climbing into the casket several hours earlier, Gemma truly breathed. Baz put an arm around her and held her to his side. She leaned against him, exhausted, trying to feel relieved but knowing they weren't out of the depths yet.

"We'll have to wait until dark to sneak out," he whispered. "I don't know how long the onlookers intend to stay."

"I'd rather sit in a shed than lie nailed in a coffin." She sighed. "This'll do for however long it's needed."

"I was having a lot of trouble prying the lid off. I was afraid you wouldn't be able to get out," Baz said.

"It were harder to do than I'd expected, but I've pried a few lids off. I knew I could do it. And if I could get out, I could get you out. That were all the motivation I needed."

He pressed a kiss to her temple. "Do you ever wonder how we went three years without even seeing each other, without being together? I can't imagine doing that now."

She twisted and kissed his cheek. "If we can manage to hop the jig out of this churchyard, we never need to be apart again."

His embrace tightened. "And *that* is all the motivation *I* need."

She closed her eyes. Though they were far from safe, she felt much of the fear and tension ease from her. They'd managed the trickiest bit of it. What remained was to wait.

CHAPTER 31

Night had long since fallen, and Baz still sat in the dingy toolshed with his arms around Gemma. She'd drifted to sleep at one point, but he suspected she wasn't truly at ease. He certainly wasn't. He wouldn't feel relieved until they were back at the Dread Master's safe house with their deaths having been confirmed to anyone hunting for them. And he likely wouldn't feel truly at peace until they were settled under false names somewhere away from London and free from the reach of Gemma's murderous family.

It had been hours since he'd heard anything from the outside.

The time had come.

Moving carefully and quietly, he woke Gemma from her fitful rest. They rose from the spot they had occupied for hours. Hunger, fatigue, and thirst were taking a toll on him, and he was certain Gemma felt it as well. But they couldn't stop yet. Not until they were safe.

He opened the door of the toolshed, careful to make no noise. She slipped out beside him. He closed it again. They were alone. The small slice of moon hanging in the cloudy sky provided just enough light to carefully navigate by but not enough to illuminate them. They followed the edge of the wall, which would take them behind the chapel but also spill them out onto the street eventually. They were one dim walk away from freedom.

They hadn't gone more than a few steps, placing them behind the chapel, when the sound of tools stopped Barnabus short.

"Sounds like a shovel," he murmured.

"The church's gravedigger ain't going to be working at this time of night," Gemma whispered.

"Would a resurrectionist ply his trade this early in the evening?" It was dark, yes, but it was hardly the middle of the night.

"Not unless they ain't got any other choice."

The sounds of digging continued. Barnabus didn't want to think overly much about what that meant. Whether he put a name to the danger or not, he couldn't deny it was past time to get out of the churchyard.

They inched their way along the wall. As they emerged from the back end of the chapel, keeping to the darkest shadows, Barnabus searched the churchyard, dimly lit by moonlight. He didn't need to look long.

Two men stood over a grave, a pile of dirt beside them. They had made a lot of progress. The dirt appeared loose, not clumps like it would have been if the grave weren't a very new one.

"That's ours," Barnabus said in a tense whisper.

"The wall, Baz." Gemma's strained whisper was filled with worry. "On the corner of the chapel."

At about waist level, smudged in black was a single, long vertical line followed by a *K*, then a shorter vertical line and another *K*. Barnabus had never seen the Kincaid mark look that way, had never heard Gemma describe it like this.

"What does that mean?" he asked, keeping his voice low.

"They're both here. They're digging me up."

He'd thought the biggest obstacles were behind them. They'd managed to escape closed coffins and a hearse that was being watched. All of that would be for nothing if Silas and Arlo were nearby.

"They are going to discover there is nothing in those caskets but sandbags."

Running now would get them away from the imminent threat, but the Kincaids would know they were alive. The hunt would never stop.

"We cain't just run," Gemma said. "There's a bit of the wall up ahead that ain't in shadow. We'd risk being seen."

"We'll wait here," Barnabus said. "They'll find an empty coffin and go searching the streets. We can leave after they do."

"And go where?" Gemma asked. "They'll start hurting people again. All this, and it won't change nothing."

He had no words of reassurance. They had to stay where they were, waiting and watching while all the effort they'd made was undone.

The shoveling stopped.

"They've reached a coffin," she whispered. "I don't know if it's yours or mine."

Wood splintered. Resurrecting a corpse without fully digging up the coffin meant breaking the lid. This wasn't an endeavor they were attempting to hide, then. Since the Mastiff did this sort of thing to send a message, it made sense the Kincads wouldn't have been careful about their work.

The taller of the men watched as the other tossed aside his pry bar.

"They have it open." Gemma's voice quivered. "They're seeing an empty coffin. They know."

The taller brother fetched what looked like a length of rope from a bag. The two of them lowered it into the hole they'd created.

"That don't make sense," she said. "The rope's for hooking around the arms of the body and pulling it out. But there ain't a stiff inside. Are they trying to pull out a sandbag?"

"Unlikely," Barnabus said.

"But that's our plot," Gemma said. "And that soil's fresh. It cain't be any coffin but one of ours, and we're not in 'em."

They were at a distance and an odd angle, which made it difficult to see exactly what was happening at the grave.

The Kincaid brothers pulled something out of the ground. Whatever it was landed at their feet with a thud. In the next instant, cries of horror sounded from the hardened criminals. They ran. Two men feared by all of London ran screaming from the grave, leaving behind every tool of their trade and whatever had come out of the coffin.

"Sandbags wouldn't scare 'em," Gemma said. "They'd be angry, raging, but not scared. And they wouldn't run."

"Much as I would love to follow their lead and run off," Barnabus said, "I think we need to know what sent them heading for the hills. It's somehow connected to us and the price on our heads now that they'll know we're not dead."

"Oi." She didn't sound any happier about it than he was.

With the churchyard empty and quiet again, he inched toward the disturbed grave, Gemma keeping pace with him and holding fast to his hand. She could probably hear his heart racing. His medical schooling had included morgues and corpses. He'd treated gruesome injuries. It wasn't the possibility of discovering something grisly that worried him.

The Kincaids weren't afraid of anything. So what could possibly have terrified them? A feeling of foreboding washed over him with increasing force as they drew nearer the grave.

They reached the other side of the mound of disturbed dirt and saw what had emerged from that hole.

It was a body.

A body covered in dried blood, pulled from what was supposed to be an empty coffin.

"Blazes," Baz whispered.

"Is that who I think it is?" Gemma asked.

He nodded. "That's the Mastiff."

CHAPTER 32

The *Mastiff.*

The corpse at their feet was the man the DPS had been chasing for months. He was the one the Kincaids were working for. The criminal who'd hired them to undertake this resurrection had just been pulled from what should have been a corpseless coffin.

"I don't understand," Gemma said in a frantic whisper. "Why was he in that casket? How did he get in there? Who killed him?"

"And why?" Barnabus added.

From the shadow of a nearby tree, a woman's voice answered the question. "Because he was no longer useful." A silhouette in a dress stepped forward, but not far enough to be seen in any detail.

"Who are you?" He didn't bother whispering. He took Gemma's hand and pulled her the tiniest bit behind him, unsure of the threat they were facing.

"I am the maestro," the woman said.

"I ain't heard of no one that goes by that name." Gemma stepped up next to Barnabus.

"It is not my name," the woman answered. "It is my destiny."

The maestro. It was her role. "The Mastiff answered to you." Barnabus felt a chill pass through him.

"*Everyone* answers to me," she replied, calm and unperturbed but also fierce and intense. "Mine is power without limit, vengeance without end, an inescapable nightmare. All who oppose me fall."

She sounded familiar.

"Is that why the Mastiff was in this casket?" Gemma asked her. "He weren't supportive enough?"

"He craved power, which I offered him. And he adored me, which was exceptionally useful. But I no longer need him."

"And so you killed him?" Barnabus demanded.

"People die all the time," the woman said, unemotional, unconcerned. "You're a doctor, Barnabus. You know that."

"They don't always mysteriously end up buried in another person's grave," he said.

"A little surprise for the Kincaids. Was that not terribly fun to watch, Gemma?"

Barnabus held tighter to her hand, not liking the sound of Gemma's name on this murderer's lips.

"What could you possibly gain from terrorizing the poor and vulnerable people of London?" he asked.

"What have I gained?" She laughed humorlessly. "I have gained an army."

"If you're amassing an army, you must mean to go to

war." He hoped if she kept talking, he could sort out who she was and, more important still, a means of escape.

"People like you, weak fools that you are, address your family pain with good works and rescues," the woman said. "Vengeance is far more satisfying."

"What is it you're meaning to do with us?" Gemma asked. "Wouldn't do to miss a prime opportunity for bloodshed."

"Do not be dramatic, sweetie. You're both still useful to me. You will deliver a message."

"What message?" Barnabus asked. "To whom?"

"Tell your friends that 'the poor and infirm, the hopeless and voiceless' will tremble before me." She stepped from the shadows, lit by the gray of cloudy moonlight.

Gemma gasped as Barnabus's heart froze in his chest.

"Tell them I do not relent. And I never forget. I am the Tempest," Serena said.

Barnabus held fast to Gemma's hand as they raced down the dark London streets toward DPS headquarters. He had to warn them. He had to tell them that the enemy they thought they were fighting was not the real threat.

All this time, Serena had manipulated them into searching for her, looking for her, reaching out to her, saving her. And in so doing, she had met many of the Dreadfuls. She knew so much more than they likely even realized. And she, not the Mastiff, was the head of London's criminal underworld. She was, as she so aptly put it, a nightmare come to life.

He pushed his way through the familiar blue door and slammed it shut behind him, Gemma at his side.

Nolan was not on his bench. The door to the parliamentary room was wide open, and raised voices, echoing in chaos, sounded from inside.

To Gemma, he said, "I will explain all of this to you, I promise. But we have to tell them now."

"I trust you."

He rushed into the parliamentary room. Most of the DPS members were there, and everyone was talking at once. This was not the friendly gab they often had before a meeting. Everyone looked worried and confused.

Barnabus didn't have time to slowly get their attention. He popped two fingers in his mouth and whistled as loud as he could manage. They all turned. Surprise, shock, even horror appeared on a few faces. Most of the DPS had not been told that his death had been staged.

"What are you doing here?" Fletcher asked.

"The Kincaids came to resurrect our graves. We hadn't been able to get out of the churchyard without being caught, so we were waiting."

"They discovered the empty caskets?" Brogan guessed. "That might explain why we're all getting warnings from every urchin in our network."

Barnabus shook his head. "The coffin they opened was one of ours, but it wasn't empty. They'd pulled a body out."

A heavy and uncomfortable silence settled over the room.

"Who was it?" Fletcher asked.

"The Mastiff."

He could see they all meant to ask questions, but there wasn't time. "The Mastiff was not the mastermind we believed him to be, pulling the strings and giving the orders. All this time, he was answering to someone else. He was acting on orders. And that someone was waiting nearby, watching the resurrection, enjoying the whole thing."

"Did you figure out who?" Stone asked, obviously understanding the significance of that.

Barnabus nodded. "It was Serena. We were all convinced she was a victim, but she is the head. She is directing all of this. And she knows everything. She knew the coffins would be empty. She knew when we would be escaping."

Barnabus looked around the room. "As Serena, she learned where my safe houses are and who runs them. She knows Hollis is in the DPS because she saw him at the gambling house while she was pretending to be held captive there. She knows Ana and Fletcher were part of that operation. She knows Brogan's involvement and that Vera is connected to him, which could easily lead her to Mr. Sorokin. And"—he swallowed against the lump in his throat—"she quoted the DPS's creed. She knows it by heart."

"How could she possibly?" Elizabeth asked.

"She knows too much to not have someone on the inside here. Someone in our meetings. Someone part of us," Barnabus said.

That sent all their gazes to everyone else in the room.

"The Mastiff said his network overlapped with ours," Fletcher recalled. "There's a traitor among us."

"Baz." He turned at the sound of Gemma's quavering

voice. She held out a slip of paper. "This was on the bench by the door."

He took the paper and, with a trembling voice, read aloud the four words written there. "The Tempest is here."

Silence filled the room.

"Nolan," he whispered.

"He was gone when we started pouring in," Fletcher said. "That ain't never happened before."

Was Nolan the one reporting to her? He knew them all by sight, knew their schedules, their missions.

"Serena told us that she is the Tempest. If Nolan was her eyes on the inside, she knows who we all are. She knows *everything*."

Fletcher barked out orders on the instant, instructing the DPS members to go secure and safeguard their families. He sent Elizabeth to shut down her school and keep her students safe. As the room emptied and the DPS scattered like leaves on the wind, he turned to Barnabus and Gemma.

"Get yourself to safety. Knowing how much you know, you likely will be the Tempest's most pointed target. You were planning to leave London, and now is the time to make good your escape."

"To abandon everyone now, when the danger is so—" Barnabus began objecting.

"Nothing is simple anymore. You both are certified and recorded as dead. You have the means of escape."

Barnabus looked at Gemma. "We are ready. We can get out of London before anyone catches up to us. I will go wherever you want to go, do whatever you choose."

She nodded. “We are dead, Baz. We have some anonymity. We could help.”

“We would be in danger,” he reminded her.

“We are already in danger,” she said. “But neither of us is the sort to abandon people when they need us. Neither of us will be happy if we ain’t helping.”

He lifted her hand to his lips and pressed a quick kiss there. “We’ll go invisible, then? The bachelor and his bride, slipping through London’s streets like ghosts?”

“People’s lives are on the line, Baz. We are going to save everyone we can. Together.”

“Together.”

CHAPTER 33

In the quiet of the abandoned house, once the center of this network of authors and philanthropists, Fletcher Walker set his hat on his head, straightened the lapel of his coat, and turned to face the chair he'd sat in for years while guiding the efforts of the Dread Penny Society, acting on behalf of the Dread Master.

He took hold of a spindle on the back of his throne and pulled it, activating a lever only he knew about. In the wall directly behind the chair, a panel opened. He stepped through, taking up the lantern and matches set there for precisely this purpose. He lit the lantern as the panel closed behind him.

He followed winding stone steps down farther and farther into a subterranean passageway. Down he walked, his footsteps echoing around him.

He stepped through the door at the end of the passageway and into a room that in any other location would appear to be nothing more than a library belonging to a merchant or a well-settled member of the gentry. It was lit by candles. A cabinet to one side held weaponry of various kinds. Shelves on the walls held copies of penny dreadfuls, likely all that had ever been published.

A large desk sat along one wall with a tall chair turned away from the room, its occupant, no doubt looking out the high window that was curtained with translucent fabric, allowing lamplight in but obscuring the view from outside.

He often reported to the Dread Master in precisely this way. Never before had his report felt so dire.

"The Mastiff is dead, killed by Serena, who calls herself the Tempest. She has been the mastermind all this time. Nolan has fled, and we've reason to believe he's a spy. The Dreadfuls have scattered, rushing to safeguard their families. The Tempest is preparing for a battle that is nearly at our doorstep."

For so long, he'd forced himself to not even think the Dread Master's name, to not allow even the tiniest indication of identity to enter his thoughts or slip free of his lips. He kept even his silent, mental references as neutral as he could. But it was time this organization fell under the leadership of the only one capable of seeing them through this war.

"I'm turning over the DPS to you. I will do all I can, whatever you ask of me. But they need to know they have you. With you at the lead, they can have some hope of survival."

The chair shifted, and the Dread Master rose. A light fall of heeled boots clinked against the stone floor. A swish of fabric broke the silence.

Fletcher looked into the face of the only person who could give them a chance of emerging victorious in the coming war. "We are in your hands, Móirín."

ACKNOWLEDGMENTS

I could not possibly have written this book with any degree of accuracy without the preservation of and access to

- *The Science and Practice of Medicine v. 2*, written by William Aitken in 1866.
- "The Evolution of Light from the Living Human Subject," written by Henry Marsh and published in *The Provincial Medical Journal* in 1842.
- *The Medical and Physical Journal: Containing the Earliest Information on Subjects of Medicine, Surgery, Pharmacy, Chemistry, and Natural History, Vol III*, published in 1800.
- The 1880s publications of the Folklore Society of Great Britain.
- *Passing English of the Victorian Era: A Dictionary of Heterodox English, Slang and Phrase* by James Redding Ware, published 1909
- The (modernly published) and invaluable works of lexicographer Susie Dent.

I further owe many thanks to

- Jolene Perry, for cheering on this series.
- Esther Hatch, for checking my use of Russian.
- Annette Lyon and Luisa Perkins, for encouragement and accountability.
- Jesse Perry, for being a proofreading lifesaver.
- Liz Swick and Jonathan Eden, for invaluable assistance juggling everything.
- Pam Pho and Bob Diforio, for being the best team an author could hope for.

Discussion Questions

1. Fear and significant trauma prevent Gemma and Barnabus from confessing their feelings for each other. Which other characters do you think are being held back by pain and worry?
2. Both Gemma and Barnabus come from difficult family circumstances, suffering from poverty and danger as they grew up. How do these similar experiences help build a bond between them? Do you think they are ready to trust that their marriage is something more than an unwanted necessity?
3. How might Gemma and Barnabus being declared dead prove helpful in the coming battle with the Tempest? How might it complicate things?
4. Gemma's family now knows she was not buried in her coffin. Do you think they will continue searching for her? Do you think they will assume Barnabus is also still alive?
5. Why do you think Stone has kept his sweetheart a secret from his friends? How do you think that will impact him moving forward?

6. Did you correctly guess the identity of the Dread Master? Who else did you feel could have filled that role?
7. What role do you think Parkington might play in the coming conflict with the Tempest?
8. What theories do you have as to why the Radlett murder is of so much significance to the Mastiff and/or the Tempest?
9. With their secrets known and the danger growing, the DPS has scattered. How do you think the organization will function moving forward?

About the Author

Sarah M. Eden is a *USA Today* best-selling author of witty and charming historical romances, including 2019's Foreword Reviews INDIE Awards Gold Winner for Romance, *The Lady and the Highwayman*, and 2020 Holt Medallion finalist, *Healing Hearts*. She is a two-time "Best of State" Gold Medal winner for fiction and a three-time Whitney Award winner.

Combining her obsession with history and her affinity for tender love stories, Sarah loves crafting deep characters and heartfelt romances set against rich historical backdrops. She holds a bachelor's degree in research and happily spends hours perusing the reference shelves of her local library.